Running W

Dedication

To all the friends young and old I've made throughout the years while running on the roads, up and down the trails, and circling many an oval track. To all those who encourage others to follow their hearts, chase after their dreams, and to never settle for anything less than the very best this world has to offer. To my family for always believing in me, even in the face of the steepest odds. And to Bill Priest, for teaching me how to love, one day a time. May your hometown marathon continue to thrive.

"My pain is self-chosen. At least, so the prophet says."- Mad Season, *River of Deceit*

Chapter 1

"I want to break three hours in the Boston Marathon." Those were the exact words spoken by Denny to his Uncle Mike.

Ten years ago, that would have been unimageable, for Denny had come to the end of the road...

He was crouched in the living room, with arms curled so tight around his legs that any feelings in his fingers were gone. They were ghostly white, drained of blood, and almost matched his face, itself ashen white and gaunt, with eyes partially sunken into the bony visage.

If he released his iron grip in the slightest, his hands would begin to shake. In the pervading silence, Denny swore he could hear his heart still beating inside his chest; for a few moments it was in sync with the ticking of a clock hung on the wall, invisible somewhere within the cloak of darkness. The time may have been two a.m., or three, or four by then? But time, as measured by clocks and calendars, had ceased having any sort of meaning in the discourse of life. Except for perhaps one last date, to be engraved into marble somewhere.

What did trouble Denny, was the lattice-like wooden framework of the two large windows across the living room, which separated each of the windows into nine individual panes of glass. For such a design potentially posed an impediment; but the woodwork was rather thin, and would likely just shatter along with the glass upon impact. Or so he hoped. A clean break was much more the preference.

A break from the misery and torment, sleepless nights and horrifically long days. From the thoughts-the terrible tragic, heartbreaking thoughts that were always there.

Freedom from the prison that had been systematically constructed around him.

And so, Denny crouched, and waited, coiling up his energy into a centered mass in the belly. He waited for something to click in place-a trigger, a cosmic vibration to thrust the whole body violently forward across the room through the windows and out into to the unforgiving blackhole of the night where he'd lurch and spin and eventually fall, fall, fall, fall until the threshold would be crossed seven stories below.

Denny felt a chill course through his entire body. He rocked onto his backside and let his head hit the carpeted floor. Denny took his arms and crossed them on top of his chest, as his eyelids infinitesimally began dropping over his eyeballs, cutting the field of vision into narrow slits looking up at the white tiles of the ceiling. He took one deep breath, and exhaled; the next thing he knew something was kicking at his feet. Denny opened his eyes-a young woman was standing over him. And there was light, a lot of bright light.

"Are you alright?" she asked. It was like being questioned by a phantom. Denny sat up, and realized he was sprawled out on sand beneath a swing set. He ran his hands through the sand, almost mechanically, allowing the grains to fall between his fingers. It was real. He was alive. The sun was angled almost directly behind this person; Denny had to squint in order to try and really see her.

"Yes. No. I must have fallen asleep," he stammered. Sand was all over his clothes, which Denny began to brush off, cognizant suddenly that his actions were being minutely scrutinized. And he had no idea where he was, though an innate sense dictated that emitting such a vibe should be avoided at all costs. Though there was a tenuous familiarity about it, like one of the playgrounds at a nearby elementary school.

"Are you sure?" The stranger queried Denny again, with what seemed to be a degree of concern in her voice, though she didn't appear to be all that startled by the pathos that must have been emanating from Denny's persona, despite his efforts at subterfuge, albeit born out of a precept of basic survival.

"No, I'm okay," he quickly and rather curtly answered as he stood up. But Denny hesitated briefly before leaving, and added, "thanks though."

Instinct and adrenaline had begun to kick in; he knew getting the hell out of wherever he was the proper recourse. The rear of the back wing of the school was visible just beyond a grove of trees, which served to confirm the physical location; how he had gotten there and why he was there though, Denny didn't have the damnedest clue? In a flash, he was gone.

Once he got back on the sprawling gardens where he lived, Denny quickly became disoriented. A wave of panic gripped him. His mouth became all cottony and dry, and sweat began forming on his forehead. Denny's hands he noticed were trembling. There were numerous buildings on the property; block like numbers were painted above the framed double door entrance ways. But he could not recall for the life of him the number of the building in which he resided. They all looked the same. Panic morphed into terror. It was like being trapped in the clutches of a nightmare, where everything was being transmitted on a frequency Denny couldn't tune in to. The brain was losing the ability to perform rudimentary tasks like recall, similar to what dementia patients must have to endure. The more Denny tried to get his wits about him, the further his mind seemed to float away.

He sat down on a curb, and managed to bring the short rapid breaths under control; after a few minutes a look upward at the surrounding oak trees, swaying delicately in the springtime breezes, provided solace and a sense of direction, for it dawned upon Denny, like rediscovering a divine revelation in the depths of one's soul, that such trees were visible from the bedroom window, and therefore the entrance to his apartment was on the other side of the building nearest to where he rested. He jumped up and headed forthwith in such a direction, keeping his head hung low, lest he pass someone who might know or recognize him.

Though a similar incident had transpired recently, a painful reminder of which was brought forth when one of the retention ponds was spotted adjacent to a parking lot. It was that very pond where Denny had stopped to ostensibly rest at the water's edge, while in route on foot to a nearby convenience store to buy more beer. In this harrowing instance, Denny came to while being prodded in the chest by some trampy-looking homeless guy, who in response to receiving a bug-eyed, startled look, replied rather coolly, "good, you're still alive."

And then the madness was on Denny; it felt like millions of leeches were crawling all over his body, so he dove fully clothed into the drainage pond itself. But not before snarling at the man, "quit fucking bothering me."

When he came out of the water whoever it was had faded wisp-like off the scene, leaving Denny to question whether or not he had been real to begin with. A few days later, however, the same bum was seen rummaging through a dumpster behind one of the gas stations on Market Street. Right after Denny had returned home then, all the fence posts on the edge of the property had morphed into short, squat Mexican men standing perfectly erect and perfectly still; they all stared directly at him like they knew every sick secret inside of him. And Denny knew without a shadow of a doubt who had sent them all, but he dared not go back to find that dirty vagabond again.

But he knew what would fix it, and distill the mind back to what had become a toxic homeostasis. It had been purchased and carried back home, despite the fact that his right arm had gone numb from the wrist to above the elbow, likely related to the deep crimson colored splotches all over his forearm, and both of his legs for that matter. Denny didn't even bother to use the refrigerator anymore; he set the case of beer down, ripped open the box, and pulled out the first twelve-ounce can which he'd probably puke up anyway…

The blare of the tractor trailer's horn caused Denny to jerk in his car seat. His hands reflexively grasped the steering wheel tight, as out of his peripheral vision the sight of the big truck appeared in the passenger side windows. He had been so absorbed in thought, that apparently, he had been on auto-pilot in the car, and in the left-hand lane to boot. Denny flipped his right hand up in the air and waved an apology to the truck driver. The phone conversation earlier with Uncle Mike had catapulted his mind backwards, since it was suggested that before he begin a new challenge, to bear in mind with clear vision, where it is, he had come from.

He had been fidgeting mentally with such a lofty undertaking for awhile now; perhaps as measured on some biological scale, the time had come for Denny to embark on a new vision quest, as he liked to term such grandiose projects. Another chance to peer behind the veil? The perpetual yearning to chase after something, to put himself out on the edge, where Kurt Vonnegut once said is the place where you see all kinds of things you can't see from the center.

"Hey," Uncle Mike had said a tad forcefully into the phone, "the memories of our depths of despair often make the best jumping off points. Not only for running."

"For sure," Denny agreed.

"Filter your expectations thru such a prism."

"I'll see you soon wise one," was how Denny had concluded the conversation. The words were taken to heart, and carried a little extra poignancy, considering the circumstances their speaker was facing.

Up ahead was the large road sign welcoming travelers on Interstate 95 to the state of Virginia; Denny checked the clock on the dashboard and was pleased that he was going to exit the state of North Carolina in a few minutes shy of three hours elapsed drive time. Not bad for the first big leg of the trip. And not that there was any particular cause to hurry or any constraints being imposed; it was just a little game Denny liked to play when traversing longer distances on the road, in order to leaven the dull monotony ubiquitous to long periods spent behind the wheel. He was debating stopping anyway in Maryland, and going for a run up in the Catoctin Mountains. If so, it would end up being dark by the time eastern Pennsylvania was reached. Denny surmised that temperatures would be much colder up in the elevations to the north; he had left out of his home in Carolina Beach in a pair of shorts and a light weight sweatshirt. He could have checked such particulars on his cell phone, but it wasn't all that important.

Later as the highway approached Washington D.C. traffic began to clog and slow south of 485, or the Beltway. Denny hoped since it was a weekday, that the commute wouldn't be too problematic, but this section of concrete always seemed to serve as an unwanted chokepoint. The cars did come to a complete halt, but fortunately not for long. Denny took advantage and rolled down the window and stuck his arm out to gauge the atmosphere. It was noticeably cooler. Soon the signs indicating what routes to take to Baltimore, New Jersey, and New York City became visible; such landmarks never failed to fascinate Denny, for they served as catalysts that spung the mind forward, to what experiences might lie in store in the keystone state. For no matter how far one may stray, there will only be a solitary, single spot on the vast curve of the land, that every one of us has sprung forth from. And in Denny's case, he would be there in a few hours' time.

Chapter 2

The trail was rather rocky, and continued to vertically climb. Denny was already breathing with a pronounced effort; he leaned his six-foot lithe frame slightly forward, and cut the pace back to a gentle bound, since there was no particular reason to be attacking the terrain with such a display of vigor. Maybe close to six hours in the car had balled up some of his nerves, making falling nearly into oxygen debt five to ten minutes into the run appear to be a novel cure for such angst. But all Denny desired to do was get some easier mileage in and time on his feet, while enjoying the scenery at a place he hadn't run at in a couple years. The Catoctin Mountains always fascinated him, though usually their marvel was confined to views from the car while travelling through central Maryland. They were an integral part of the Appalachian Mountains; those old rugged vertical land masses that held within their confines' mysteries dating back to the prehistoric times. Quartzite veins that jutted at all angles out of the ground, or the immense, jagged rocks protruding all about the gloomy, dense forests, all seemed to whisper about tales of fire and brimstone, as they were remnants of Jurassic upheavals from a world long forgotten, yet preserved for millions of years in places such as this.

Denny's Garmin watch beeped a mile into the run; he had covered the distance in 12:18. He almost had to laugh at such a pedestrian time. A quarter to a half of a mile later, the single-track trail did flatten out some, as it wound deeper into the virginal woods. The atmosphere was much chillier and raw, especially amongst the sweeping shadows. Denny was glad that he had put on a beanie atop his curly brown head of hair, and a pair of gloves on his bony hands, in addition to a long-sleeved shirt. But it was a clean, pure country cold air that enlivened the spirit, even if the physical body took some time to warm up. The overall pitch of the terrain began to incline upward again, as the trail would rise sharply for say forty to fifty meters before leveling off, or even descending a little, before rising up and over the next section of the mountain. Denny guessed he was somewhere above three thousand feet in elevation by now; according to the trail map at the State Park's Visitors Center, the run had commenced at about twenty-two hundred feet. The quadricep muscles were certainly feeling all the climbing that had been done the last forty minutes or so, and Denny's feet were also a tad sore from having to land on a lot of uneven rocks. Though there were long stretches of trail where the surface was predominately hard packed dirt; but since all the leaves had long since fallen from the trees, Denny had to still be meticulous with his footfalls. Somewhere hidden in these parts was the famous presidential retreat Camp David.

    After another long, slightly elevated climb, and one more rather precipitous incline which passed right aside of what looked like a cave made of quartz, Denny came to a peak in the range, and a vantage point that offered a stunning view southward into Maryland and beyond, perhaps on past Washington D.C., and into northern Virginia. He stopped and sucked down a salted caramel flavored gel, savoring the sweet taste as the gooey, gelatinous mixture slid over his tongue and on into his throat. Denny gazed in an almost child-like wonder at the miles upon miles of woods which rolled down the mountains, before eventually smoothing out and bleeding into the farm country, with its quilt-like pattern of now barren fields, dotted with sporadic barns and houses; all of it appeared idyllic and tranquil stretched beneath the afternoon sunshine. He was happy the decision had been made to stop and partake in the run, not only for the views that lie before him and the challenge of getting to such a remote locale, but perhaps more importantly, the excursion was serving to take the mind off the reason the trip had been undertaken to begin with, and what may lie in wait to the north and east. Up on top of a mountain, the concepts of sickness and death held little sway. Denny took a deep breath, practically feelings the molecules of air that filled his lungs; a silent prayer of thanks was offered, as a wave of gratitude dropped down through the scattered clouds above. For in the moments just then, his own life seemed so viscerally real and brimming with potency, that the bead of sweat trickling out from beneath his knit hat and rolling down the front of his cheek was acutely felt in every pore of the body. And then in an instant Denny was gone, headed on back down the mountainside.

A half hour or so later after getting back on Route 15, the large, blue Welcome to Pennsylvania sign appeared on the right side of the road. Denny snapped a picture. He found this independent rock and roll station near the bottom end of the FM dial that he dug; with volume turned up, Denny imagined throngs of teens and young adults jamming out to metal and punk music in old barns and abandoned farm houses, many of them drinking beer, smoking cigarettes and plotting eventual escapes from the vast rolling nothingness that stretched out indefinitely in all directions. The collective dreams and energy of youth, fueled by six-string guitars and copious amounts of cheap alcohol. Daylight waned in the rear-view mirror; twilight washed softly across the eastern sky with its attendant hues of deep blue and purplish black. Neil Young's "Hey Hey My My," started to play. For a few precious minutes the scene almost seemed too perfect-Denny felt like he was cut adrift and floating weightlessly in the ether. Soon nightfall would be upon the fields and houses and all the cows that lazed about. Some of the buildings already had lit up their Christmas lights and ornamental displays, full of bright festive colors on strings that also wrapped around fences and trees in the adjacent yards. For a long stretch of the highway Denny sort of forgot what he was doing or where he was going; some of my meditations must be bearing fruit he did think, as he began to approach the more populous Harrisburg area.

The traffic was also noticeably heavier on Route 581, which snaked through the western and southern sections of the state capital. Atop the long bridge which crossed over the Susquehanna River and basin, Denny looked southward to see if he could make out Three Mile Island's infamous nuclear cooling towers. In due course Denny was exiting off Interstate 78 and onto Route 61, which headed northward and away from most any civilization and into the heart of darkness of rural, eastern Pennsylvania. Coal country. The road wound through a steep valley, formed by one of the Susquehanna's many tributaries, hidden somewhere close in the pitch-black shroud of the evening.

The small town of Port Clinton was situated somehow in the floor of the narrow valley, with its clapboard houses and old-time mom and pop businesses tightly clustered along a few streets wedged between the looming hillsides. In the light of day, poverty hung in the air like dense fog that had become trapped in the foreboding landscape; the community, like many others, was an unfortunate part of the opioid crisis tragically swallowing up some of the inhabitants. Usually those too young to ever realize that alternatives existed. Though Denny did imagine, on a somewhat unrelated note, what it would be like to reside there as a runner, running into the hills and mountains on any given day, where one could likely find themselves miles away from the nearest signs of any other human life, except perhaps during hunting season. A girl he used to know from his high school track team lived there, or used to live in the community. But such a trivial fact held minor importance to Denny, as the road began to climb up and over another small mountain, before winding through New Ringgold, another sparsely inhabited town, situated beside a set of railroad tracks, and along the banks of a fast moving, little river. Then it was into the village of South Tamaqua a few miles later, as Denny drove by Leiby's Family Restaurant, located at the intersection of Route 443 and 309. The once-popular place had been closed and shuttered for a long time, but was rumored to be re-opening next year. For ages it had been known for some of the best handmade ice cream in the state.

From there it was less than a half of an hour's drive. Denny had become a bit punch drunk from being on the road for ten hours, and craved the concept of not being inside a moving vehicle much longer. Soon though he was proceeding through the Mahoning Valley on 443, driving by landmarks witnessed hundreds of times-some of the environs over the course of a couple decades had changed, but there were enough vestiges, even in the dark, to tug at something deep inside Denny, as perhaps jumbled memories long since forgotten stirred within the subconscious realm, trying to bubble to the surface when particular remnants were spotted. For the moment, a throbbing ache in his left shoulder that extended up into the neck, had succeeded in manipulating most of Denny's attention. He massaged the troublesome area with his right arm, and temporarily some of the discomfort abated. Denny was also quite aware of the fact he was hungry again too.

Finally, he entered the town of Lehighton, right after driving by his friend Trent's house. Denny saw his car parked in the driveway in front of the big garage where he raised all the pigeons; the two had plans to get together and run Saturday morning. Denny got stopped at the traffic light to the main entrance of the Carbon Plaza Mall. He had a brief flashback to sitting there at a red light one night about two years ago, when he had last been up for an extended period. Tonight, he fondly laughed at the memory, recalling the wave of panic he had experienced then, unsure of at the time why he was in his old hometown, and for just how long he intended to stay. And it had been a few days after randomly bumping into Jennifer in the lobby of the middle school. As the light turned green and Denny placed his sore right foot back on the gas pedal, all of that stuff seemed so far off; but then again, as he got stopped at another traffic light at the base of the Ninth Street Hill, was it perhaps as far off as he thought it all was?

A few minutes later Denny pulled off the road for good, and into the parking lot of the Country Inn and Suites, located on Route 209 in Franklin Township, three miles east of Lehighton. It was five minutes after seven o'clock, and he was relieved that the drive was done, and completed in a relatively pretty good overall time, taking into account the trail run in the mountains of Maryland. The legs cramped up pretty tight as Denny got up and out of his vehicle, causing him to hobble like an elderly man the first few steps towards the front entrance of the hotel. Inside the sliding glass doors, was about a ten-foot-tall Christmas tree in the back of the lobby, which was set up sort of like a living room nook with a sofa and chairs just off the main floor, and across from the reception desk. A fire was lit inside the fireplace; stockings were even hung from the mantle, which made the scene look all peaceful and welcoming, especially to the road weary traveler like Denny, who was cast into a bit of a holiday unknown himself. Some of that would likely fall into place tomorrow he imagined; for now, the objective was to check in and unpack, and then find something easy to eat for dinner.

"I hope you enjoy your stay with us," the young woman said from behind the front desk, as she handed Denny his room keys.

"Thank you," he replied. "It's good to be here."

Chapter 3

Denny pulled open the thick navy-blue curtains and let the light of the morning come into the room. After brewing a cup of hot coffee, he opened up his copy of *Daniels' Running Formula* book, which was bookmarked to the training plan being used, and doublechecked the particulars of the workout that would be done today. Jackie would probably write the thing on her hand he thought, as he tossed a few gels and the room keys into the outer flap of a backpack, then headed for the door. She had started her Boston Marathon plan last week as well, and was probably half way through a run today somewhere back down in Wilmington, North Carolina, where it could be safely surmised it wasn't nearly as cold. The details on the weather channel indicated locally that it was 29 degrees outside, with a wind chill of 23.

The gravel and dirt parking lot at the D&L trailhead was deserted, save for one other lone SUV. Denny pulled in and hopped out, and got right into his normal pre-run routine consisting of legs swings and lunges. While doing so he debated shucking the pair of tighter fitting running pants being worn, but thought better of and kept them on. The sun's rays did manage to cast some warmth, but the temperatures weren't forecast to rise all that much during the day.

The plan for the morning was to run the first eight miles of the workout through the town of Lehighton, which he was currently on the outskirts of, and on up into the heights, as the areas to the north and west of the town were referred to, at least in the running circles Denny had grown up in. Then the route would bring him through Mahoning Township and through the center of Lehighton, after which he would enter onto the D&L Trail to run the next eight miles, with six of those to be put down at an adjusted lactate threshold pace, on much leveler ground.

Within the first mile, the topography became quite hilly. Such as with the weather, Denny was hard pressed not to form comparisons with what he was primarily accustomed to in North Carolina; terrain wise most of the area was predominately flat, with the exceptions being the downtown section of Wilmington that sloped abruptly away from the Cape Fear River, and several of the bridges spanning the numerous waterways in the region, at least those that had not been constructed as draw bridges, and had to be tall enough to allow decent sized boats and small ships to be able to safely pass beneath. There were also several steep, though rather short hills that Denny often ran in the Carolina Beach State Park. But nothing like what he was currently climbing on Coal Street, along the northern side of Lehighton, which Denny was forced to take block by block, even at such an early stage in the run. The grade did abate after about a half of a mile, before the route being taken wound up the ridgeline that extended westward form the town, and helped from the upper boundary of the Mahoning Valley.

Denny looked around and absorbed the views back down into Lehighton, and of the rolling hills which swept southward towards the Blue Mountain. To the north, and obscured from his sight, the elevation continued to climb up into the Pocono Mountains, and all of its immense tracts of mostly undisturbed and untouched wildlands of old growth forests, abundant with natural, clean streams, ponds, and lakes. It was all so refreshing simply to ponder, and again very familiar too; Denny could always seem to hit the ground running around here, and almost feel as though he had never left, or at least the part of him shaped through the thousands of miles that had been laid down on foot. All of it never failed to welcome him home, in a silent, stoic manner, befitting the esoteric scope of the land.

And the hills, despite the extra effort required to surmount, did not bother Denny; on the contrary, he savored the challenges they laid bare at his feet. Plus, today, pace was not much of a concern the first half of the run, though Denny did check his watch when it beeped after each elapsed mile, more so out of curiosity, and habit. He figured that overall, the first eight miles would average somewhere in the low to mid eight minutes per mile range, as the sharp descents and numerous downhills tended to offset some of the slower tempo run on the climbs. After about forty-five minutes into the workout, as he was headed back into town along Route 902, Denny began to feel slightly warm, so a decision was made to lose the outer long sleeve shirt being worn when he returned to the parking lot. Which is precisely what Denny did back at his car, throwing the light weight shirt on top of the vehicle, before taking several swigs from the water bottle, whose contents fortunately had not frozen. Then it was time for the real work to commence, as Denny jumped onto the D&L Trailways, named for the Delaware and Lehigh Rivers, along which the rails to trails network mostly followed.

Thus, came the crux of the training run, which got under way with three miles at threshold pace. To be repeated a second time, following an interval of rest. In this case the rest would three minutes standing, or completely stopping between the sets. On the surface, a few of the aspects of the workout went contrary to what Denny was accustomed to doing, and came off as being a bit diabolical. But necessary? Sometimes though prudence dictated just doing and not questioning. He focused on ratcheting the pace faster, though for now the watch was not looked at, as the idea was to try and locate a sweet spot based off perceived effort, at least initially. The hope was to be able to lay down such miles in the neighborhood of 6:30s; a bit beyond where the Mahoning Creek emptied into the Lehigh River, and the surface changed from asphalt to dirt and finely crushed stone, Denny went through the first threshold mile in 6:41. It's fine he thought. Experience had taught him that his pace was likely to be very gradually increasing, within an ongoing effort to try and settle into a somewhat tight confine between not running quite hard enough, and at a speed that slipped across an invisible line, where the body couldn't clear lactate as fast as it was being produced. There was a certain refined art to it all, based off of science.

Denny periodically shot glances over at the Lehigh River, visible through the stripped deciduous trees. The morning sunlight glistened off her waters, which meandered lazily along. The base of the Mahoning Mountain also kept company, a few feet off of his right shoulder. Mile two was run in 6:38. Denny shook his gloved hands to create some movement in his arms, and reminded himself to keep it steady. In six minutes, a reprieve would be coming. He'd suck down one of the gels that were being carried in his pants pocket then. Salted caramel too. That would make for a sweet little treat. He hadn't taken any yet; for some reason the thought hadn't entered his mind. Denny never ate before he ran; a cup of coffee would sort of fill the belly up and suppress any appetite, though at times on a morning run he could become really hungry. Then again, often the same feeling might pass. Most runners he knew did eat something beforehand, especially if it was to be a longer run or workout. He really wanted to look at his watch, not only to check the pace, but to see how much farther was left in the mile. But Denny didn't, opting instead to focus on each successive chunk of trail ahead. He knew too that his watch was going to beep for the third mile a little before the wide trail way intersected with Route 895. A green metal gate would be visible at such point-recollections from runs with Trent supplied such detail. And runs with Suzanne. The path spoke without speaking. Under the turnpike bridge, itself way up above the ground, then around the bend in the river. Over the two short foot bridges that allowed runoff water off a steep hill to pass underneath, and not flood the D&L. The last section of woods. Denny had to be coming close; maybe a tenth of a mile remained? The watch beeped. 6:26. Nice, Denny remarked to himself, as he eased into a slow walk, before stopping altogether. He ripped open a gel packet with his teeth, and squeezed the goo into his mouth, all while continuing to count to one hundred and eighty in his head.

  It felt pretty darn good to simply stand still, in a small patch of sunlight too. The wind was barely noticeable either, unlike the pesky, cold headwind encountered in the heights. Denny did wish though after ingesting the gel, that he had access to a few quick sips of water. But he knew the deal all too well; it was the byproduct of not being able to find the means to comfortably carry fluids while running. Not that he ever had invested much effort into perhaps discovering an efficient, non-bothersome means that could work for him. Denny would manage today, like he always did. When on his traditional turf, all sorts of sources of water, such as fountains, sinks in public bathrooms, hoses attached to buildings, had known locations. This was obviously different. Colder temperatures helped though to reduce the need to intake liquids. The time had arrived to begin the next three mile segment anyhow; Denny wheeled around in an exaggerated motion, then stood perfectly still for a five count facing northbound on the D&L, before pressing the start button for the second time on his watch today, as he propelled the body back on into the forward motion of running again.

The first mile of the second set of threshold miles felt much easier than anticipated; the standing rest must have worked wonders, which was something Denny was loathe to do, preferring instead to slowly jog during the intervening spaces in harder intervals. He was enjoying the sublime serenity of the environs, getting lost for short spells simply watching the infinite flow of the river, as the water found its way naturally between larger rocks or snags of low hanging branches that could impede the journey. The river didn't need to think, it merely did. Denny himself started to think about being in Pennsylvania, as it had been a rather hasty decision to travel on up, based on a set of circumstances beyond the purview of his control. But he felt the correct call had been made, especially within the spirit of continually working on becoming less selfish. He didn't need to be reminded that his uncle had always been there for him. And he didn't like to second guess things too much once an operation had begun to the executed.

After passing beneath the turnpike bridge and on by the sparsely inhabited hamlet named Parryville, nestled in a hollow across the river, the watch beeped and displayed a time of 6:43. Denny realized why the pace had felt a tad too easy after the rest and turnaround; a conscious effort was then made to shift gears and increase the speed by a quarter to a half click, which sufficed to make the run feel more like a grind again, as he found himself back in the province where the entire system was being pushed close to the brink. Up ahead, the Mahoning Mountain became visible. Denny knew it would be right beside him for the majority of the middle mile; for whatever reason, such knowledge came peppered with mental relief. Anything helped, for a more intense, pinpointed focus was required to maintain the physiological necessities to run the last two miles in the 6:30s. He needed to slip back into the realm of becoming comfortable with being uncomfortable, and ride the beast all the way to the trailhead; any slight drift would have to be caught early, and summarily corrected. This is where the money is made. Talking about it is just talking about it, and doesn't mean a damned thing out here, unless one can, and does do it. Words are only words. Goals are just goals. All of it has to be worked for, and subsequently earned. Denny's thoughts had become really clipped again, but at a much earlier juncture then they had in the initial set. He was in the void; the only way out was to hammer straight ahead. By now almost a half marathon had been run, and Denny had been on his feet for over an hour and a half. But the little old mountain threw off some solace; why was not known. Nor did it matter. The watch beeped. 6:31.

Such was to be the life for the next sixteen to seventeen weeks, the running part that is. Not every run of course, but there would be many, many more like the one today. Some would be easier; others would be harder. Some weeks would be easier, others harder. For that was the natural law, as it pertained to marathon training. Denny had done it before. He'd probably do it again. If you were to inquire as to why, it's doubtful a sufficient answer could be proffered. Or maybe one could? A lot of it was primal, driven by forces that existed on a molecular level too microscopic for human eyes. It just had to be done. For people like Denny, who responded to the call. So much of it could be classified as spiritual. But even that would likely fall short of the mark. Long, wordy, technical books based on the principles of psychology, sociology, and religion could be written about it; or the whole matter could be succinctly summarized with a few choice words. Take your pick. All the blather helped Denny continue to chew up ground, as his mind must have slipped behind the shortness of thoughts that had mirrored the shortness of his breaths. The flow had scooped him up, and almost before any realization had crystalized, it had delivered Denny under the bridges connecting Lehighton to the other side of the Lehigh, and the village of Weissport. Two people on bikes rode by headed southward; Denny flicked a small wave with his right hand, tacitly acknowledging he was on the wrong side of the pathway, as he ran the final bend before the last quarter mile straight shot to the parking lot.

All sorts of graffiti art were painted on a cement wall below the backside of a row of houses well up above on First Street. One particular image caught Denny's eye; it was a cartoon character of a woman running, which bore a striking resemblance to Suzanne. It was within the realm of possibilities that whomever had created such a picture, had used Denny's friend for inspiration, as it was conceivable, they would have seen her in these parts, since it was her favorite place to run. There was also what looked like a spray-painted depiction of the old railway trestle bridge that used to cross the river. But Denny couldn't be sure. About any of it. He was though about to pop out of the other side of the void, in less than a minute's time. The throttle was kept down. The legs dutifully kept churning. Denny could see his vehicle up ahead. Right where it had been parked. And the water bottle. Setting in front of the back tire. It was all being sucked forward. Straight at him. Closer and closer. And then, it was over. Only a two-mile cooldown jog remained.

Chapter 4

As he drove southward on Route 248, Denny glanced, with a modicum of satisfaction, down the embankment towards the D&L Trail nestled across the Lehigh River. He hadn't been sure how his legs would handle the harder, long run after the drive and challenging trail run the day before. Plus, the adjustment to the cold weather, coupled with the much hiller terrain. Albeit the tempo miles had been run on flatter land. Nonetheless, as he passed by Bowmanstown, with her couple of well-worn macadam streets, lined with older houses creeping up the hillside towards more forested land, it had been a solid effort, and Denny could hope, perhaps a positive indicator of how the training might unfold and play out over the duration of the next several weeks, though a good chunk of the fall season had been spent methodically constructing a solid base of mileage, with the intention of building further upon. And there had been periodic, harder efforts mixed into all those miles, most of which occurred during workouts with the faster kids he coached in cross country. An athlete never could surmise beforehand how these things were ultimately destined to develop; injury, illness, burnout, psychological stress, major life upheavals to name a few, could all beset even the most prepared amongst the running tribe. Then again, the element of chance was baked into a big part of why so many of Denny's ilk relished setting lofty goals and chasing after them with the seriousness of children at play; there were no guarantees in any of it.

Denny parked at the top of the long macadam driveway that led down into the Hackenberg Family Farm. He got out in front of one of the two old barns, situated on either side of the entranceway and which looked like large gate posts, and slowly walked on towards the stone farmhouse. He inhaled the crisp, clean nighttime air; it filled his lungs with some more of that pure, crystalline goodness like up in the Catoctin Mountains. Chickens quietly clucked in the large penned in coops located off to the one side of the house; as Denny got near the front porch, he was greeted almost ceremoniously by a plump, fluffy white cat with black streaks. He bent over and rubbed its head while the feline purred; "it looks like you lead a good life around here," Denny remarked.

A set of three wooden steps leading up to the front porch creaked as Denny walked on to the large, sheltered porch. The sound of a bare first knocking on the wooden door seemed to echo far into the dark, stillness of the evening. The cat had followed up onto the porch as well, and rubbed up against the bottom of his legs. The front door to the house opened and Denny was greeted by John Hackenberg, with a warm, earnest smile etched on his weathered face. The man extended his two arms outward from his big, six-foot three-inch frame, and grabbed Denny up into a bear hug. "It's great to see you young man," he said softly, as he released his powerful grip.

"How are you Mr. Hackenberg? It's such a pleasure to see you as well."

"Come on inside and get warmed up. I trust you did indeed find the place okay after all this time? I almost texted the address this afternoon, but figured you'd call if lost."

"No problems. Just had to jog my memory a bit to find that turn off of 873 south of Slatington. I knew it was near that little church which sort of sits between two roads."

"Saint Mark's."

"Yes. Once I found that I knew it would be smooth sailing. Though for the life of me I don't recall that house across the street up on the hillside."

"You wouldn't have seen that before. Was built in 2008. A family from Indiana bought the land a long time ago and finally built on it."

"Must have been an adjustment of sorts after all these years to finally have a neighbor relatively close by?" Denny asked.

"It was a little different to actually be able to see another house from this part of the property," Mr. Hackenberg agreed.

While the two longtime family friends amicably chatted, Denny stole peeks into the dining room and kitchen areas, which were located through an archway and opening that separated the back part of the house from the living room they stood in. A decorated Christmas tree was in one of the corners of the living room, and there were white plastic candles in the windows, which Denny had noticed from the outside were in all the rooms. The interior of the home also seemed to congruously align with the visual remembrances Denny had, formed by countless days and nights spent in the place while growing up. Now the only remaining question was where was Uncle Mike, of which Mr. Hackenberg apparently sensed such a thought, for he said, "your uncle is upstairs right now. He usually takes a nap for an hour or two after his nurse leaves. We'll get him down for dinner soon."

"Yes, something smells good. How is he today?"

"In good spirits mentally. Physically….," his voice trailed off for a brief moment, but he continued, "well let's just say there are good days and bad days."

Mr. Hackenberg put his arm on Denny's shoulder, and lowered his voice to almost a whisper. "It means a lot to him that you've come up here for the holidays. Seems to have put a little bounce in his step. Well, figuratively speaking of course."

Denny smiled, which eased the slight tension that Mr. Hackenberg had felt for accidentally employing such a metaphor.

"I know what you mean about the good days and bad days. Such is the nature of having cancer. As we know. But let me say so in person as I have over the phone." Denny was aware that his voice had become choked with some emotion as he spoke. "I mean I don't even know how to even begin to thank you for all that you are doing here."

"You're welcome Denny. Our families' history extends so far back." Mr. Hackenberg let the remainder of the sentence evaporate into thin air; neither of them needed the thought to be formulated into words anyhow. "But I do need to check on the kitchen. Go ahead and sit down. Make yourself comfortable."

Mr. Hackenberg ducked out of the room and into the kitchen, and Denny followed a few seconds later and pulled up a chair at the table in the adjacent dining room, which had a view out the large windows into a part of the yard that extended all the way on back up to the road, about a football field or so away. The light from the rising moon, which was close to being full, illuminated the outside faint enough for Denny to be able to make out some of the contours of the property. A grassy place that many, many games had been played in; whiffle ball and kickball games during the long, endless summer days, followed by games of scout at night, which was their own variation of flashlight tag. Sledding during the winter months down the pathways that bisected rows of Christmas trees on the monster hills, before eventually coming to a stop in the yard below. And so much more in between, that was buried beneath the sands of time. But it was as if all of it was preserved in some kind of magic time capsule, able to be viewed at will, only though in instances such as it was for Denny just then there at the table. He was so absorbed in the concept that he hadn't even heard his uncle enter the room, until he felt something poke him on the back of his neck.

"Hey boy you drifting off into space?" Uncle Mike asked, with a devilish grin on an otherwise haggard, grizzled face. He put the cane back underneath his body, in order to support his weight. Although his rather short, squat frame was not holding nearly as many pounds as the last time Denny had seen him in person. "It's good to see some things never change," he added, before Denny could reply with any sarcastic rejoinder himself.

"I was sitting here pleasantly watching one of my past selves out in the yard playing ball. I was rather talented in those days. Did I ever tell you that I invented a pitch called the hover craft?"

"No. I don't believe you ever did. But I'm indebted to the fact that your pro career fizzled before it even got off the ground, so you could spend some time with this old man. Come here Denny," Uncle Mike said, as he motioned with his free hand for him to get up.

After they embraced for several moments, Denny added that even if such a statement were true, that by now he'd likely be retired anyhow from playing ball.

"Geez I forget how old you are," replied Uncle Mike. "For the life of me you don't look but a day or two over thirty."

"Compared to us everyone looks much younger," Mr. Hackenberg remarked from the kitchen. "It's funny how certain definitions change over the years too," he added, while opening the refrigerator door and taking a few items out, including a plastic pitcher which Denny guessed was filled with the family's famous iced tea.

Uncle Mike sat down at the dining room table. "So how was your run today? What was the workout again?"

Denny sat back down as well. Every time he did, it felt good to be off his legs. Something kept nagging at a muscle in his thigh, like he had never felt before. "Sixteen miles. With six at threshold. Mercifully broken into two sets of three. Went alright."

"What was the rest? Between the sets."

"Three minutes. Standing. Which I ended up appreciating. As opposed to slowly jogging. Felt like I was able to attack those last three miles a little harder." It always felt good after the fact to discuss what had been done. For it was as if some of the latent energy in the stated distances or times had shifted, from being something that had the power to generate a certain amount of foreboding when looking ahead at what was to be done, to something that once completed, now contained an underlying current of satisfaction, with degrees of pride mixed in too. Maybe it was a glimpse into what soldiers or war correspondents must feel after returning from the front lines? Of course, it was a real stretch to compare the level of danger and fear in the two.

"Sounds like this training plan has you diving right into the deep end," Uncle Mike opined, with a look of chagrin in his eyes, that looked as intelligent and alert as ever behind a pair of thick lensed glasses. "Heck it's not even Christmas yet."

"Yeah it was tough Mikey." Denny did somewhat agree with what had been just said. "But I think it must be designed to really callous a runner over time to the demands of trying to run faster when tired. Like today. I had already done eight miles before even starting any of the tempo miles."

"I should think so," said Uncle Mike, as he took a drink from a cup that Mr. Hackenberg had set in front of him on the table.

"Last week I had a workout with threshold miles where I ran three of them early on into a seventeen miler, followed by sixty minutes of regular running. Then another two T miles." Denny took a drink himself from the cup that had been placed in front of him. It was the iced tea too, just as lemony and robust as he had recalled from his youth.

"Do you need any help in there?" Denny asked Mr. Hackenberg, who was over in the kitchen again.

"No thanks. Carry on," he replied. "I'm getting out of breath just listening," he added with a laugh from in front of the stove.

"What kind of pace are you running these in?" Uncle Mike queried.

"The tempo miles? Good question. Last week I knocked those last two out in 6:17 and 6:18, which sort of surprised me to be honest. Especially considering that the first three weren't as fast. About eight to ten seconds slower on average." Denny paused and rubbed his left inner thigh. "Today I was thinking if I could average in the 6:30s I'd be happy. That's around on the scale where I should be, when factoring in the amount of time I was going to be spending at threshold pace beyond twenty minutes. Plus, it was coming off a bunch of climbing in the eight miles before. I ran up through Lehighton and into the heights from the D&L." Denny took another drink. The recap had made him thirsty.

"That'll put some wear on the tires," Uncle Mike stated. "We used to come down out of the heights as you call it past the Packerton Dam. Then head up into Jim Thorpe on some of our long runs. But the traffic wasn't nearly as bad on that stretch of 209 and mansion house hill. Now days it would be a suicide mission!" He banged the table with his fist to emphasize the point, then laughed out loud after realizing he had hit the table rather hard. Uncle Mike's voice had the endearing habit of rising an octave or two near the end of certain sentences, when some affectation was apparently deemed as necessary to accentuate what was being articulated.

"Mike's still got a fair amount of strength left as you can see," Mr. Hackenberg said, as he lowered a crock pot onto a heating pad in the middle of the table. "I assume you're hungry," he said to Denny.

"Yes sir."

"Well you've come to the right place kid," Uncle Mike said. "In fact, it's almost as if John has been fattening me up for the slaughter." He smiled the smile of a person who seemingly had not a trifling care in the world.

Denny knew, or thought he knew, that this could not possibly be true, for considering the circumstances, how could it be? But the man had always been a bit of a strange bird, self-admittedly too, though not in any negative way. He just had a unique way of seeing things, and apparently had adopted a rather gallows sense of humor as part of his attitude towards his sickness, though many folks can be relatively gifted in donning their own hand-crafted veneer when amongst the company of others. This rather enlightened outlook, seemed to mesh naturally with Uncle Mike's personality, and he tended to live outwardly in unison with whatever core beliefs were held within, at least from what Denny had witnessed throughout the years. So, the acceptance of his lot was likely rather genuine, and warmed Denny to see in person, which also aligned with what he had been told by Mr. Hackenberg the last several weeks, after he had graciously taken Uncle Mike into his home.

Mr. Hackenberg laid a basket of bread on the table, and finally pulled out a chair and sat down himself. "Would you do us the honor Mike?" he asked.

"I'd be humbled to do so. Bless us father for the food we are about to receive. Bless us for such wonderful friends gathered here before you tonight. We rejoice in the warmth of your everlasting love. Amen."

"Amen," the other two men both solemnly remarked in unison.

"Alright," Mr. Hackenberg said, as he smiled at each of his dinner companions. "All of this we are about to eat comes from right off of this farm. Including the venison in the stew. Which is from a deer taken by Lou during archery season."

Mr. Hackenberg turned to Denny and told him that his son Lou and his family would be here in a few days. And he had added with a gleam in his eyes, "he actually took the shot from the front porch. About sixty yards. Almost directly across from the pond."

"That's impressive. And we get to reap the rewards."

"Dig in. The beets in the salad we preserved sometime in October. I'll show you where we grow much of the produce around here when you come during the daytime."

"Yes, for sure," Denny replied.

"He's never seen the new barn down the hill off the backyard, has he?" Uncle Mike asked Mr. Hackenberg.

"No, I haven't," Denny answered. "I do remember all the raspberry bushes over in that area. And the blueberries too. Kind of near where all the rows of corn used to be planted, if I'm not mistaken?"

"Yes. Where the land levels off before the lower woods," Mr. Hackenberg said.

Denny had dug into the stew, and was eating bites of bread between each spoonful. "This is delicious," he remarked.

"Yes, it is," agreed Uncle Mike. And so they ate, and conversed. And ate some more. It was nice too for Denny to have a home cooked meal, or a sit-down type of meal in someone's house. He felt like it had been awhile, but didn't want to bother to think of when the last occasion would have been. And he most certainly was hungry too; according to the data extracted from his Garmin watch, 1,847 calories had been burned during the run. Some of which had been replenished when a hearty late breakfast at the hotel had been consumed. Denny had rekindled that symbiotic relationship of eating a lot to support the quantity of running being done. Calories out, calories in. Run to eat. Eat to run. Or something to that effect. It was a mighty fine set-up he thought, as he swirled a piece of bread inside the bowl of stew, allowing the broth to soak in. Last week sixty-two miles had been run; this week the totals would likely eclipse sixty-five.

"Have some more," Mr. Hackenberg instructed. Once again, Denny felt like the guy was privy to his thoughts, which was not only amusing, but comforting as well. The kind of feel-good comfort one tends to derive from the generation ahead of them, even when not originating from their own parents. Denny rarely saw his own father, who was currently somewhere in the remote reaches of Alaska. And his mother, Uncle Mike's sister, had been deceased for many years by now. Denny ladled out more of the stew into his bowl.

"I can send some home with you too. You got a refrigerator there right?"

"I do," Denny replied. "I would greatly appreciate that. Leave some for yourselves though."

Mr. Hackenberg had practically insisted that he stay at the farmhouse while in Pennsylvania; but Denny, being the type of person who hated to feel as if they were ever imposing at all, and also one who when possible, desired a decent amount of privacy, even at the tradeoff of having to spend their own money, had politely declined several times, though he did agree to stay over Christmas eve, when Lou and apparently Mandy and her family were also slated to descend upon the farm. Denny was looking forward to all that, no matter how chaotic and cramped it might become. It would be much better than being alone.

~

Later that evening, after Denny had returned to the hotel, he put on a heavy sweatshirt over the top of a long sleeved shirt, donned a knit hat and a pair of gloves, and walked out one of the side doors of the building, and into the frosty chill of the night. A dirt road was located off to the west side of the property which led to the Pohopoco Creek. A short hill deposited him at the banks of the water, which spanned a good hundred feet or so across, despite being named a creek. Denny sat down on matted, dead and dried weeds, crossed his legs in front of his body, and placed the palms of his gloved hands on his thighs, just below the knees. He sat there and watched the slow, methodical flow of the water, and listened to the soft sounds the creek produced, as it gurgled and slipped its way towards the ravine to the left, partially visible beneath the moon which had climbed half way up into the sky, until it all vanished around the bend through the woods.

After awhile Denny closed his eyes. He attempted to concentrate on nothing but his breathing, feeling the cavity of his chest expand ever so slightly as fresh air was almost imperceptibly pulled through the nostrils of the nose and the slight opening of his mouth, and then into the lungs; a few seconds later the relatively benign process reversed, as air came on up from the diaphragm and then left the body, as his chest simultaneously returned to a prone position. He tried to be acutely aware of all of this in the least conspicuous manner as possible, by being cognizant of each cycle as it occurred, while remaining as disconnected as possible, from any acknowledgement of what was naturally taking place. In....................and out. In....................and out. Occasionally the holy silence was broken by the sound of a car or truck crossing the bridge on the highway. But after a bit, it was hardly noticeable.

"Ask for nothing. Refuse nothing," Denny whispered into the night sky. Fittingly, there was no response, for none was needed. Both of his thighs now began to throb a little, so he paid heed and gently massaged them with his hands. They had been through a lot the past two days. Denny opened his eyes, and the Pohopoco appeared virginal and clear, brimming with its own tangible energy; for a few fleeting moments, the veil had been lifted.

Chapter 5

Snow had already begun to lightly fall as Denny left through the lobby of the hotel, and got into his car to drive a few miles to the high school track to meet Trent. It was definitely cold enough, with temperatures hovering around thirty degrees, for whatever fell to accumulate on the ground. By the time he arrived at the school grounds, most everything exposed had started to become coated in white. Denny took another sip of coffee from the hotel cup, and looked out at the football stadium and track and field complex, as he waited for his old buddy to pull into the parking lot. The Mahoning Mountain, about a half a mile to the south, had become partially shrouded by the greyish white clouds and snowfall. The top of which, though only about a thousand feet higher in elevation, had by now almost entirely vanished into the elements.

Two quick, successive beeps of a horn alerted Denny that Trent had arrived; he was driving the old blue work van of his which had been utilized a few summers ago to transport kayaks they had ridden on the Lehigh River. An excursion that had begun north of Jim Thorpe near Glen Onoko State Park, and had ended a good ten miles or so downriver near Palmerton. As Denny ambled out of the car, the wind picked up a touch; he pulled his beanie snug on his head to almost right above the tops of his eyes, and tucked the sleeves from the outer shirt and water-proof jacket being worn into the bottom of his gloves. Winter had apparently arrived in eastern Pennsylvania, and would do so officially in three days. The contrast in seasons was much more pronounced than it was further to the south, something of which Denny offhandedly remarked to Trent before they began running. And about how he did like to see snow, but was rarely afforded the pleasure in his part of North Carolina.

Trent led the way as the two former teammates fell into a rhythm; he suggested running their alma mater's cross-country course, which had been altered numerous times since they had been harriers wearing the school's maroon and white colors. More new construction in the past year led to a different design this past season, Trent informed Denny. The whole area though was nothing like when their teams had competed, as most of the land then was comprised of open fields and scattered groves of trees that ringed the perimeter of what was then the county fairgrounds.

In addition, there was a three-kilometer course that the middle school used, which overlapped a section of the five-kilometer course. Denny knew that Keith and Suzanne's daughter Nicole had run on the middle school team the last two years, and so had one of Trent's stepsons. Denny told him that a middle school cross country program had just been started in the public schools down in the Wilmington area, but the season had gotten all messed up by Hurricane Florence.

"And now you're up here running in snow," Trent quipped, as they cut around and behind the outfield fence of the girls' softball field. "First time we are going to get any kind of accumulation," he added.

"God I miss running in the snow."

"Probably not as difficult running in a hurricane I imagine. If that's even possible."

"Both present their own unique challenges. It is possible. Yes. But not right when the center is near you, or if it was a major one like a cat three."

"Yeah for sure."

"Did I ever tell you about the run me and my friend Xander did while Florence was still going on?"

"I don't think so. I would remember that." The two runners headed behind a soccer field, and threaded their way along a tree line that demarcated the far southern border of the school grounds. Trent and Denny were moving at a steady clip; the snow on the ground didn't act as much of an impediment yet, as only a half inch, to about an inch had accumulated, but it was enough to be able to clearly see footprints being laid down, when Denny looked behind them.

"Well as you may recall. Or more than likely don't recall, the storm lasted for several days. So, I believe this run took place on day two or three of the rather epic event." Denny's watch beeped as he was finishing the last sentence, which somewhat interrupted his train of thought. It read 7:39.

"Almost spot on. Mile mark is parallel to the soccer goal," Trent stated.

"That's good," Denny said, before regaining his thread and launching back into the story. "So, by now the wind wasn't as bad, but it was still blowing pretty good. I'd estimate thirty to forty miles per hour sustained. Gusting higher. We tried to run onto Wrightsville Beach. The town that is on the island, not the beach itself. But the police stopped us before the drawbridge."

"That's where it made landfall?"

"Yes. Came ashore real early in the morning the day before there. But by now it was sort of meandering off the coastline a little to the south, and not really moving much."

"Which was pretty unusual right?"

"Yes. But not even a mile into the run this awning that had blown off a restaurant's patio wrapped around my leg. Like a boa constrictor. Literally knocked me down! It's funny now to think about, and my buddy always reminds about it."

"I'm trying to picture this all," Trent said, as a smile crept across his face.

"So, we took the road then that parallels the sound. The waves were coming off it so high that water was starting to come onto the street. It was wild man. Everything seemed to be under water. Or about to be under water. And there were all these powerlines down. Whole poles had been knocked to the ground. And the wires were all in the water. We were scared shitless in a few spots of being electrocuted. But we figured by then power was completely out everywhere. Ours had been off for like a day and a half already."

"Jesus. Like something you only see on the news."

"Yes. Airlie Road looked like a warzone. Or like a tornado had gone right up the road. Huge old oak trees all down everywhere. Had to run into people's yards to get around. Or in some cases crawl under the trunks."

"Sounds crazy," Trent said. "I've never seen anything like that."

"Plus, it had started raining really hard again. Stuff comes in sheets. Sideways at you. Like someone throwing little rocks in your face. And unbeknownst to us, all these tornado warnings were being issued."

"Do they have those loud sirens? They sound eerie."

"No. Not then at least. But they were popping on cell phones constantly that night too. The warnings. Scare the crap out of someone if you're say sleeping at the time. Or are prone to be jumpy." Denny chuckled out loud.

"How far did you guys end up running?" Trent asked. He was keeping the pace pretty honest, well down into the sevens. They had almost finished the first, larger loop of the two-loop course.

"We ended up going I think fourteen miles," Denny answered. "Looking back on it, it was kind of an insane thing to do. Lots of people gave us shit about it afterwards. From a safety standpoint."

"I can imagine. Though I probably would have done the same thing." Trent glanced at Denny, who nodded slightly, a tacit acknowledgement of the brotherhood inherent in the sport.

Denny, despite the long oratory, was most aware of the tempo Trent was keeping the pair locked into, and conscious of the fact that it was being accomplished with little outward effort on his friend's part.

Finally, he said, "you're in half decent shape."

"Yes," Trent replied. "I'm feeling pretty good."

"Nice."

"Closing in on a thousand miles for the year. Be higher too if not for missing some time in the spring and early summer." Trent had wrenched his knee bad, while loading a couch for delivery at his furniture store. The injury had caused him to miss about two months of running. But since he had gotten back at it in earnest, he told Denny that he had also started to eat healthier, cutting back on sugar, and also on the consumption of beer.

Which was apparent to Denny; despite all the clothing being worn, Trent looked trimmer than the last time he had seen him. Though his musculoskeletal composition was more like a running back on a football team, or a strong safety. Trent's height was a few inches less than Denny's, and he took shorter, more compact strides when he ran, as opposed to the longer, loping ones his pal ran with.

By now the snow was coming down at a moderate rate; it was sticking to both of their beanies, and reduced visibility to several hundred yards. When Denny looked at Trent, he saw that there was also some snow sticking to his dark brown goatee, but he didn't say anything. Not that it mattered. The forecast was calling for three to five inches, which Denny did mention to Trent, as the pair of runners made their way past a huge rock, partially covered by snow. What was still visible on the sides and front face was painted in a variety of colors, with all sorts of writing scrawled on it.

"Chloe likes to paint lines from poems or song lyrics on there," Trent said. "Put these Beatles lyrics on last week she told me."

"Apple never falls too far from the tree. How is she?"

"Doing well. Gets good grades in school. And got a part-time job at Arby's. Did the whole thing on her own. We had no idea she was even looking for any work."

"That's just awesome. All of it," replied Denny. Then as he was wont to do, he began singing to Trent, "Chloe dance on tables in the French Club. She's always been given…"

He smiled. Trent was proud of his daughter, and still pleased with the decision all these years later to have named her after a Mother Love Bone song.

"We're hanging a right here," he said. "Course goes around the new elementary school on the second trip. Then ends on the track." They ran in silence for a bit, both absorbed in the beauty of the snow that fell, as it transformed the landscape into an idyllic winter scene; the only noise heard was that of running shoes gently mushing in the snow, and the din produced by all the landing snowflakes, which sounded like a chorus of fingers delicately tapping the earth.

Trent suggested a loop through the upper part of town to get a few more miles in; as they ran adjacent to the alley behind Ninth Street, he pointed and said, "right up there is the house Franz Kline lived in. The big white one behind those pine trees."

"I've seen that house so many times. But always from the front."

"Me too. For the most part. Winnifred Benfield used to live there when we were growing up. Her family. I've got the book in my van. Don't let me forget," he said. "Just finished last night for the second time."

"You've got me intrigued of late. I even went on-line last week to look at some of his paintings."

"Right on. I went down to check out some of the land past the D&L parking lot. Which used to be the old railroad station. You'll see some of the pictures in the book and recognize the land."

"I guess the trains would go all the way to Philly then?" Denny asked.

"Yep. Pretty much the same route that the trail uses," he answered. "There was another rail line that also went to New York City. Kline took that one a lot."

Denny's watch beeped again. 7:12 he told Trent, who used an app on the cell phone to record distances and times. The phone was in his pants pocket, but for some reason he couldn't get the audio function to work this morning.

Trent continued then, stating, "I walked on down behind Dunbar's to try and find where a baseball field used to be. And also, the approximate whereabouts of the first Gnadenhutten settlement along the Lehigh. But it's so different today with the woods in there. Makes it hard to tell exactly where things may have been."

"That's cool. Must be where my grandfather would have played baseball. He was a pitcher on the high school team. Charles Blose. He was really good too." Denny was trying to picture the area, and what it may have looked like in the 1920s.

"How's Uncle Mike?" asked Trent.

"In pretty good spirits. Giving me a little crap about my running. Can tell he's lost a bunch of weight, but I didn't say anything to him about it." Denny paused, and wiped some snow off his knit hat. "We didn't talk about the cancer. Last I knew he probably had a few months left. But you never know with that stuff."

After Denny gave the brief update, he was acutely aware of the moments of ensuing silence, and again the muffled, steady sound created by the two runners' shoes making brief contact with the snow, this time on the sidewalks.

Trent did reply, and said, "Jill and I made a prayer altar for him. We found an old picture of him running too. And Chloe did some drawings with biblical verses in a calligraphy style. Some nights we even light candles too."

Denny almost didn't know what to say; at first only a few barely audible mumbles came out of his mouth. He started, and said, "wow, that's..." but couldn't complete the thought. Finally, he did state, "I'll let him know. He'll be really touched. Thanks that is very kind of you all."

The pair ran in silence again for a little while. Snow continued to increase ever so gradually in intensity, as cars occasionally drove by, going slower than normal. The smoky, charcoal white dome of clouds by now appeared to be hovering just above the town. Despite being a tad cold, Denny was immensely enjoying the run, and offered thanks in silence to God for such a serene morning. Trent, in his own personal way, was deriving just as much pleasure out there too.

"This is what's it all about," he exclaimed, rather animatedly. "And it's so freaking awesome to be running with you again. Though I wish it was under different circumstances," he added, with a little more solemnity.

"Ahh it's all good," Denny replied. "Such is life. We all gotta just take it a day at a time."

While rolling along the slight decline on Coal Street headed eastward, Trent asked, "how many weeks is it until Boston? Race is in April, right?"

"You got it hoss. April 15th," Denny replied. "Sixteen weeks to answer the first question. Actually, to be precise, it's sixteen weeks from this coming Monday."

"Right on. Gives you plenty of time to get ready I imagine."

"I'm on an eighteen-week plan."

"Wow. That's some incredible dedication," Trent said. He suggested a route back to the track, cutting down Third Street past Saint Peter and Paul's Catholic Church to Iron Street, then back down Ninth. Denny concurred.

"Yeah I guess it is a certain level of dedication. And discipline. If my math is correct that's over a third of a calendar year," he said to Trent. But Denny didn't have to be reminded that it was a hefty commitment, that required a substantial amount of devotion, though it was nice to have it acknowledged by a fellow runner and friend. And Denny also knew for him that there was much more below the surface to it, even if he was again hard pressed to articulate some of it what it was. So, he stuck to the facts, and the numbers.

"I'd love to break three hours. Kind of a bucket list running accomplishment. To break three in a marathon."

"Damn. That would be phenomenal."

"And what better place do it then at Boston right?" Denny paused, perhaps for a little dramatic effect, though the whole notion didn't really require anything further, for the declaration could support its own weight so to speak. "I think I can do it," he went on. "It'll be harder to pull off on that course. Because of the hills. Not that there are that many. More because of where they are located in the race."

"Near the end, right?"

"The latter part of the course yes. Between sixteen and twenty-one."

"You've been studying the map," Trent said.

Denny glanced at his buddy and saw the wry smile on his face. "Yes," he replied, "I have. And there are videos you can watch too. I've heard it's hard to PR there. But people do. I've got a bunch of friends in Wilmington who have run it before. Some many times."

"That first-hand knowledge helps a lot I'm sure. Like us knowing our own cross-country course."

"Exactly."

"Oh shit. I almost forgot. I made up this long run course that I want you to run while you're up here," Trent said. "You'll get plenty of hills too."

"Where at?"

"Mahoning and East Penn Township. And a little bit of West Penn too."

"Tell me more amigo." Denny wiped moisture off his face with the back of a glove. As they ran on Third Street and passed the downtown Borough Park, the snow was coming more at them directionally as it fell. Plus, when the wind whipped a little, it seemed to kick the snow fall rate up a slight notch or two.

"It starts past my house by the old Farmer's Market. Then goes up Gilbert's Hill all the way into East Penn Township. That's a hell of a climb. Then it basically follows the ridgeline. Eventually you'll end up going by the West Penn Elementary School. After that it loops back around then down onto 443 by the school academy. Or whatever that thing is called."

"Oh, that building that used to be the car museum?"

"Yes. I've drawn a map on notebook paper. Hits a bunch of different roads but I think it should be fairly easy to follow. But of course, I know those roads much better."

"Why don't you just come with me?"

Trent laughed. "I'm not there yet."

"What's the distance on this bastard?"

"I clocked it on the odometer at 18.2 miles."

"Yowser."

"It ends with a straight shot back 443 to the starting point," Trent added, knowing though that such a detail only softened the blow a bit from the overall severity of the course.

"Can you run on there?"

"443? Yes. There's a decent amount of space on the left side," Trent answered. "Left facing towards Lehighton. Remember we ran part of that a few summers ago on that one run I do a lot? We parked at the Free Church."

"Oh yeah that's right," Denny said, as he did recall what Trent was referencing. "We saw Sally Freeman's mom's tombstone in the small graveyard."

"Yep," Trent said. "It's strange what we remember sometimes isn't it?"

"The mind works in mysterious ways."

"It'll be a good challenge for sure. I'm curious to hear what you think. And how it goes. I'll be able to give it a try soon." There was an air of resolve in Trent's speech when he said the last sentence.

"I'll do it Monday. Or maybe Tuesday," Denny stated. "See what I can lay down on your bad boy." He winked at Trent.

"Days like this I wish we could run forever."

Chapter 6

Keith sat at the top of the stairs and ran his hands delicately over a pair of running shoes, trying to recall the last time he had strapped them on, for it most certainly had been quite a while ago. No, it wasn't all that long ago; there were those few days in late October when it had been super mild out, a real Indian summer, and he had gotten some runs in then. Yes, right after Niki's last cross-country race, when she had podiumed in the league meet by coming in third place, outkicking a rival from Schuylkill Haven in the last fifty meters to secure that last coveted spot by six tenths of a second. Keith had been so elated and inspired and proud that immediately after getting home he had laced up his running shoes and busted out the door to do the Ukes run, though he had ended up walking most of the hill on Beaver Run Road, and all of the menace known as Spring's Hill. But he had loved getting out, and all of that did feel like a ways back now that he pondered it over for a minute. That was almost two months ago. Heck it had even snowed. Keith slowly slid the Asics over his socks and onto his feet and tied the laces into a double knot; if I don't go this moment, I'll never go he thought, as he walked down the staircase and into the sun room to put on some additional clothing.

"Hey have you seen my watch?" he hollered to no-one in particular; the only response obtained was from his oldest offspring Ron who said no.

"Damnit, I swear it should be in this drawer," Keith said, with a tinge of impatience and frustration. Now that the biggest hurdle had ostensibly been surmounted in the operation, that being the shift mentally to bring himself to start running again today, he didn't need any impediments to crop up that could potentially derail the worthy prerogative. But then Keith recalled Suzanne had been using his Garmin the past week on her runs, since the strap had broken off hers, and she was still waiting for a new one to arrive in the mail. She had most likely put it in the wicker basket on the kitchen counter top where they kept all the keys. It helped at times like this to be intimately familiar with some of Suzanne's ingrained habits.

"Got it," he announced rather loudly, and again to no-one in particular; this time there was no response from anyone who may have currently been somewhere inside the two-story house. And with that he was out the door and onto the streets again. The thought of simply not wearing a watch had never crossed his mind.

A few miles around Lehighton seemed like a sensible objective, based on the assumption that the necessary stamina to tackle the Ukes run was not currently present, coupled with the fact that it was almost dark out anyhow, and there wasn't too much light up in the heights. Therefore, Keith headed along Second Street, through the blinking traffic light at the intersection with Iron Street, on past the police station and Borough Park, then up the hill towards Coal Street, where he took a left and proceeded into the northern section of town. About a mile and a half into the run, Keith was pleasantly surprised that he was able to maintain a decent, steady pace, albeit much slower than if he were in any kind of aerobic shape. But it was encouraging to say the least. He had been walking a fair amount with the family's one dog, a chocolate brown lab named Ramey, and also lifting weights with Ronnie in the rec room above the garage, though not as much once the wresting season had begun a few weeks ago. So, he lumbered forward, knowing too that he had gained weight since summertime; the last time he had stepped on a scale in the bathroom, the number 187 has summarily greeted him on the digital screen. Then again, some pounds of muscle had been added, and on his six-foot one-inch frame, which was a bit wider to begin with, he didn't feel like he was that much overweight. Keith knew it was also a product of age, and if pressed he'd admit to being more concerned with how much more grey colored hairs kept appearing in his thick, black beard. But when back out on the roads, all of that seemed a little vain and trivial.

The cold air actually felt invigorating, as it was being drawn down into the lungs. Keith caught sight of the moon which had already begun to ascend through the purplish, deep blue hues visible above the hills to the north and west, the last part of the sky holding on to any color before the black tar that stretched out like elastic from the east overtook it within the next several minutes. It was such a tranquil evening to be outside, and to be outside running, even if the pace wasn't all that swift. But then again how fast or how slow he was currently moving didn't matter so much; maybe I'll see if I can pick up some speed on the way back Keith pondered, as he crested the gradual incline on Coal Street, and crossed over Eight Street.

Keith knew Denny was in town, and the skinny little fucker would be getting on his case if he weren't running, in that sort of passive aggressive way he had of telling you how far he had run, or how many miles he had already run in the week. A wan smile managed to appear, as Keith mulled such thoughts over, and wondered what his friend had likely done himself today, but he then recalled that Denny had texted him that he was planning to run some route in Franklin Township he used to take when growing up. Damn guy has probably run more miles in the last few days than I have since I was last getting out more regularly over the summer, though he hadn't really talked about it much since arriving back in the area. There always was something a tad peculiar concerning Denny's whereabouts; Keith couldn't quite put his finger on it, though he suspected sometimes the guy wasn't all too sure why he was back home to begin with, as was the case a few years ago. He didn't always press him on it either. Certainly, this time though it was understandable to an extent that Denny be here. Suzanne said maybe he also had another girlfriend stashed somewhere in town. That had brought forth a hearty round of laughter at the family dinner table the other night.

    Keith turned onto Ninth Street and headed downhill. For some reason he opted to run behind the old high school, and down the alley which went right smack behind what used to be the home set of bleachers at the football stadium. It was pretty dark in there, making footing precarious as some of the snow and ice pack hadn't melted in spots yet. Keith gingerly picked his way down the hill like he was on eggshells; he did slip once, but mercifully was able to right his balance before falling. The brief rush of adrenaline though from nearly breaking his neck served to energize him, like receiving a shock from an electrical outlet; when he cleared the alleyway and got to the sidewalk next to Mahoning Street, Keith upped the pace. He then crossed over Ninth Street at the traffic light and ran to Eight Street, where he went right, and headed towards the Community Grove Park. This feels good he thought, this feels real damn good.

    Work had been progressing well for him of late. It was such a nice perk to be able to perform the bulk of his job duties, consisting primarily of creating and then testing software simulations, from the privacy and comfort of his own home. By meeting a year-end project deadline early, Keith would be able to enjoy an extended period of time-off through New Year's. But all of that being said, some of the old stressors had started to creep back inside of him, especially when he had to commute into the office building in Bethlehem for meetings with clients, or attend the bi-monthly roundtables, as they were called, with his boss and the rest of the tech staff. Not to mention the quarterly evaluations with the head of the human resources department, one of the conditions that had been agreed upon, as a prerequisite for his re-hire by the company last year. Though Keith understood from a rational standpoint the necessity of most of it. After all it was he who had a breakdown. Maybe some of the subtle, nagging fears stemmed from the reminders that such interactions brought forth? And of the darkness which had pervaded the mind and soul, and the destructive pathways he had been led down? What was it that his psychiatrist had said recently about recognizing triggers in their embryonic phase? Keith couldn't recall exactly how she had phrased it, but the words spoken had all made perfect sense to him, and had reinforced the importance of establishing a consistent routine again on the roads, if that was to be the chosen place to physically stimulate endorphin production.

    A bottle of gin, a bottle of pills, and a loaded gun pointed at his temple were no longer viable fallback options; Keith intrinsically knew this, as he continued to slowly increase the tempo along Iron Street, holding his speed steady on the gradual incline towards Fourth Street. He pressed a button on his Garmin to illuminate the watch face; a little shy of two and half miles had been run, so Keith reasoned that he ought to see how fast three miles could be put down in, which would bring the run to a close right around where his house was located on South Second Street. Around the corner he flew onto Fourth Street; the legs churned, and Keith was aware of the swinging motion of his arms, making sure to pump them in a cadence that matched the legs, something he would always hear Niki's coach yelling to her and her teammates near the end of races. Races! Yes, races. He started to think about how cool it would be to enter a local 5k in the next few months. Training could be done in the evenings like this; maybe speedwork on Saturday mornings at the high school track like Suzanne sometimes did. Niki would probably go with too. She could start preparing for track and field season. Perhaps a longer run on Sundays? Like those he used to do when he was training for the Richmond Marathon. A marathon. Wow. Keith's imagination was being stretched out of its bounds now. But who knew what was possible again? He could feel his chest constricting; breaths had become labored and contracted, much more rapid then they had been earlier, as his legs continued to thrash through space and move forward, pushing through the heavy, leaden feeling that seemed to suddenly be flooding downward all the way into his feet. Damn, I'm really doing this he thought. Just push through to the next block. A car came up the street, forcing him to move closer to the one side of the road. Almost simultaneously, someone got out of the driver's side door of a parked car; "whoa," Keith hoarsely yelped as he adjusted his stride in midflight just in the nick of time to avoid crashing into the person.

"Jesus man," returned a female voice from inside a hooded sweatshirt.

Keith however was nonplussed, and kept the throttle on maximum as he took the left turn across from the gates to the cemetery, and pounded the asphalt down Alum Street as fast as he could will the body to move. Another couple hundred yards he told himself. His brain was being depleted of oxygen. Good lord I'm going to pass out on my first run back. What a story that would make. Ronnie will eat it up. Some kind of karmic payback he'll theorize. For pushing him so hard with the weights. I can see it now. Have mercy. Second Street. Finally. Keith's mind sputtered out fragmented thoughts, as his body was in a state of near collapse. It had been thrown headlong into the throes of demanding labor, and the heart was about to flatline. Or so it felt. Keith counted the houses which remained until he got to his. Eight, seven, six; fortunately, the watch dinged for three miles with a few left to spare, and with that, the mission had been accomplished.

He slowed into what likely appeared to any casual observer as some sort of drunken stupor of a shuffle. Keith used his right arm in an attempt to steady himself on the black iron fence that formed the front boundary of the small yard. He stopped, and turned around to look back up the street, like one surveying the carnage left on a battlefield. The totality of the effort started to sink in, in an ethereal realm beyond the dictates of language.

Later in the evening, while eating dinner at the kitchen counter, Keith asked Suzanne what the name of the website was which listed all the upcoming local races and contained all the results. Suzanne walked into the room and put her arm on his shoulders and replied, "welcome back superstar."

Chapter 7

The map, drawn horizontally on an eight by eleven-inch sheet of lined notebook paper, laid on top of the desk in the hotel room. It contained a fair amount of detail, including approximate locations of houses where people that Trent and Denny knew had grown up at. Which for the most part Denny would have to take the word of his friend on, since he was not nearly as knowledgeable with the rural areas of the two townships the course traversed, though it was all part of the same school district as the town of Lehighton and Franklin Township were to the east, where Denny had lived as a kid. The map was also not fully drawn to scale, which in and of itself would have been quite an artistic feat of cartography; Trent had duly reminded him to bear this kernel of information in mind, before setting out on the actual roads themselves, via the shoe leather express. But having the distances measured and subsequently marked between turns that would be made onto different roads would likely be of tremendous assistance. Denny had looked at the map's app on his cell phone to sort of synchronize internally what was on the hand drawn map; he had also been unsure about two particular spots, of which Trent explained to his satisfaction over the phone. And Denny had decided it would also be a prudent idea to carry the piece of paper in a pocket when he ran as well.

The first thing to do was to drive himself out Route 443 about a half mile past Trent's house. Denny pulled off the road and parked in front of the entranceway to the Mahoning Valley Farmer's Market. There was a closed gate in front of the dirt parking lot, which was next to the big, long desolate wooden building. It was a cold, raw, dismal morning; a low layer of gray cirrus clouds dominated the sky, though there was but a slight chance of snow flurries in the forecast. The kind of day that Denny could recall as being pretty much the typical norm for the next few months in eastern Pennsylvania.

Before he had left from the hotel, Denny texted Trent and asked him for a predicted time on the course; details were added to the message that the hope was to get in several miles at goal marathon pace, which was in the high sixes, but he was unsure with the undulating terrain what he might be able to sustain. Thus, he may end up running the bulk of the thing at a moderately hard pace; the specifics of the workout were six miles, followed by ten at goal pace, then two more easy miles. As Denny was about to close the door to his car and embark on the adventure, a text reply came from Trent that simply read, "2:20."

The run began ominously with a sinister climb up Gilbert's Hill Road, which seemingly cut straight up the Mahoning Mountain until it finally crested the ridge, before heading in a more southwesterly direction a little over two and a half miles into the run. Denny knew that he would have to lay up, to borrow terminology from the sport of golf, the first few miles, as there was little to be gained from any attempt to run faster early on the course. The smart thing to do was to merely survive the inclines, using the least amount of energy possible. Which is what was done. Soon though, he was able to open the pace up on a two-lane country road that weaved its way through barren corn and wheat fields, with their ubiquitous washed out yellows and browns that dominated the palette used by mother nature in the farmlands this time of the year. Interspersed were tracts of forested lands; one of those was Zeppelin Woods, named by Trent and his cousin Matt way back in the days of loading up cars with cases of beer and cruising some of these very same roads, trying to stay one step ahead of the law, and one step ahead of everyone's parents, many a halcyon night. Denny loved it that Trent had drawn the location of the iconic Zeppelin Woods on the map.

To the south was a view of the Blue Mountain, a few miles beyond some additional rolling hills that swept into East Penn Township. Denny soaked in the sight of the mountain, named for its bluish tint, as it sat there, forming the northern boundary of the Lehigh Valley, which extended towards the cities of Allentown and Bethlehem. There was a connection on a deeper, mystical plan with the mountain, itself nothing more than a small geological ripple created a few million years ago. But it had framed a part of the backdrop of Denny's youth, since it was visible from the bay windows in the living room of the house he had been raised in, as well as from the window of the bedroom he had slept in every night for eighteen years. The mountain was a constant, immovable presence; today it looked exactly as it had looked all those years ago, a rarity in the ever-changing perceptions humans carry within, as they ride through the tides of their lives.

The road dipped into a hollow, and the view was lost, as had the feeling of being numbingly cold that Denny had experienced when initially beginning the run. In fact, he had become gradually, almost imperceptibly warm; Denny took his gloves off and could feel that his hands were a little moist from perspiration, as was his forehead when he briefly took off the beanie being worn. He realized that he was over-dressed, and now might be a good time to actively address the transgressions that had been made prior to hitting the pavement. So just past the East Penn Township Municipal Building, Denny stopped on the opposite side of the road by a telephone pole next to a chained off dirt road leading up to some farm fields. There he slid off the pair of shorts being worn over a pair of tighter fitting track pants, and took off the lightweight hooded sweatshirt that was atop another long-sleeved Tec shirt. Denny carefully placed the garments behind a hedgerow of bushes in back of the telephone pole, in order to prevent anyone driving on the road from seeing them, and to have a landmark for him to use when returning later to retrieve. The gloves and knit hat were for the moment put back on; all of this was accomplished in less than thirty seconds, and done so without stopping the elapsed, running time on the watch. There are no timeouts in this sport, Denny said to himself, while quickly getting back up to speed on a short, but rather steep downhill. And almost immediately he felt better, knowing that the correct decision had been made to lighten the load. The competitive juices had kicked in too. What to wear when running can be a delicate balancing act, to say the least. Denny was accustomed to fighting the heat. By its own nature this was on the simplistic side of the equation; wear as little as possible. Cold weather, however, presented much more of challenge.

All of which served to bring Denny's mind around to Uncle Mike and the reason he was in Pennsylvania in the first place. Last night when he visited, there was an underlying sense of sadness, or perhaps resignation in the demeanor and spirit of his uncle; though he tried like the dickens to hide it, his words spoken seemed to be emanating from a far-off place, somewhere foreign to both the speaker and listener. Denny had also talked for a good bit with his nurse in private; she had tried her best to explain in basic terminology that certain blood cell types and counts were lower recently than what should be expected, caused probably by the changes in some of the medications being administered, though it wasn't all that unusual with such an aggressive form of lung cancer. And how it wasn't necessarily an indicator that his life was in any immediate danger, though it would more than likely have a rather egregious effect on Mike's overall physical condition for the next few days. Naturally all that could also have a deleterious influence on one's temperament.

For the interim, there wasn't much that Denny or anyone else could do except to tend to his daily needs, show as much love and empathy as possible, and continue to pray. A long time ago Denny's mother Ellen had shared with him that if one truly believed miracles can occur, then it was just a matter of carrying such faith along at all times, in the face of any and all evidence suggesting otherwise. For what existed in the outer world could be seen as mere impediments attempting to peel us away from what we felt to be true inside our hearts. Tests. The devotional silence of the landscape provided all the testament needed, as Denny kept on running on the side of the road.

A check of the Garmin revealed in about a minute's time the pace would have to be increased, as the scheduled marathon simulation miles were about to commence, ironically into the teeth of what looked to be one long hill looming up ahead. Despite the topography, Denny had been averaging only a few seconds over eight minutes per mile, ducking well into the sevens the last two miles, though they had contained more of a net downhill. Overall, a cursory check of the systems revealed that things were in good shape; the legs were turning over without hinderance, except for some very slight discomfort in the right knee, but that was bound to occur at times. Breathing was good. No stiffness of any note in the neck, shoulders, or back area. Denny had ingested a gel about forty-five minutes into the run as planned; he wasn't thirsty, and since unless he came upon an unexpected water source, there wouldn't be any chance for fluids until around mile thirteen, where he had stashed a water bottle last night, near where the route would dump him back onto 443. And last, his core temperature felt to be just about right, validating the earlier decision to drop clothing. Right before the watch was about to beep at the six-mile mark, Denny lost his gloves as well, tossing them by a mailbox at the end of a long driveway, located amongst a cluster of scattered driveways leading to houses well off to the right side of the road. A mental note was made that there was a bald eagle painted on the mailbox. Hopefully the gloves would be there later too.

After Denny finally crested a hill that had climbed through some densely wooded land, he was able to lower the pace downward close to seven minutes per mile, as he ran on a fairly level section of roadway that passed by another cluster of homes and yards, this time on both sides of the street. On a long, gradual decline, Denny opened his gait up even more, uncoiling his legs and letting things fly; a Christmas tree farm marked time, before a narrow bridge at the base of the shallow valley. A small but fast-moving stream ran beneath. The first mile at pace registered on the watch at 7:03; Denny knew the splits could be erratic, influenced in large part by the continual changes in elevation and terrain. Another long, but this time winding, moderately sloped downhill comprised a healthy chunk of the second pace mile, although there was a small hill going up thrown in; all of this brought Denny to the front of the West Penn Elementary School. It was a bit of a surprise then when his watch revealed a slower split of 7:16.

The map was pulled out of a pants pocket again to verify what was thought to be true; the school was situated at about the western most point of the course. Denny folded the piece of notebook paper and put it back inside his pants, memorizing the name of the next road to be turned onto. He told himself that he would eat another gel when he got to the junction; the guess was this would be in ten to fifteen minutes. There was still a decent distance to run before the water bottle and the chance to drink any fluids; a foreboding thought popped into Denny's head just then. What if someone had found and picked up his water bottle, thinking it was just discarded trash? Such negative conjecture though was dismissed as fast as it had cropped up; long runs always contained measures of the unexpected, and it was wiser from a psychological standpoint, to simply deal with any incidents if and when they transpired. Things can, and do go wrong; it's an inherent, adverse byproduct of spending a couple hours out in nature, whether alone or amongst a group. But there was no need to get worked up over something that may not even occur in the first place. Thus, Denny ran on, and tried to focus his attention on the next mile in front of him.

And the mile in front of him rose sharply up through another section of woods, before eventually coming to Orchard Road, where Denny was to take a right-hand turn, and begin the trek back down into the Mahoning Valley, towards Route 443. For whatever reason, Denny had the notion that once the forthcoming turn was made, the terrain would level off on the ridgeline, and then begin to fall; however, the reality was that Orchard Road continued to climb even more, and at an even higher pitch then the road which was just left behind. He ran by another farm, where dozens of cows lazed about in the brown, dry, grassy meadow behind the fence line. Denny was becoming a touch frustrated as he looked over at some of the cows, a few of whom returned his gaze without a trace of pity or care. Nope, he was on his own, that much was abundantly clear. It was his battle to fight. And what was that about negative thoughts and the folly of engaging in them? The road mercifully dipped a little as he ran past a big red barn, but then it abruptly rose up again out of a ravine. At some point the Garmin beeped; Denny didn't even bother to check the mile split, for he wasn't so much running now, as he was simply surviving. A few hundred meters going downhill would be just enough to allow some feeling to return to his legs, but each subsequent climb would punch it back out of them. Denny intrinsically knew that he had to come down off the mountain; he clung to the thought in the back of his mind, as the war continued to rage on. He clung as well to the words from something Jane Chantal had written several centuries ago in a letter; "this way is very narrow, but it is solid, short, simple and soon leads the soul to its goal…"

The goal at this juncture had spiraled to merely finishing the run in one piece, time be damned. This wasn't too far removed from part of Denny's philosophy on long runs and workouts; the primary objective was to always get the requisite mileage in no matter what, and whatever else was prescribed, be it marathon pace miles such as today, threshold miles, VO2max intervals, assumed a secondary role to the principal cause. But he wasn't fully sure if all of it made a whole lot of sense from a performance objective; that was the domain of those who held the advance degrees in kinesiology and exercise science, or had spent considerable time coaching in the marathon field. Practically speaking, however, the formulation worked for him, and for others he knew who subscribed to similar theories. And nine times out of ten, the workout would actually be completed close to how it was intended to be done. One could argue in spite of, or perhaps because of such a mindset.

Finally, the road Denny was on did begin the descent off the mountain, as evidenced by the drastic changes in topography encountered through another vast section of thick, wooded land. A small farm was snugly nestled into the surroundings, whereby the road did flatten out for a short span, before plunging downward, and back into the forest. The next two miles were clocked in 6:28 and 6:34; Denny felt too like he had been extended a lifeline, though he chided himself for becoming a bit too distraught earlier. The road eventually spit him out of the woods, and off the mountain, as the angle of drop abated; ahead Denny could see out to Route 443, about a half to three quarters of a mile in the distance.

He took the last gel out of his pocket, a salted caramel flavored one that had been purposely saved; Denny ripped the top off with his teeth, then sucked down the yummy contents and twenty milligrams of caffeine in two swallows, right before coming to the white fence that extended along the side and back of the car museum's property, or learning academy as the place now was. The water bottle was propped up against one of the posts, exactly as it had been left. Denny bent over and scooped the bottle up, twisted off the cap, and took several swigs of cold water as he continued to run. The fluids were much needed, and refreshing as the water rolled over his tongue and into his mouth; Denny took one final gulp before putting the lid back on top, and tossing it beside the parking lot. He swallowed some of the mouthful a few seconds later, and spit the remainder out right before crossing over 443 in order to run on the left-hand shoulder, such as Trent had instructed him to do, for the last remaining miles to the end point.

The first thing noticed was not the increased volume and speed of the vehicular traffic, but the biting chill of a damp breeze, blowing directly into Denny's face. But it wasn't his face that quickly became cold, it was his exposed hands, since the gloves that normally would be protecting and insulating the extremities, were sitting somewhere on the ground by that damn mailbox with the eagle on it. Denny was forced to tug on his sleeves and pull the outer shirt as far down his arms as possible to at least cover part of his hands. His upper body began to feel rather raw too. Not a good sign when there was still over thirty minutes of running left to be done, all of which would be in an eastward direction, directly into the wind. Now the decision to shed clothing, and especially the decision to lose the gloves, was coming back to haunt Denny. He questioned himself as to why he hadn't just shoved them in his pants' pocket instead? Though had he done so, the extra bulk would have ended up bugging him at some point later on. Looking back on it, were his hands really all that warm? Could he not have simply tolerated the minor inconvenience for the time? Since the route had headed predominately westward all those miles the wind, albeit not much more than what a student of meteorological terminology would call a zephyr, had not really been noticed much. But the mistake was that Denny hadn't thought ahead, that he might be in need of such articles of attire at a later juncture in the run. What was done was done though; he periodically blew on the uncovered parts of his hands, and continued to grind forward, chewing up chunks of the road section by section.

Denny went through the next mile in 7:04; good, yes, but it left him to wonder how in the hell was he going to be able to run twenty-six miles at a pace that would have to average 6:51, in order to break three hours? For again that was the magic number pace wise required to accomplish the goal; slip back one second per mile to 6:52 and the finish line time would begin with the number three, and not a two. Maybe on a good day he could hold the pace for sixteen, seventeen miles? Perhaps, just perhaps 6:51 could be maintained for a whole twenty miles. But for the entire duration of a marathon? Denny wasn't fooling anyone out here. Not today. Then again, today was today. Not April. That was months away. He was just getting started on the training plan, and besides which, experience dictated that once race day arrived, a runner could sustain set paces for much longer than previously thought possible. Or what seemed to be beyond the scope of one's athletic ability while in the midst of heavier volumes of mileage and intensity, appeared to actually be within reach come the day of the big event, once all the training had been done, and the proper taper and proper rest, had been taken.

All of that was so far off though. To Denny's left, the Christ Evangelical Free Church appeared, as did one of the roads Trent had taken them running on. He thought about him, in the context that Trent was at work now, awaiting a text with the details of the run. Someone had eyes on this thing, and a vested interest in it besides Denny, which fed some motivation to keep the hammer down, and finish the run under 2:20. He guessed he was a little under pace to do so, but didn't check the elapsed time on the watch. Denny didn't want to know. Instead he thought of Lydia Mandalay. She used to go to the Free Church. Was very active there too, and quite religious. She tried many times to get Denny to open his heart to the possibility of God, and to perhaps believe in something a little larger than his own ego and intellect, and his own notion of infallibility. But he wasn't listening. Or wasn't ready. All of that seemed so very, very long ago, as Denny continued to turn his legs over almost mechanically through the charcoal greyness of the December morning.

The final few miles everything went numb; body, mind, and soul, as Denny's line of sight stayed perpetually fixed on the slice of roadside fifteen feet in front of him. He was all too familiar with this part of 443, and pretty much knew were things were without having to see the surroundings; the approximate distance left to be run could rather accurately be gauged, without having to consciously process any information. At times like this the runner knows without knowing. Denny almost felt like laughing out loud by the time he was approaching the Mahoning Valley Speedway, whose dirt track lie off and behind the far side of the Farmer's Market; the last quarter mile of the run was going to be uphill, an apropos conclusion to the affair.

After a brief walk around the grounds to allow the internal systems to return close to equilibrium, Denny took a long drink out of a water bottle from the car. He threw on a jacket, and then figured enough of a space had transpired to cap the buildup to checking the final time on the Garmin. 2:16:37 the numbers read, besting the target Trent had given by over three minutes. A well-earned smile formed on Denny's half-frozen face; I slain the son of a bitch he thought. Now it's your turn Trent. Now it's your turn.

Chapter 8

The flames danced inside the fireplace to a silent beat; some leaped in pairs and audaciously stretched out in an almost violent symmetry from the center of the fire, while others appeared content to remain in a delicate, less ostentatious sway near the pile of stacked logs. There was an occasional crackle, or pop, when an individual flame shot up a little too fast; a small wave of invisible heat would be omitted, and felt by Denny who was sitting comfortably on a plush, soft reclining chair in the lobby of the hotel. He casually sipped from a cup of dark roasted coffee, as he sat there in an almost benign trance, transfixed for the moment by the visual artistry of the fire burning a few feet away. The Christmas tree in the corner stood silently, decorated tastefully with strings of small white lights, and an assortment of hand-crafted ornaments, many of which were made to represent local places of attraction, or contained the names of small businesses in the area, of which many were recognizable to Denny. Silver and red balls also adorned the real, live tree; an angel was delicately perched on top, and kept vigil over all. A couple conversed with the attendant at the front desk; from what Denny absentmindedly overheard, they were looking for a place to ski tomorrow.

Denny reached his free hand and massaged his quadriceps; he could feel them quivering through the black pair of track pants being worn. It was understandable. Those muscles had taken one heck of a thrashing today, and were bound to be pleading for help now that they found themselves in a state of repose. Over eighteen miles worth of ups and downs, but the entire network of muscles, tendons, joints, and tissues had performed admirably while in the breach. Denny's lower back felt slightly sore as well, probably as a result of all the elevation changes, of which the body was not used to. The two ibuprofen swallowed earlier would help alleviate the microscopic swelling in the muscles, and reduce the discomfort. The longer he sat, some of the highs generated in the afterglow of the long run had begun to wane, and instead, a certain melancholy began to permeate Denny's disposition that evening, the feelings of which he had unfortunately become accustomed to, especially of late. He downed the last few swallows of coffee, which had become lukewarm by then, threw the cup into a trash bin, and headed out the sliding glass doors into the oily black darkness of the night.

 A drive through Franklin Township, and around Lehighton, revealed that most everyone was absorbed in the holiday spirit, as least as measured by the number of outdoor Christmas displays and colorful lights, which were ubiquitous to just about every house on every street or block. In the Borough Park, a giant Christmas tree proudly stood all brightly lit and well decorated for all the townsfolk to admire. The lamp posts along First Street were all adorned with either illuminated Santa Clauses or candy canes; a giant wreath was hung way up high on the ten-story retirement building, which was by far the tallest structure around. Though why the scene may be any different than any other small town at this time of year, Denny didn't know, but it was the first time he had been here during the holidays in about twenty years. "Crazy," he exclaimed aloud, as he turned by what used to be the 7-11, and headed up Iron Street.

 Denny drove a few more blocks, then parked his car in an empty parking lot in front of what had once been one of the town's elementary schools several decades ago, but was now an office building, across the street from Lehighton's largest cemetery. He thought of some line in a Jack Kerouac novel about pretty girls making good graves, but couldn't recall the specifics, or where exactly it originated from. Denny zipped up his outer jacket tight, for there was an icy chill in the night air.

The rumors were true; he was most certain of that, though it was deriving from second hand accounts. And to use the word rumor was sort of stupid to begin with, since it connoted something more on the nefarious side, or that was transpiring in secrecy, or on an amoral basis. At least when used in the context of relationships. No, it simply existed as it was, and did not warrant any linguistic labeling that might imply otherwise, though perhaps by muddying the thing up in his mind this way, it helped Denny to feel like he was being aggrieved on some deep, fundamental plain, that could in particular circles, invite a little sympathy to be cast his way. Not that he was looking for any, or that such considerations would be of any help, for in the long term, didn't all of it serve to just keep the chains attached in an unhealthy manner? Of course, maybe it helped justify his presence, slipping as he was like a ghost hidden inside the dark crevasses predominate in the night.

Trent had seen the guy with her at a wrestling meet again last week; Denny could tell his friend was hesitant to provide much of a tangible follow-up, to any sort of questions that might have been asked about the sighting. And it had been months since Denny and Jennifer had spoken; the two had drifted apart, again. A couple of years ago it had all been so very different when he had been in Pennsylvania on an extended indefinite stay, fulfilling what he had called part of his vision quest. Their relationship had been rekindled a second time, some twenty years later, after both had been married and divorced; but evidently there was not enough magic to overcome all the things that laid between them, which had organically grown in the intervening decades, despite the couple's enormous, heartfelt efforts to bridge such divides. Such truths, and half-truths, were a tangled mass that was supposed to be buried, yet it still lived and breathed within Denny as he slowly walked up Fourth Street, past many of the houses that had once seemed to welcome his persona, like friendly neighbors waving from their stoops. But tonight, those very same houses retreated into the shadows; no trespassing signs hung from their cold, iron gates.

    Denny slowed even more as he approached her house; he was walking on the opposite side of the street, partially invisible in the saturating darkness of the evening. A tingling sensation gripped his body, similar to the nervous anticipation felt right before the gun fires at a road race; as sore as his legs felt, Denny suddenly wished that he was standing on a starting line, instead of staring down at the evenly spaced, straight cracks that separated the individual cement blocks of the sidewalk. He shuffled a few more steps, turned and looked across the road just as his line of sight was directly across from the house that so much time had been spent inside of; a string of multi-colored, blinking lights was wrapped around the bannisters, and extended along the perimeter of the porch. The curtains were parted; inside and up against the far wall of the living room was a decorated Christmas tree, full of more colorful lights and ornaments. And suddenly she was there, Jennifer, standing in front of the tree, reaching upwards to put something on it, or maybe move a decoration. Denny was too far away to specifically see. But he could see her curly blond hair moving ever so subtly, as it fell over her neck and shoulders and half way down her backside, as she leisurely turned around as if in slow motion to face towards the front windows and the porch and the street and Denny…

And then Denny saw him too. In the living room. As the guy must have stood up from the sofa, and walked over to the tree, to also hang something on it. She was smiling now. Laughing. So was he. Denny turned and, in a flash, began jogging down the sidewalk and back down Fourth Street; it felt as if tears were going to well up in his eyes as the stride length was opened up further, despite all the stiffness in the legs. In a mere matter of seconds, Denny was practically sprinting, like a petty thief fleeing the scene of the crime. The cemetery gates came into view; he crossed the street in a couple of erratic bounds, not even bothering to look for any traffic behind him. Denny fumbled in his pockets and pulled out the car keys, his hands were visibly shaking as the door to the car was opened, into which he practically leaped onto the seat, and then turned the keys over in the ignition, put the two ton machine into gear, and got the hell out of there as fast as humanly possible. For it was all a little too gut wrenching, and a little too heartbreaking. None of what had gone down on Fourth Street had been anticipated, nor had any possible scenarios been reasoned through. What had he expected to find there tonight? Denny didn't know. He didn't care. It was over. It all made him kind of angry. But most of all sad. And a bit lonely. All he did care about at that moment, was to return to the warmth and safety of his hotel room in Franklin Township. Denny wanted the images he had just witnessed to be burned out of his eye sockets.

Perhaps a good night's sleep would help? Who knew.

Chapter 9

"She could do it for sure. What was her time again at Saint Luke's?"

"1:54 and something. I think?"

"Yep. That equates to about a low four-hour marathon. Plus, the course from what I recall Suzanne telling me is pretty hilly there?"

"It is," Keith confirmed. "Though not quite as bad as this." The two of them were climbing up Beaver Run Road and into the heights; the pace had slowed considerably. Any slower, and they might as well be walking.

But Denny was just content his friend was out running again, attempting to lay down some miles on such a fine, December day. He intuitively sensed a smidgen of what might be on Keith's mind right then, so Denny said, "you know how it is the first few runs back. Gotta give it a little time to get on into shape like before."

"I know," he managed to grouse between audible breaths.

"Anyhow. Let's calculate this in my head. She's what, fifty-one years old?"

"Suzanne? Yeah. No. Fifty-two," Keith corrected himself.

"Okay. This means she'd need four hours exactly to qualify." Denny paused, then added with a touch of emphasis, "see, she's right on the cusp."

Mercifully for Keith the hill was finally crested, and a left turn was taken, as the run headed along the ridgeline into Mahoning Township. Somewhere around the area they had just trudged through, Franz Kline had painted his large, abstract-looking mural of Lehighton, from one of the vantage points where he would have able to see a large swath of the town. Or he had at least formed the mental pictures there to reproduce later with paints and a brush. Denny had been reading the book Trent had lent him, entitled *Franz Kline in Coal Country*, written by Rebecca and Joel Finsel. Though Denny knew very little about the art world itself, he was thoroughly captivated. Ironically, he knew someone in town who did know quite a lot about art, but he didn't want to go there today, inside his mind that is. It was a new day. Last night was done for.

The sun was shining; its rays bathed the landscape in luminescent light, and temperature wise it was almost what one could term as mild out, relative to the locale. Denny had even taken the opportunity to leave the long pants behind in the hotel dresser; he ran while wearing a pair of shorts.

Keith managed to laugh a little, after what Denny had said apparently settled in. "Well it's one thing to race a half at a decent pace. Whole other to do a marathon near the same pace."

"True," Denny agreed, in principle. "But she's tough. I don't doubt with a lot of training she'd get there."

"Probably a moot point anyhow," stated Keith. "I doubt she even wants to. Run a marathon that is. Or try to qualify for Boston. But what do I know?" he added with a snort. "We've only been married for eighteen years."

"Still figuring it out."

"Always."

The road, after a series of smaller rolling hills, plunged sharply into a hollow, with woods that extended further westward, and scattered, open fields to the east and north which climbed up and over another hill. Part way up, the two runners took a right on to another road that led past the bottom-side of the Ukrainian Homestead, which, though unlikely unbeknownst to anyone associated with the mysterious, secretive property, lent its name to the route Keith and Denny were running. A route that had been established sometime before Denny had run track and cross country in the early nineties, and had been handed down if you will, from one class of scholastic runners to the next; it was simply known as the Ukes run. Though the true course would have begun and ended on the school grounds where the current middle school and old track was located, and not in front of Keith's house. Such trivialities, were of scant importance at the moment.

Though it did spur Denny to recall a specific run the two had taken a few years ago. "Twas in about these very same environs I delicately and deftly placed the marathon bug into your feeble soul. You remember that?"

"Oh yeah," Keith answered. "Turned out to be my one and only."

"Well you never know my man." The pace overall was rather easy and pedestrian for Denny, but steadier and little more up tempo when descending the sloping road towards Spring's Hill. "Guess I have to work on Suzanne now if you're out of the mix," Denny added.

"She's a much better runner than I will ever be. Dedicated. And disciplined. Personally, I'm just glad to be getting out here today," said Keith, with perhaps a slight petulant twinge.

Denny took the cue and didn't want to say or do anything that could potentially disrupt the conviviality of the combined efforts on the asphalt; he changed the subject, and asked his friend how his job was going, and how the kids were fairing in school. Over the past few months, Keith had filled him in over the phone that things in general work wise and life wise had been much more copasetic than they had been in some of the relatively recent past. A marked improvement from where much of it was the last time Denny had been in Pennsylvania for any notable length of time, and had spent quality time with Keith in person. Some of the changes did not merit acknowledgment on either's part, yet were unequivocally understood by both.

Keith conversed a good deal about Ron, especially after the two began rolling down hill back into Lehighton, after successfully surmounting the diabolically steep Spring's Hill Road. He was a junior now, and off to another solid start in the wrestling season.

"Ronnie won his last match a minute fifty-two seconds in," Keith said, while the town began to reappear in front of and below them as the pair ran down off the ridgetop. "Got the guy in a hold up top and was strong enough to take his legs out from under him. Once he had him on the mat it was all but over. Solid pin." In Keith's voice was the pride a father has for his own flesh and blood.

It was well deserved too, in Denny's opinion. "Nice," he remarked.

"Yes it was. His third win by pin already on the season. And the guy he just defeated ended up pretty highly ranked last year at 176. Placed third in States in 3A."

"What does Ronnie weigh now?"

"He's been wrestling at 185. But can bump up or down a weight class depending on the opponent. Or the team. Sometimes there'll be forfeits in certain slots if a team doesn't have anyone who can compete."

"Damn. He must have really been hitting the iron with you," Denny remarked. "And the dinner table too." This time Denny laughed out loud, as he glanced over at Keith.

"Six and one so far and the only loss was to the state runner-up last year in Quad A. Wrestled him in the finals in a tournament at Northampton the other weekend."

It was a much smoother and easier run heading down Beaver Run Road, and down Ninth Street then on the way out of town, most especially for Keith. Not that the climbs didn't do some damage on Denny as well, but by now he was becoming acclimated again to the hilly terrain.

Keith continued on rather animatedly. "He finally bought into a lot of what I've been trying to tell him about the importance of regular weight training. Particularly during the summer and fall leading into the regular season. And of course, cross-country helped. Though as you know Ron isn't super-fast. But it was good for his legs."

"Yes. You obviously sold him on the benefits that running would have for his wrestling."

"Yep. As did the coaches."

"I try to do that with some of the kids I coach. Or shall I say with kids that we try and recruit out to run cross from other sports. Like soccer players."

"His strength has exploded over the past year or so. Started to notice a big difference late this summer. Which carried over into the fall, and right up to the start of mandatory practices. I keep telling him the key is to stay disciplined and stick with it no matter what."

"Like running."

"Yes of course," Keith laughed, with a hint of disdain. Furthermore, he added, "I see you still have a one-track mind."

Denny took some small measure of offense at such at a remark, though he probably shouldn't have; one of his failings of character was that he tended to be a bit too thin-skinned at times when elements that made up the core of his persona were challenged, even if it was being done in an off-handed or humorous way. Such encounters seemed to occur from time to time with Keith. There also was an almost invisible antipathy just below the surface that existed between the two, who had nonetheless, remained very good friends for over half of their respective lives. And all things being considered, the whole matter was rather minor, and not that different than the dynamics inherent in many relationships. Neither of them ever professed to be on the road to sainthood either; so, after a brief moment of silence, Denny asked, "when's Ron's next meet?"

"The twenty-seventh. There's a dual meet with Panther Valley at home," Keith replied. "Then they go to a huge holiday tournament in Bethlehem. Supposedly over eighty schools entered. Bunch of the top dogs from New Jersey. And a couple of other states too."

"Wow. Sounds cool. And competitive," Denny added.

"And very long. But yes, they'll get like eight, ten, twelve mats going all at the same time in the gymnasium. Might even have a second gym being used for loser's bracket I think."

"Dang!"

"Starts that Friday morning and lasts all weekend." Keith paused, and stipulated, "well all weekend if you keep on winning. It's double elimination."

"I'll come out to the Panther Valley meet."

"Great," Keith replied. "Ron will like that too. Though that's one where he could have a forfeit win. Depends on if he gets moved up. They have a kid who's undefeated at 194."

"He'll have his work cut out for him then."

"Yeah. That dude is tough. Saw his final match in Northampton. Pinned his opponent in under thirty seconds."

"It's going to a good old-fashioned street brawl," commented Denny, with a laugh.

"Varsity starts at six thirty."

A few minutes later the two runners were back inside the sunroom of the Druckenmiller's house. Denny pulled the details of the run up on Strava, and gave props to his compadre for knocking out over five miles with him, in lieu of his recent lapse in active participation in the sport. The details that the run was done at well over ten minutes per mile pace were not of primary importance; Denny reminded Keith to just take it as it came out on the roads and to exercise patience, and that things will gradually start to click again.

"Cheers," Keith replied, as he handed him a cold Gatorade from the refrigerator in the kitchen.

~

Several hours later, Denny drove out to Trent's house to watch the Eagles game. It was a 4:25 kickoff in Dallas. Beforehand, the two of them hung out on the blacktop driveway and shot some basketball hoops at an old rim attached to the front side of the free-standing garage. The promises the morning had first hinted at of a delightful day had come to fruition that afternoon; temperatures had soared into the fifties, and there wasn't a cloud to be found in the cerulean blue sky. A real rarity for this time of the year, and also bound not to last. Jill was in the backyard digging out some dead weeds that she said had been in the bed where the sunflowers and pumpkins had been grown. She asked Denny how long he was going to stay in town, and if he wanted to stop over Christmas Eve.

"Thanks. I'd love to but I'll be in Slatington through Christmas night," Denny replied. "South of Slatington to be more precise. At the house where Uncle Mike is staying. Most of the family is coming too."

"That's right. Trent told me. How is he doing?"

"We talked on the phone last night and he sounded alright. But it's hard to tell you know?"

"Yes. We were talking about him the other night. How Mike would always stand by each of the goalposts and call out splits during the meets." Trent dribbled a basketball as he spoke, then shot and missed; the ball caromed off the back rim and started to roll down the driveway towards the road.

"Oh yeah. He always wanted to make sure we heard the correct splits every four hundred meters." Denny hadn't thought about any of that in a very long time, but the memories came on rather vividly. "Yes. He'd bounce from the goalposts by the high jump to across the grass by where you'd be waiting to long jump. Then on over to the far goalposts in turn three and four." Denny spoke excitedly, picturing it all in his head. The track all of them had run on was unique in that it was five laps to the mile; hence each subsequent four hundred meters was passed a quarter lap further around the track than the previous.

"I never ran anything longer than the 400," Jill said. "But hey Sam ran the mile this year for the middle school track and field team."

"Missed the school record by three seconds," Trent said, after walking back up the driveway with one of the basketballs in hand. Sam was the youngest of Jill's two sons.

"Yes. That's awesome, you must be a proud track mom. 5:24 right?"

"Twenty-two," replied Jill. She looked up from the ground and smiled at Denny. Her dirty blond hair was pulled back in a pony-tail that stuck out from the back of a tied-dyed bandana on her head. A little bit of sweat on her forehead glistened in the sunlight. "Don't be cheating him out of any seconds," she added.

"How's Silas doing" Denny asked.

"Hopefully okay," Jill said, with a bemused countenance. "They're over at their Dad's until Christmas. He did well in Cross Country this fall but I'm guessing you already know that."

"Got into the eighteens," Trent concurred. "Not bad for a sophomore."

Silas was classmates with Jennifer's oldest son Micah, and had been pretty good friends for a while, especially when they had wrestled together. But Denny wasn't sure if such was the case nowadays, and didn't bring the matter up or ask about it. He hadn't mentioned anything to Trent or anyone about going by her house, and certainly did not feel any urge to do so now. It would remain his little secret. Instead he picked up a partially deflated basketball from the yard and took a few foul shots, standing behind the piece of white tape affixed to a spot on the driveway, which did appear to be fifteen feet away from the rim. Denny sank the first three shots he attempted, walking under the basket to pick the ball up each time as it would sort of thud to a stop near where it fell through the net.

"I'm going in to check on the food," Jill announced, as she opened the side door to the house and headed inside. "Hope you're hungry," she added over her shoulder, presumably to Denny.

"You fish this morning?" he asked Trent. Denny knew that every Sunday morning in the fall he habitually went somewhere on the Lehigh River, and usually dropped a kayak into the water at the park near Bowmanstown, which was also right off the D&L Trail. Sometimes the excursion would include a run. It would help take Trent's mind off the upcoming game for a few hours.

"Yes. Met Joey. He cut out a little after twelve for the Steelers game." Trent pulled his cell phone out of his pants pocket, looked at it quizzically for several seconds as he ducked into the garage and out of the direct sunlight, then added, "I'm down thirty-two now. Shit. Looks like Ryan just threw another td pass."

"Bad time to be playing against him. He's hot," Denny said. He shot again, and missed. An airball too from around three-point range at what would be the top of the key.

"Thirty-eight now. I'm down to a forty-four percent chance of winning," Trent stated as he held the phone in his hands, hoping perhaps if he stared at the screen long enough without blinking something would change in his favor. He was playing in the championship game of the fantasy football league they were in named the Lehighton Mob; Denny's team had failed to make the four team playoffs this year.

"I ran with Keith this morning. Did the Ukes loop from his house."

"Right on. I did a hard three miles on the D&L towards the gap after Joey left. Last mile I got down into the six thirties. Felt like my chest might explode," Trent said.

"You animal."

"How's Keith? Saw him at the meet last week but didn't get a chance to say hi. His son looks really good."

"Yeah he was telling me on the run. I'm going to go to the meet Wednesday night."

"For real? That's cool," Jill remarked. She had come back outside and was dragging a large box of what looked like old junk. Her dog Carly dutifully followed alongside wagging her tail.

"Yes, I'll be there."

"I'll see if I can get there after work. Depends if any deliveries," said Trent. He grabbed on to the other end of the box and helped Jill set it down inside the garage. "You want any gourds to take down to North Carolina?" he asked.

"Let's just chuck these," Jill said, before Denny could respond.

"We grew a whole bunch of hot peppers again this summer," Trent said as he walked across the driveway. "I pickled and canned a lot of habaneros and cut the chilis and ground into a powder. And I have some more drying on strings upstairs in the garage. I'll give you some of those to take back. They'll keep anywhere."

"For sure. Thanks."

A few minutes before game time they headed inside. Trent had a flat-screen television set up in a small room off to the side of the interior garage and recreational room in the downstairs level of the house. There were only two chairs in the room, one today for each of them, as Trent did not like to be distracted whatsoever when watching Eagles games, of which Denny was quite familiar with, either in person, or through anecdotal evidence relayed to him throughout the years. House rules were house rules, and certainly Denny had no objections, for he felt the same way. There was a replica player's locker up against one of the walls, that contained numerous jerseys; Trent solemnly and studiously opened it up and leafed through a few, before pulling out a green Randall Cunningham jersey, which he pulled on over top the shirt he was wearing.

"Your turn," he said.

Denny walked over and checked out what was all inside the locker, then decided he'd don a black Brian Dawkins jersey, as he had always been one of his favorite professional athletes, let alone Eagles players. The two uniformed fans took their respective seats; Trent cracked open a can of a beer, and Denny twisted the lid off of a Dr. Pepper bottle, just as the football was about to be kicked off.

Chapter 10

Denny arrived at the Hackenbergs at twilight; there was always an indescribable touch of magic and anticipation in the air on Christmas Eve, and even more so to him this year up in the colder climate of his home state of Pennsylvania. Unfortunately, there was no snow on the ground, and none in the forecast for that night or the next day, though temperatures had returned to where they should be for early winter, which did serve to make the occasion feel more festive, in an almost sublimely religious way to Denny. Whatever sadness was felt a few nights ago, he prayed would remain behind for now.

A purple, cobalt blue haze hung just above the hills to the west, the final remnants of daylight. Denny noticed two other vehicles parked near the bottom of the driveway, and figured they belonged to Mr. Hackenberg's offspring. Two of them were expected to come, along with their families. Uncle Mike's own son would not be attending, as he and his wife and two children were going to his in-laws who lived in the same area of northern New Mexico that they resided in, near the city of Santa Fe. Cecelia, Mike's own wife for well over thirty years, and Denny's aunt, had passed away several years ago. Denny was about the only flesh and blood Uncle Mike was still close to. There was a long-standing feud, for lack of a better word, between his son Roger and Mike of which Denny was not aware of the particulars, as it was just one of those things that was never discussed. Not much thought was ever given to it by Denny, except of late because of the situation that had materialized with his uncle's deteriorating health.

Smoke could be seen rising out of the chimney, the smell of which wafted towards Denny as he approached the farmhouse. He lingered in the yard for a bit, with a backpack slung over his shoulder, watching and listening to the sounds of the chickens busily scurrying around in the large pens; did they know what day tomorrow was, which celebrated the birth of Jesus over two thousand years ago?

"You going to stand there all evening in the yard like some misplaced stage prop that fell off the truck a little south of Quakertown?"

It had to have been pushing twenty years, but the sound of Lou's voice was unmistakable, as was the uncanny, original wit which used to entertain and amuse Denny to all hours, all those years ago. "I thought it might prove to be interesting to see how long I could remain motionless out here until someone perchance finally took notice of my presence. Perhaps, I would merely blend into the natural scenery?"

Denny walked over and shook Lou's hand. "So good to see you old sport."

Lou grasped his hand and pulled him into a hug. "You as well Denny," he replied. "Gosh you look like you've only slightly aged over the years. Though it relieves me to some extent to see you're losing some of your hairline too."

"Ahh you had to remind me."

"Happens to even the most debonair of the lot," Lou said. Though he still to Denny seemed to have a nice thick mop of black hair that fell over his ears and back of his neck. The glasses Lou always wore were now a smaller, more sophisticated looking pair. The devilish glint was still in his light blue eyes, apparent even in the relative darkness of the yard.

"Let's go inside. I want to introduce you to my better half. And our son."

"Sounds good to me mate." Denny followed Lou into the toasty confines of the house, which was already abuzz with activity, in anticipation of the evening, and the big day ahead tomorrow. He met Lou's wife Michelle, and their son Rene who was six years old, and had been adopted and brought to the United States from a refugee camp for orphans in the country of Haiti. Lou's sister Mandy was there in the house as well with her husband and their two daughters; Denny was told they were ten and twelve years old, and in fourth and sixth grades, and that the oldest was attending a brand-new middle school in the Lower Merion School District. Uncle Mike sat on a reclining chair in the living room, taking in all the boisterous gaiety with a slight grin on his face, happy to entertain any of the kids when they actually dared to cease moving for a few precious minutes.

In the kitchen, Denny and Lou resumed their conversation over glasses of iced tea from a freshly brewed pitcher; it seemed the two of them had much in common still, some two decades later. Lou was a writer for a newspaper in central Pennsylvania, and also moon-lighted as a self-proclaimed ghost hunter and historian, which was quite the eclectic mix Denny told him. He had also recently published a book, and had written several magazine articles about the paranormal. A subject that Denny found fascinating, since he knew little about; he asked Lou what a typical investigation was like.

"Most of the time, what we are essentially doing is assuring say a homeowner that everything is fine," Lou said. "Those weird noises they're hearing in the middle of the night actually have a logical explanation. Like a pipe expanding when hot water flows through. Or a tree in the yard creating an eerie sound when some of its branches rub against each other in a particular way."

"What about when someone claims to be seeing apparitions?"

"I ask them if they have a drug problem?"

Denny laughed so hard he almost choked on his tea. "So, it's a little different than depicted in the movie Ghostbusters I guess?"

"Yes. Though you are not alone on such sentiments," Lou replied. He was wearing a black Clash tee shirt underneath an opened, button-down flannel shirt, which Denny just then happened to take notice of.

"Hey remember when we went to see it at the theatre?" Lou asked. "We all piled into Mom's purple station wagon and went to Becky's Drive-In."

"Heck yeah!" Denny exclaimed. "Must have been why the movie popped into my head. Bridgette got sick after the first movie from eating too many milk duds. Or maybe it was buttered pop-corn?"

"Or both. Gosh you're right. Totally had forgotten that. It took your sister years to live that whole infamous episode down."

"I know. We'd always have to ask her if she needed to bring a barf bag any time we went to the movies. Or out just about anywhere for a while," stated Denny. "We were mean," he added too.

"Yes. We could be unmerciful," Lou agreed. "But it was a whole lot of good times too. How's Bridgette doing these days? I see she's out in sunny California."

"Yes. Loving life out on the left coast. Got a promotion as some kind of account executive near West Hollywood," Denny answered. "I was just there to visit them in August. Which reminds me I have to tell your sister later about some of the trail running I did in the San Gabriel Mountains. But I digress. I'll send her your regards."

"Please do." Lou's son wandered into the kitchen and tugged on his arm, as if to try and drag him into the adjoining room.

"Rene don't be so shy. Why don't you show Denny your new race car?"

Rene looked up at his Dad, then looked at Denny rather inquisitively, as if to judge the merits of such an endeavor, before scrunching his face up all tight and running into the small play room, which also doubled as a library and computer den, loosely speaking. The room had seemed so much bigger when they had been kids themselves, Denny remarked to Lou, who concurred with the observation. They ducked into the room as well; sticking out from one of the shelves built into the wall, and facing forward was a copy of Lou's book, *The Untold History of Lock Haven, the Underground Chronicles*.

Denny took the book into his hands, and said to Lou, "man this is super cool. I must admit it's been a sort of secret ambition of mine for some time to have my own book out one day, which will hopefully adorn a bookshelf like this." He started casually flipping through the pages after looking at the back cover, that included a picture of the author standing inside an old jail cell.

"Thanks. And I know exactly what you mean. It's safe to say that at least two homes now have this book in their private library collections," Lou said, as Denny handed him the book.

"And the other one is in my own house," he added, with a good-natured laugh.

"Well good for you. I can only imagine all the work that went into it. And you have to start somewhere right?"

"Hey it's a labor of love. Like playing in a garage band. This thing here took almost four years to bring to print," Lou held the book in the air as he spoke.

"Move it Uncle Lou," came a friendly, yet serious request from Mandy's youngest girl Sophia, as she came careening into the room driving Rene's race car. Denny had seen the approach coming out of the corner of his eye, and had wisely taken a step or two backwards.

"This guy is a celebrity," he said as he pointed at Lou.

"What's that?" she asked, before leaving the room and wheeling herself into the kitchen, well before any type of a response could be proffered.

"Fans are tough to cultivate."

"So I've been told," mumbled Denny, above his glass of iced tea. There was work for him to be done, lots of work, though he rarely spoke to anyone about it. The whole enterprise mostly germinated inside of his mind, in some dimly lit nook; he fed the idea just enough nourishment to keep the thing alive, while mostly idly dreaming about a day that he could class himself amongst those who were published authors like Lou. Denny did make a verbal note to his old friend to solicit advice at some juncture down the road; for the time being he let the matter ride, and walked outside at the behest of Mr. Hackenberg, who was carrying a large tray of venison steaks that had been marinating in the refrigerator since the night before.

Out behind the house, and up a small hill, there was a fire pit that had about two-foot-high stacks of cinder blocks on three of the sides, and a black metal grate on top, which all had been constructed to cook food upon. In response to Denny asking about the effects of cold air, Mr. Hackenberg slid some kind of home built aluminum contraption over the whole thing, demonstrating how the heat from the fire would be mostly trapped inside, similar to how an oven bakes food, or a portable gas grill when its lid was closed. The deer meet smelled delicious even before it began to be cooked. Denny helped pile up in the pit what he was told was pecan wood that an old hunting buddy had dropped off sometime in the fall; the wood itself was from northern Florida. Mr. Hackenberg struck a kitchen match on one of the cinder blocks and dropped it into kindling that had been placed on top of the wood; a fire swiftly came to life.

Once they had carefully laid the steaks one by one atop the grating and closed the pit, Mr. Hackenberg turned to Denny, and without any verbal pretense, told him that the outlook for Uncle Mike was not good; he attempted as best as he could to explain much of the latest medical prognosis given from the primary physician yesterday. The rather grave sounding details meant little in and of themselves to Denny, thus he queried what it all meant in practical terms, and what all he or anyone could do for him.

"I would say there is scant chance of him beating this. Which of course is what we all thought all along." The voice delivering the sober news was serious, yet soothing. He continued, "so it's probably looking like he's got several more weeks. Maybe a few months. But it's highly doubtful for anything much beyond that."

After a short pause, Mr. Hackenberg opened up the covering and carefully flipped the steaks over, with the deft touch of one who takes the art of cooking as a sincere pleasure. The meat was sizzling; its juices replied to the ebb and flow of the fire. Denny was captivated by the optics and acoustics of the culinary show. Plus, the aroma was intoxicating. He was hungry too. All the distractions served to briefly take him away from the news at hand; Denny did agree that what he had been told now was pretty much in line with his own thoughts at this point, and had been all along, though it was human nature to still cling, even if tenuously, to the chance that some sort of miracle was to still come about. Whether or not his uncle thought along such lines Denny did not know; the man appeared to be maintaining such a wondrous state of levity and grace daily about his circumstances, almost beyond comprehension to those in his affectionate orbit. So many of his uncle's long-time friends continued to reach out and, in some cases, stop by as well; it was safe to say that he was never all that alone in any of this.

Mr. Hackenberg echoed Denny's observations with a few of his own, and added that we could all ultimately profit from such an example of dignity. But it had to contain its fair share of difficulties as well, many of which Uncle Mike bore in silence, or in the counsel of his maker.

Both of them had lost immediate family to cancer; it was going on fifteen years since Mr. Hackenberg's lovey and kind-hearted wife Maggie had passed. And Denny's mom had succumbed to the disease as well. The two men seemed to simultaneously catch themselves from their own morbid thoughts; the conversation shifted to other topics, something of which Mike would have insisted upon rather vociferously, had he been present in the backyard with them.

By now the farm was enshrouded in darkness, and save for the sounds of the fire and the food being cooked, a silvery, holy silence had enveloped the entire hollow. Denny took his bare hands out of his pockets and blew on them. Overhead, countless stars glistened in the jet-black sky; the moon, not even at a quarter crescent, had begun to rise in the western sweep of the horizon visible above the not too distant wooded hilltops. Somewhere well off to the north, Saint Nicholas was preparing to venture out on his sled, pulled along by all his trusted reindeer, for yet another journey to deliver joy and mirth to the multitudes of good little boys and girls scattered all over this big tender world of ours.

~

    The Christmas Eve meal was divine, almost too much if that were at all possible. Venison steaks, broiled trout, sweet potatoes, green bean casserole, a tossed salad, fresh baked buttered rolls; most of it all originating from the farm. Blueberry and raspberry pies, from the preserves that had been canned and stored in the root cellar beneath the house. Denny could barely move after he finished eating, a solid hour and a half after the dinner had commenced. Uncle Mike looked at him from across the table all the adults were seated at. He leaned back in his chair and rubbed his belly, and with a beaming, playful grin on his face exclaimed, "get ready to do this again tomorrow kid!"

    Later in the evening and after all the young ones had been put down to sleep in various bedrooms upstairs, Denny, Uncle Mike, and Mandy found themselves an interlude to talk shop. Denny had carried forth with keeping his uncle updated almost daily with his running, but many days it was more just a numerical accounting of what had been completed on the roads or trails; tonight though, he was able to elucidate in depth as to how he was feeling and handling the various aspects of the training plan. He welcomed his uncle's input; after all, the guy was a veteran of many marathons himself, and had been an active runner for decades, up until he had first started getting ill a few years ago. Plus, Denny knew, and certainly his uncle knew that he knew as well, that being intimately involved with his nephew's running was a vital and welcome outlet amidst the battle being waged by himself. Though if Denny had couched this aspect of their relationship in such verbiage, a friendly rebuke would have likely been forthcoming, since words like fight and battle weren't a part of the lexicon being used, on the rare occasions when the cancer was more overtly discussed. For Uncle Mike felt that to employ such terms formed an unhealthy relationship with the malady itself. Perhaps that didn't make perfect sense to Denny, but it did to his uncle, and that was what mattered more.

"How many miles are you running per week?" Mandy asked. The two of them were seated on the couch next to Uncle Mike, who occupied his usual spot on the reclining chair nearest to the fireplace. She was an accomplished and very dedicated runner herself, having gotten into the sport big-time with a Team in Training program after her mother had passed away. The last few years she had led scores of runners through the requisite rigors needed to complete marathons of their own. By now Mandy had run well over twenty road marathons herself, and a bunch of ultras too, which Denny knew she had been pursuing more the last several years. He always enjoyed viewing her pictures posted on-line, as well as reading many of the subsequent race reports on her blog. She was real wiry and lean looking in person, and probably stood about five-nine; her almost girlish looks belied the fact that she was also over forty years old.

"I've been topping out in the sixties, close to seventy," Denny replied. "I started cycling the miles upward in the fall. After we got rid of a good bit of the heat and humidity."

"Oh yeah that summer weather could linger well into October." Mandy had lived for a few years in Charleston, South Carolina after college. "Impressive numbers too," she also said.

"Yes, they are," Uncle Mike chimed in. "Boy I sure do recall those days too," he continued, without any trace of resignation in his voice. He did have on a heavy wool sweater over top a long sleeve shirt, despite all the warmth being thrown off by the fire. But apparently another symptom was the feeling of always being cold.

"What did you used to do back in the day?" Mandy asked. "I've heard and read some stories about how hard core all of you were in the seventies and eighties." She raised the volume of her voice when speaking directly to Uncle Mike, like one would do with someone who is hard of hearing; both Denny and his uncle found this to be charming and amusing, since his hearing had not been affected in the least, though neither of them had the heart to inform her. Denny suspected maybe Lou had pulled her leg a little, instructing her to speak up when talking to their long-time friend. The two siblings had a history of playing practical jokes on each other.

"Oh golly Denny was just asking me about this the last time he was here. Honestly, I wish we or I had written some of it down." Uncle Mike took a drink of water, and carried forth. "Actually though I do recall keeping journals or running logs at certain times of my training. Or so I seem to think. Anyhow, my best guess is that our mileage peaked out between sixty and seventy miles. But I know some of the guys were hitting close to a hundred a week. Maybe more. There were a bunch of studs in the area back then."

"Yeah, I do recall a few of them," Denny interjected.

"We would do a couple of twenty-five milers leading up to the marathon. On Sundays. And then a second longer run during the week. Maybe fifteen miles. Which I did most of the time solo. The fifteen milers that is." Uncle Mike was a shorter man; he stood only about five and a half feet tall, and his weight was likely down to under a hundred and thirty pounds by now. But when he spoke about his own running, it was as if an aura developed around him that made him appear bigger than any physical dimensions; there was a twinkle in his darker shaded eyes, that emanated out from behind a pair of well worn glasses, and there still appeared to be an abundance of life left within the contours of his rugged face. The streaks of whitish hair in his customary grey beard served to add gravitas to the spoken words, as his small hands gesticulated animatedly about, matching the excited pitches in his voice.

"You guys were animals for sure. I remember Bud Coates. And who was the real fast runner from I think up in Lansford? Always won the Switchback Scamper?"

"Oh, hold on," Uncle Mike said, as he looked downward. "Bob Thomas. That guy could fly like the wind. Be close to thirty minutes every year."

"That's moving for a 10k."

"He wasn't the only one," Uncle Mike stated.

"I bet our ultra-runner here might find twenty-five miles to be a bit piddly?" Denny leaned over and lightly slapped his uncle on the leg.

"No way," Mandy quickly replied. "Twenty-five miles is twenty-five miles. I guess that was more a part of the conventional thinking back then as far as long runs. In preparing for marathons?"

"True. Most plans don't have runs that go over twenty."

"Well you have much more information at your disposal. Which like anything in life, can be both good and bad," Uncle Mike mused. "Maybe our generation of runners were all just blissfully naïve. Or we just thoroughly enjoyed doing a heck of a lot of really long runs!" Uncle Mike's voice raised an octave or two with the last sentence; he then busted out laughing. So did Mandy and Denny, almost in unison. The fire continued to periodically crackle away in the background.

Mandy's husband Anthony popped into the living room and asked if any of them would like a cup of coffee, as a fresh pot had been brewed by Mr. Hackenberg in the kitchen. Despite looking rather fit, he was not a runner himself, though according to Mandy after he left the room, was unequivocally supportive of her adventurous pursuits in the sport. She went on to tell a story about how he had to take care of their daughters all day while she completed a forty-mile trail race in the Allegheny Mountains in western Pennsylvania, which included an unplanned visit to the Johnson County Hospital's Emergency Room, after the youngest had fallen off a jungle gym in the local park where the race began and ended.

"I'm not sure which of us had the more difficult day," she concluded, with a wry smile.

"So, what's next on your agenda?" Uncle Mike asked Mandy. "We all know what Denny here has coming up."

She adjusted herself on the couch, and pushed back a few strands of her shoulder length brown, frizzy hair behind one of her ears. "Well it's not quite as well known as Boston, but I'm planning to run in a hundred k ultra in northern New Jersey in early March."

"That's a hundred kilometers there Uncle Mike," Denny said, partially in jest. He loved to rib his uncle, particularly when in a good mood, such as tonight.

"Thanks for the edification junior. Sixty-two miles. Right Mandy?" he responded, without missing a beat. Uncle Mike whistled, and said to Mandy, "my my, that sounds like one heck of a challenge. Good for you!" He raised his coffee mug up in the air, as if to toast her.

"Thank you, kind sir. Actually, I've got sort of a bucket list thing I've begun to chase after." As Mandy spoke, she clasped her hands together, and leaned forward a little on the couch. "I haven't ever told anyone except Anthony, and my bestie running partner."

She glanced at Denny on the other end of the couch, then back to Uncle Mike, as if awaiting confirmation that it was safe to proceed forward.

"Do tell!" Uncle Mike blurted out, as he abruptly shot himself upright, spilling a few drops of his coffee onto the arm of the chair.

"Well it's been a dream of mine for years to one day run in the Western States 100."

"Holy shit that's awesome," Denny instantly replied. "And excuse my language, hopefully the kids are asleep. That's some pretty crazy stuff!"

"Yes, it is. And I know it's a pretty crazy ambition and who knows if I'll ever get into the thing."

"I've read several books about the race. Or parts of books I should say that write about it," Denny said. "That's a hundred miles too Uncle Mike."

"Yes, that's what I thought. I've heard of it too. And good for you Mandy. I don't doubt you'll get there one day. Not for a second."

"Thanks Mike." She explained to them the basic gist of the process involved to actually qualify to participate in the world-renowned ultra-marathon, which because of its very nature of utilizing a lot of single track trails in extremely difficult terrain, had to set fairly strict limits on the number of entrants allowed in the race each year. And similar to the Boston Marathon, more runners desire to go, than can be accommodated. Plus, not just anyone can be permitted to run the unforgiving course; an athlete has to essentially prove that they are capable of being able to finish such a daunting, demanding event, before even being granted a chance to enter the lottery system. Which consisted of successfully completing other ultras under specified parameters, within time frames allotted during each calendar year. Which is what Mandy was setting out to do.

Denny did know a little something about the deal too from first-hand experience; once he had been on a trail run with several people on the rather technical single-track trails of the Brunswick Nature Park, and one of the runners in the group was also attempting to get into the Western States and had broken down the process, and where they currently were at with all of it.

After some more discussion, mostly running related, Uncle Mike said, "well I must be the most blessed old-timer in the country right now to be sitting here with you two outstanding and ambitious runners. It truly is a treat."

"The treat is ours cowboy," Denny replied. This time it was he who initiated a faux toast. "Your wisdom and guidance are invaluable. We love you."

"And I love you guys too."

Chapter 11

    He was walking on a long pier, that had an elevated hump like some kind of bridge built into it part way out, and over water. It was raining like mad, and was all gloomy and grey out. The wooden boards themselves seemed to be rather slippery; Denny felt a discernable measure of trepidation with each step taken, especially when climbing up and over the raised part of the pier. He then heard frantic screams from what sounded like a young girl off to his left, but when Denny peered out into the choppy waters, all he could make out was a man sort of flailing around on the surface. Though he appeared to be alright, and not in any danger. Maybe there was a brief moment of hesitation, it was hard to tell, but the next thing he knew Denny had leaped into the open waters himself. He was fully clothed, but there was little sense of whether it was warm or cold outside, or if the water was warm or cold. Denny still could not locate any girl, so he dove under water to about the area where he thought the screams had come from. When he surfaced, he saw a small girl thrashing about violently and in an obvious panic; Denny quickly swam over and grabbed ahold of the child, and told her that everything was okay, and that he would...

    Something was gently tugging at his arm. Denny opened his eyes and was greeted by Sophia and her big puppy-dog like brown eyes staring back at him, visible in the dim light created by the candles in the windows of the living room. For a split-second he was utterly confused; how had he gotten out of the...? But it was Christmas morning. Or in reality, it was still the night before Christmas, and dear, sweet Sophia had awoken in the middle of the blessed night to make sure Santa Claus had not forgotten that she and her big sister were at their grandfather's house on the farm, and that he had remembered to deliver their presents under the very tree which stood in the far corner of the living room. Denny assured her that he had seen Santa, and had even spoken to him, and that everything had been taken care of, and she should probably go on back upstairs and go back to sleep, for she surely didn't want to be sleepy tired for the big day tomorrow. Fortunately, Sophia relented, and apparently accepted the credence of Denny's words, though not before checking to see that there were a bunch more wrapped presents beneath the tree. He could hear her feet pitter patter on up the wooden staircase, as he rolled over on the couch, and pulled the heavy comforter back over his body. A few minutes later Denny drifted off to sleep again; this time he didn't have any unusual dreams.

But what felt like an instant later, the alarm on his cell phone was sounding; Denny turned it off almost right away, dropped his legs onto the carpeted floor, and walked into the kitchen to brew a cup of coffee in the separate Keurig machine, which he had set up before going to bed the night before. All that was required of him was to press a solitary button. The homestead was almost entirely dark and perfectly silent, like in the famous poem which went, "all through the house, not a creature was stirring, not even a mouse." Denny couldn't recall the lines that came next. Through the dining room windows, all that the outside world revealed to him was more darkness, and what he presumed was rather chilly air, though the lowest branches on the big pines by the chicken coops appeared to be almost motionless, indicating there was little to no wind blowing.

The Green Mountain brand dark roast coffee was silky smooth and warm to the taste, as was the mug when held with both hands. Denny began to dress himself in the living room, with a minimal amount of noise and light. After double lacing his running shoes, a glance upwards revealed Mandy was standing almost right in front of him, as if a hologram had been beamed into the room, for he had not heard her descend the staircase.

"I'll be ready in thirty seconds," he whispered.

"Hey," she replied. "Merry Christmas."

Denny stood and smiled. "Merry Christmas. Let's rock."

Out the front door they went, and slipped into the frosty early morning that had seeped into the natural depths of the terrain. The two started at a light trot up the driveway and on out onto the roads. Behind, the sound of a rooster calling out from its pen filled the silence of the immaculate, immense void stretching infinitely in every direction. They wound on foot down the road, further into the hollow, until the song of the rooster faded into nothingness, and all that remained was the soft thwapping of shoes striking macadam. The first initial traces of daylight began to filter through the trees that grew atop the crests of the hills to the east; a faint orangish, pink glow at the farthest edges of the horizon started to become visible to the naked eye. Denny and Mandy ran without speaking much, until after two miles in when they summited a long, steep hill which offered a view towards the Lehigh River, itself hidden in the basin of the valley just beyond the next hillside. But the top of the fiery orange sun could now be seen above the landscape that rose up from across the east side of the river floor.

The two runners, perhaps unconsciously, slowed in rhythm to absorb the scene, like bearing witness to some new beginning in time; undoubtedly the poignancy of what was being seen and felt was magnified by the day itself. Mandy suggested they even stop for a moment at a bend in the road, and say some type of prayer for peace and goodwill. Denny agreed, so they walked on to a patch of frozen dirt off the roadside, just in front of where the hill fell off precipitously a few feet away.

"Dear God we ask that you bless all of your living creatures here below on this most glorious of days. As we celebrate the birth of your Son." Mandy had begun spontaneously, and extemporaneously speaking a prayer. "Allow us to accept your grace and mercy, and bask in your radiant and heavenly glory today."

Denny had knelt down too, beside Mandy, who continued, "we say a prayer for those who have departed this Earthly plain and now reside in heaven. Like my dear mom, and Denny's mother too. May they be at peace. In the name of all that is holy and sacred, Amen."

The acoustics of her voice, though not that loud, seemed to resonate off the hilltop; Denny felt a warm tingling sensation inside, and when he opened his eyes back up, it was as if everything was appearing in such a striking vividness that the individual wavelengths of colors could actually be glimpsed themselves, like being in a fourth dimension, where the vision was at once wholly complete, while simultaneously separated into its attendant parts. Time itself had become suspended; huge chunks of the life Denny had lived were being condensed into one solitary frame of reference, whereby the demarcations between events had been blurred or erased. Before rising, Denny verbally added a prayer for Uncle Mike, and then they were off, moving swiftly down the hill, and towards the bottom of the basin where the river had flowed for a million or more years.

Denny filled Mandy in on his runs in the San Gabriel Mountains, since the view had reminded him of an early morning spent in the grip of their rugged beauty. "This one particular run once I got up to about four thousand feet, I had this incredible view of the sun poking around the nearby peaks to the east. Even though it had been light for a good bit. When I stopped on the trail and turned around, there was this spectacular view of the entire area east of downtown Los Angeles."

"Right on. That sounds amazing. You ever hear of the Angeles Crest 100?"

"Yes," Denny replied. "I looked it up online when I was out there. Since somewhere I had heard of it."

"It's supposedly harder than the Western States," Mandy said, as the two of them emerged from the woods, and crossed a small bridge above a stream. Up ahead was the lower section of Slatington. "How tough were the trails you ran there?"

"Fairly technical single-track trails in spots. Not too rocky, like some of the ones I've run in the mountains in the east. But a lot of roots and ruts. And now that I think about it had a fair amount of rocks too." Denny chuckled, and continued, "You'd probably know more about it then I would. But I recall thinking, how in the hell would someone ever be able to run a hundred miles out in this?"

"Yes, the ones I've run in the Appalachians tend to be really rocky."

"And of course, there were some super steep climbs. I only got up to maybe five thousand feet tops on one of the runs."

"That's still fairly high up. We got to around forty-four hundred feet in one of the ultras I ran in Virginia."

"Nothing to sneeze at either," Denny said. "There's such a majestic grandeur in the Sierra Madres as they are called out there. Some of the peaks close to L.A. top out at over ten thousand feet." Denny could picture the area as he ran. "Much drier out west too," he added.

"Yes, it is," agreed Mandy. "I noticed that when I ran in Colorado."

"Good preparation for the Western States, right?"

"I hope so," she said with a laugh.

After they ran a few blocks on a residential street, Mandy led the way down a short hill that turned into a dirt road, which she stated would lead over to the D&L along the Lehigh. But after they passed by a house, the makeshift road ended in front of another small hill; however, a narrow ribbon of a trail was found that crashed through some bramble type bushes, before spilling out on to the familiar, wide gravel trail that was the D&L.

"Every time I come up here, I fumble around a bit to find that little hidden trail," Mandy said, as the two runners headed southbound. "Let's go about a mile on here and then turn around."

"Sounds good."

"My kids are probably up by now."

"And waiting patiently to open their presents."

"For sure," Mandy said. "For sure."

~

Trent knew what the gift was, and what was inside the box; that however, did not diminish the anticipation he felt while tearing off the wrapping paper, in an almost child-like haste to get at the contents contained within. He reached his hands inside the box, pushed the tissue paper aside, and hoisted the new pair of Nike running shoes out of the box, one at a time.

"Thank you, Santa," he announced, as he held the bright colored shoes up in front of him.

Jill smiled and said, "you're welcome."

Trent had not purchased a new pair of running shoes in several years; in fact, he would be hard pressed to remember the last time that he did. He always kept recycling through all the old pairs that had accumulated from his earlier, more active years in the sport. By now, Trent couldn't recall where most or any of those had originated from? Most had also been in the water too, many times. But they would eventually dry out, and be good to go, even if they did smell a little funky like river or lake water. But he had made a promise to himself that if the vaunted thousand-mile threshold could be crossed in the year, a brand-new pair of running shoes would be the reward. After hearing her husband share such a lofty goal, Jill took it upon herself to head up the endeavor, though not before consulting with Trent as to the actual make and model that was desired. And what better thing to do then wrap the suckers up and place them under the Christmas tree, since the thousand-mile mark had been eclipsed a few days ago. After all this time, would could a little extra wait hurt anyhow?

"I'll try these puppies out this afternoon," Trent said, as he carefully placed the shoes back inside of their box.

"But you also know there is another thing you're going to have to do now?" Jill asked, in the demeanor of one who already knows the answer to their question.

"No. Tell me."

"Do what you've been talking about. Go run a race man."

Yes, a race, Trent murmured to himself. The last things he had ever done competitively in the sport was when he was on his second enlistment in the Air Force, and stationed over in the Azores Islands off the coast of Portugal. He had joined the base's track team, though part of the reason was to get out of an unwanted assignment of standing sentry at funerals. Nonetheless, they had run in a few meets against some local clubs and even a high school or two, but the events were much more along the lines of something like rec-league pick-up basketball games. Trent couldn't even recall any of the times he had run, though he was fairly certain he used to race the two milers at them, and may have come in first place once or twice.

There was a flyer he had seen somewhere recently, of a new race that was going to be held in Jim Thorpe sometime in the spring, as part of a running festival or something? Maybe it was posted up under the shelter at the trailhead to the D&L? He couldn't quite remember; perhaps a mysterious seed had been planted, that would sprout forth at some point during the upcoming year?

Trent looked over at Jill, and just smiled.

Chapter 12

Uncle Mike slowly turned the pages of the scrapbook, pausing to savor as many of its contents that he could. He stopped though on one of the pages, and took the index finger of his right hand and sort of traced along the edges of the newspaper clipping.

"Dang," he said in a hushed, barely audible voice, that was nonetheless tinged with emotion. "I remember this one like it was yesterday." A contemplative tone begot from unlocked memories infused his words; Uncle Mike took his other hand and rubbed the bridge of his nose, while adjusting the fit of his glasses. The eyes remained locked on the page. The others who were gathered in the living room waited patiently for him to expand upon what it was that had stirred him so vividly. A flame leaped up from the fire, emitting a rather pronounced popping noise.

"Sixteen thousand runners brave the pouring rain to run Philly," Uncle Mike said, reading the headline from the newspaper article. He looked up and around at everyone, and added with a high-pitched whelp at the end, "and I was one of them!"

"What year was that?" Mr. Hackenberg asked.

"Well let's see. Says here in the top corner November 22nd, 1979. So, I guess it must have been 1979. Sounds about right." Uncle Mike snickered a bit at his last comments; but then he launched into some of the things about the event that made the recollection stand out so strikingly in his mind, beginning with the fact that it was only his second marathon, and had come only a few weeks after running his first, which had unfortunately unraveled into an alternation between running and walking the final eight miles of the race, in what he termed a survival death march to the finish line.

"After that humbling experience, I went into this one with much lower expectations. And I wanted a little redemption too."

"What do you always say Uncle Mike? Peace is possible once we let go of our expectations," Denny asked.

"That's it young man. One of the keys to remaining spiritually centered," Uncle Mike responded. "In all aspects of life."

"I like it," Mandy added.

"Tell us about the race Mike," Mr. Hackenberg said. He himself, from several decades spent working on the farm was still in pretty robust physical condition, considering too his age was also above seventy. Running, however, was never one of his pursuits.

"Well Cecelia and I had booked a room at the Sheraton which was pretty much smack in the heart of Center City. The day before the race she wanted to go see the Liberty Bell so we walked all the way to Independence Mall." Uncle Mike laughed to himself, and leaned back in the reclining chair, obviously enjoying a fond remembrance of his late wife. "It's kind of funny now to think back on it, but I got a little peeved at her that day since it ended up being a bunch of walking to get there and back. I told her in no uncertain terms what I really needed to be doing was resting my legs up for the race on Sunday."

"That's understandable," Mandy chimed in.

"Yes. I guess," Uncle Mike replied. Then he looked up at the ceiling and exclaimed, "forgive me sweetheart, you know how my priorities sometimes got all out of whack."

"We've all been there," stated Denny.

"Anyhow," Uncle Mike continued, "the next morning when we woke up and I pulled the curtains this stunning view of the city that we had from like the twenty-third floor had been totally obliterated by fog and rain." He paused, and took a few more moments to look over the newspaper article. Plus, just as a distance runner learns to parcel their energy over the duration of the run, Uncle Mike had to from necessity, learn to pace himself with all his activities, including conversations. At times he needed to rest, even if only briefly. Those present understood, and most certainly empathized.

"Well there was nothing to do but kiss Cecelia goodbye and tell her that God willing she'd see me again in a couple of hours. I put on as much clothing as I could, and wrapped a garbage bag on top of it all and left out of the hotel."

"Sounds downright miserable."

"It was John." Uncle Mike laughed again, and rubbed his face under his glasses. "You had to get there early to get into the corrals, and then stand there and wait like an hour before the actual race began. I was soaked to the bone before the gun even went off. And pretty dang cold too."

"I would have stayed in bed," Mandy's husband Anthony remarked, which drew a round of laughter from the room.

"You married a smart guy!" replied Uncle Mike, once again letting out a whelp, a solid octave or two higher than the normal pitch of his voice. Once some animated chatter subsided, he carried forth with his oratory.

"Anyhow where the heck was I? Oh yeah, the race. Well as the two other runners in the room already know, once the race starts and you get focused on the actual running itself you sort of block out the things you can't control. Like the weather. And besides, how wet can a person get after a while?" Uncle Mike paused, perhaps waiting for someone to offer a stab at the rhetorical question. No one did. Thus, he went ahead, "I could tell from the beginning that I felt good. You know, when everything just seems to be flowing. With not a whole heck of a lot of effort."

"Yes, yes," Mandy could be heard agreeing in the background.

"But you know, all that rain acts as a natural coolant. Which probably in retrospect helped us out there, though it was fairly raw out in the morning. I remember hitting the half in under 1:40, which could have been disconcerting, since it was much faster than what my target of around 3:30 was. But this voice in my head kept whispering go for it." Uncle Mike looked around the room. Everyone was in rapt attention, held somewhat spellbound by the narrative being woven. The insidious disease wreaking havoc inside the man's body had been shoved out of the foreground, into a depth where, at least for the time being, its influence had been curtailed. The day had been a good day all around. The notion that this was almost surely Uncle Mike's last Christmas did not escape him, after all he considered himself a realist in temporal affairs, for it helped to brush away any foolhardy thoughts, that occasionally begged to see the light of day. For those very thoughts could only serve as a temporary elixir and potentially trick him into believing that this was not the hand which had been dealt. But all that being said, Uncle Mike was sure as hell going to stay in the game until he played his very last card.

"Sounds like the running gods were on your side in the race," Denny said, in the measured tone of a runner who intrinsically understood how important such a blessed occurrence could be, coupled with the knowledge that such a thing defied most any attempt at a rational explanation, especially one that could be understood by those who don't labor in the quest.

"They sure were. I was one lucky S.O.B that day I guess." Uncle Mike looked into his nephew's eyes for a few seconds, then said, "it's doubtful I would have made it all the way if that were not the case."

"It's a beautiful thing," Mandy chimed in.

After a short silence in the room, Mr. Hackenberg asked, "so how did the rest of the race go?"

Denny had come to realize, after spending many hours at the farmhouse, that Mr. Hackenberg served at times to keep his uncle on task, in a manner of speaking. The art of which was quite subtle, and could be observed in conversations such as the one being held in the living room on Christmas night. Like a navigator reading a compass and deftly adjusting the wheel, Mr. Hackenberg kept the course, when perhaps Uncle Mike was bound to be led astray. Whether or not this was discerned, no one knew; Denny suspected though that his uncle probably did, and that he more than likely appreciated the gentle hand of a dear friend's assistance.

Uncle Mike resumed speaking. "It was going well until the long stretch along the Schuylkill River. I'd say this was about at mile twenty-two, or twenty-three. I got this terrible cramping sensation in one of my calves. I figured I was still on pace to finish under 3:20. But, and this is something the young turks in the room might find amusing, but back then we didn't have these fancy watches you all are wearing. That give out pace and all that jazz." The man had a peculiar, almost mischievous grin on his face as he looked at Denny and Mandy, who also glanced very briefly at each other with a knowing look, like one gets when they've oft heard a parent talk about how much harder things were back in their day.

After the point had been taken in to Uncle Mike's satisfaction, he picked the thread back up. "So, I had to always be figuring the math in my head. Though I'm pretty sure there were some clocks on the course. But they were timed for the fast runners who started at the front. Anyhow, I had to even stop and stretch my dang leg out at one point, since the thing was hurting like the dickens."

"Ouch," Anthony said.

"Yes. Ouch. Felt like someone was whacking the back of my leg with a two by four. But I only stopped for maybe thirty seconds at the most." He paused, and peeked again at the book in his hands. And caught his breath too. "Those last few miles were some of the hardest in my life. Like any marathon is." Uncle Mike glanced again at Denny and Mandy, who reciprocated in silent agreement.

"But those last few miles were also some of the most rewarding. And memorable. I can still recall to this day coming up that last stretch. I forget the name of the road. It goes past one of those big love statues and is a straight shot to the Art Museum."

"Yes, I know right where you mean," said Anthony.

"It had started really pouring hard again. I had to be constantly wiping water away from my eyes."

"Did you have one of those sweatbands on your head like all the runners wore back in the good old days?" Denny asked. Somehow, he managed to keep a straight face. "Lot of NBA guys too," he added, while not batting an eye.

"No Denny I did not. But somehow, I did manage to hear your aunt whooping and hollering my name out. So, I ducked over to the side and gave her a big sloppy wet kiss on the mouth. She was shivering half to death under an umbrella."

"Ahh how romantic," Mandy remarked.

"Well that was me you know. Those steps in front of the Art Museum looked like I would never get to them. Finally, I could see the Rocky Statue, and I knew I was going to make it." Uncle Mike stopped talking, looking down again at the scrap book and newspaper clipping, touching the page with his hand, as if to verify it had all been real. "Three hours and seventeen minutes. What a day," he said, as his voice trailed off with the final few words; the slightest hint of sadness did permeate his speech just then.

"Man, that's phenomenal," Mandy said. She had been visibly touched emotionally.

"Yes, it is Mike," her husband seconded.

Uncle Mike perked right back up though from the brief flight of melancholy. "You are all too kind to this old fellow. This is so wonderful," he added, while raising the book from his lap into the air, like it was an award or trophy.

"Let me see what else is in here. I'm just getting started." He continued to slowly, methodically peruse the contents in the book his nephew had put together, with the help of an old friend who worked as an archivist at a local library.

Mr. Hackenberg excused himself and went into the kitchen, not before inquiring if anyone wanted more coffee. Denny declined, as he was going to jump on the road soon and head back up to the hotel.

"Here's another one I most certainly recall. The Christmas City 10k. We ran that one several years in a row," Uncle Mike stated. He described, in rather meticulous detail, the hilly course which wound through parts of Bethlehem; the race was always a warm one too as it was staged in the middle of July each summer.

"I'm amazed you found all this old stuff," he said to Denny.

"I had a little help from Saint Nick," Denny replied in response, as he winked at his uncle. Denny's own heart was filled with warmth, the kind one feels deep inside, when experiencing the true sense of the virtuous ideal that it's better to give than to receive.

Some of the races themselves were lodged in the far crevices of Denny's own mind too; fragmented, fuzzy snapshots of events attended as a kid, in tow of adults like his uncle, and his own father, and a floating entourage of their running brethren. Like the Switchback Scamper, always held in the forested mountains near Jim Thorpe during the peak of fall foliage in eastern Pennsylvania.

He closed his eyes and could see himself waiting in a grass field behind a sports complex. Perhaps a baseball diamond, or football stadium. Denny was young, real young. Maybe five or six years old? It was somewhere near Allentown; the gang used to run a lot of races there. Denny would wait near the finish line while the men hammered away at another ten-kilometer race. He would be given a task though, of counting the number of runners who had finished, before the runners he knew made it back. A most important job indeed for such a lad. Likely his attention wandered, and the count was lost. But it really didn't matter. Denny was part of a crew, being introduced and indoctrinated into something that would eventually develop into a vital part of his own life in due time; soon he was a runner too running in his own races, while the adults like Uncle Mike cheered him and others on from the perimeter of the track. He could even hear his uncle's voice...

But it was coming from across the room. "What's that?" Denny stammered.

"What are you running tomorrow?" Uncle Mike asked, with the levity of one who fully understood where abstractions of the brain can lead, especially for those who are considered to be of the contemplative class.

"It's something with thousand-meter repeats. I have to look at it again to be exact."

"I see."

"Probably something on the order of six miles easy. Then five or six thousands at five k pace. Plus a few more miles at the end."

"Getting some speed and turnover in. Good," Uncle Mike commented. "Can't get stuck in a rut running all those miles at a slower pace. Relatively speaking of course."

"The marathon shuffle is what I believe you are alluding to."

"Hey I know all about that," Mandy said, as she walked back into the living room.

"Don't we all." Uncle Mike slapped his thigh and chuckled.

"I think I'll go to the towpath for the thousands. And loop Lehighton for the first few miles whatever they are. Take as much advantage as I can of running hills while I'm here."

"Makes sense," Uncle Mike agreed. "When are you planning to sojourn on south? I know you've got a busy life to attend to in North Carolina." There was a dash of apprehension in the query; however, the statement which had immediately followed illustrated that a complete understanding of the situation was present.

The inevitability of having to at some point depart was something which could weigh on Denny's conscience and soul; usually after spending some amount of time up in his old stomping grounds an internal, perhaps organic clock seemed to never fail to let him know that the hour was about to strike for him to leave, and to return to his current home. But it was also much different on this occasion with Uncle Mike directly involved; again, it wasn't that his uncle didn't fully grasp the dynamics at play, and of course the guy was most grateful for whatever time and energy his nephew could devote to his well-being. It just brought the idea close to the fore, that this visit, or any subsequent future one, could very well be the last time they would ever see each other again. All that, however, was not going to actually be discussed, as Uncle Mike had been insistent that any such speculation was for one, mere folly and a bit of a fool's errand, and second, it served no good purpose and could only sully whatever good vibes were shared between him, and whomever he was fortunate to have around on any given day.

"When my number is called, it's called. Simple as that." Those exact words his uncle had one said.

And Denny always thought he was just about the most well-rounded, intelligent, and spiritually enlightened person he had ever met.

Chapter 13

Trent and Denny ran along the ridgeline to the north of Lehighton, beneath the shadow of Flagstaff Mountain, which loomed just off of their left-hand side. For the first time, Denny talked to Trent in depth about the writing he had been working on periodically over the last two years, and how he hoped one day to publish a novel. He had finished reading the book Trent had lent him about the life of Franz Kline, and it had not only inspired him to push forward with his own project, but had also shed some light on a curiosity of his. And that was an innate, almost primal fascination with the area when it came to his own artistic sensibilities, and the influence this was having upon the choices Denny found himself making with the material he was creating. For Denny, that translated in to writing about settings and situations from the very enclave in eastern Pennsylvania he found himself presently running in. The similarity to Kline, was that many of his best-known paintings depict scenes from the very same environs, in spite of the fact that he, like Denny, had permanently moved out of the area as a young adult.

The authors of the book had noticed this as well, as had Trent. Ironically, not that many people in the Lehighton area knew much about the famous, and quite eccentric artist. "Maybe more people will be interested in some of the local history after this book?" Trent speculated.

The two runners moved swiftly along the road, nonplussed by the small undulations in the encountered terrain; to the south, a sightline opened up all the way to the Blue Mountain, which stood higher than the series of rolling hills in its wake. "How can you not be inspired by this?" Trent asked, as if he had accidentally verbalized a sudden thought inside his mind.

Denny though decided to respond. "Exactly. I've been trying to capture some of this pristine beauty with words. In conjunction with the emotions of someone who left it all. But finds themselves compelled at times to return. Even though from an intellectual angle the idea seems nonsensical. All tied in of course to the perspective of running." He laughed out loud, and felt the need to qualify his remarks. "I feel like I fail much more than I succeed."

"Maybe some of this all just needs to be experienced in person," Trent opined. "But I know where you are coming from with the other stuff. Its nuanced right?"

"That's a great word for it."

They ran past the house where the Denali sisters used to live; Denny told a story about sneaking in there late one night and waking up Connie, and getting her to come to a party at another house down the street.

"Nice work," Trent replied.

He was getting in some miles with Denny during the first part of his run, and digging the new Nikes as well. Trent would head into work when the two split, while Denny would get his intervals in.

A cursory look by Denny at his watch revealed a 7:05 pace was being run, as the road started to fall into the narrow gorge the Lehigh River travelled through. Gravity assisted them somewhat to increase the tempo even more, as the pitch of the landscape descended further, through a dense section of forest, before opening up into the small village of Packerton.

Once the woods were cleared, Trent pointed towards the river to where the old railyards used to be, which figured prominently in the life of Kline, and the lives of so many locally in the first half of the twentieth century. Now, nothing more than a crumbling structure, surrounded by an unkempt property of tall weeds and thickets of trees, remained. Trent also asked Denny to tell him more about what he was trying to write in terms of running, which he was more than happy to do. So Denny talked about how he had taken extensive notes about runs he had gone on while up here living in the area two years ago, and how he was using them to help construct a dialogue of sorts about much of what had been experienced, not just physically on the roads and trails, but psychically and spiritually within. All of which was being woven into a fictional story. And he added, that some of the runs had been completed with Trent.

"I hope it gets published one day. I would love to read it."

"That would be cool. And thanks."

"Hey can you imagine one day people will show up to run the very same runs that we've been going on? I mean most of them go back to when we were in school, like BZ Farms, and the snake loop through town."

"That would be a trip, to say the least. I've never thought about it in that way." Denny was rather piqued with the far-reaching concept as well.

"Yep. All because you memorialized them for eternity in print," Trent proclaimed, as they began climbing a short, but steep hill on Route 209, which would take them back into Lehighton in a few tenths of a mile.

"I feel some pressure now to get it right then," Denny said, with some deadpan in his voice.

"We could even lead some of the runs. Advertise it like come run with Denny and Trent on the eight-mile convalescent home loop. Beginning and ending from where they used to meet for cross country practices." The two were grinding up the hill pretty good; adrenaline was coursing through the runners' veins. Trent said all this too would serve as additional motivation for him to get into even better shape than he was.

"Go for two thousand miles next year," suggested Denny.

"I will. Hey we could get Coach Blakemore out as well. Lead the group in warm-up drills before we hit the roads. He works with my sister too."

"I didn't know that."

"Get Bill Keer out too. He could keep the atmosphere loose with his funny humor. Like when he bet Coach and got him to wear a wig of women's hair to a meet."

"I think we've tapped into a wellspring of unlimited possibilities here," said Denny.

"Fifty years from now a young kid will set out on a run as written about in some musty old book that he found in his grandparents' attic," Trent said. And then he added, "it's always a good thing when you're back up here."

"Thanks partner." It was a good thing indeed, thought Denny.

After Trent had left, Denny ran across the railroad trestle that spanned the river, and found the ribbon of a path that led to the much wider towpath, where he began the hard part of the prescribed workout. His legs had already absorbed a bit of a beating out on the hills, running at a fairly frisky clip with Trent; such fatigue, however, mimicked what would have to be endured in the marathon itself, where it becomes a necessity to continue to turn the legs over mile after mile, after they've already been maxed out to near their load capacity. Such a huge, fundamental part of it was mental too; Denny knew from experience, how important it was to overcome the negativity that invariably tries to poison the souls of all who labor in the marathon realm. Running thousand-meter repeats would demand some of the same type of focus needed for when the internal circuitry is being pushed into survival mode, and the messaging becomes almost binary; continue to run and risk death, or stop and live to fight another day.

Denny headed northward back towards Packerton, and Jim Thorpe. The first thousand meters were rather benign, and he was pleased it had been completed in 3:53, right about where he hoped to start out time and pace wise. The recovery period between the repetitions was four hundred meters, or a quarter of a mile of easy running.

The surface of the towpath was perfect; hard packed dirt with a little bit of finely crushed stone. It was dry too, as there hadn't been much, if any precipitation in the last several days. The weather was just about perfect as well; temperatures were in the upper thirties to low forties, and there wasn't too much wind blowing. Thin, wispy cirrus clouds high up in the sky did partially obscure the sun from time to time, but for the most part its rays shone bright upon the land beneath, though sections of the towpath usually remained in the shadows, owing to the almost vertical embankment that rose up pretty high along most of the canal's eastern edge, and to the trees that grew between the towpath and the Lehigh River, which for the most part paralleled the man-made waterway to the west.

Denny wore shorts, a short-sleeved shirt and arm sleeves, as well as a beanie and a pair of gloves. Likely it wasn't much colder here today than it would be in North Carolina on many a winter's morning. A rare treat indeed, though one more snow fall would be welcomed, before a departure was made.

The next two thousands were each run slightly faster than their predecessor, with a controlled, moderately strenuous effort. This was a good indicator of Denny's current fitness; a positive signpost that the training was unfolding the first few weeks as it needed to be, especially when filtered through the lens of all the hills being run, which in and of themselves, would also assist in preparation for the specific demands of Boston. The waters of the canal and the river aided the efforts, by furnishing serene visuals that blunted some of the pain being endured, specifically in the final few hundred meters of each long interval. A decent amount of the canal was iced over, but the river continuously flowed, providing occasional auditory distractions, like the splashing sounds small rapids created as they curled their way around the larger rocks which penetrated up and out of the water's surface.

Denny had turned around during the fourth repeat, passing twice by a wooden bridge a little beyond the canal's last lock, that led to a tiny grove, abutted by the steep, wooded hillside. There was a solitary bench there, donated by a church in Weissport, as well as numerous small rocks painted in Easter-egg like pastel colors that included verses from the Bible. He had discovered the sacred little garden many years ago on one of his runs, and had even knelt there and prayed once. Denny doubted that but a handful of people even knew it was there.

He had disciplined himself not to look at the watch during the work bouts, same as the modus operandi when running threshold or pace miles. Instead, Denny would gauge the tempo based on intuitive feel and perceived effort. Maybe some of Uncle Mike's wisdom was rubbing off; he seemed to always be ruminating about how runners today were over reliant upon technology, instead of relying on sensory data, and the subtle clues the body sent out. For the most part Denny agreed but he also told his uncle that it was pretty damn difficult to put the toothpaste back in the tube. Yes, this generation of runners, and even more so the one after, were wired into the instantaneous feedback of numerical and graphical information; if the run didn't appear on Strava or Garmin Connect, it would be like the old adage about the tree falling in the woods. Denny was old enough to recall running before the advent of satellite embedded watches, when routes or courses were measured by getting in a car and driving them and looking at the odometer. Mile marks were landmarks that one memorized. Some of the kids Denny coached couldn't seem to wrap their minds around the concept; it was like trying to describe life before cell phones, or the internet. Maybe I'm getting old myself, Denny mused, before glancing at his Garmin, which let him know it was time to begin the fifth, and penultimate thousand meters.

By now, once he had only run about a minute or so hard, Denny could acutely feel the collective toll that the workout had extracted from him; lactic acid would commence again to ravish the legs, which in turn made breathing become much more labored. Mentally, this combined to stretch the distance of one kilometer into feeling like it was longer than what it was supposed to be. Thus, Denny was forced to break it down into smaller components; in his case a tenth of a mile presented itself as a viable and logical solution to the problem, as he could convince himself that such a measured distance could be plausibly endured at the speed needed to be maintained. The idea that he was mixing the metric and American systems didn't enter into the dialogue. A new rule was also adopted; the watch could only be looked at after each subsequent tenth of a mile had been completed. It was a fun game to play, and Denny made it through number five without any premature glances, finishing in 3:38, several seconds under a six minute per mile pace.

During the final four hundred meters of recovery, Denny pondered the goal of a sub three-hour marathon at Boston. For the last two weeks or so in Pennsylvania, the dream lie latent within his running psyche, as much of his mental energy had been expended upon the circumstances that had dictated his travel northward. Last spring, he had run the Wrightsville Beach Marathon in 3:06 and change, but it was an almost entirely pancake flat course, and the weather had been conducive to producing fast times. Plus, the training cycle prior had been about as good as it could have been; sure, numerous minor injuries had to be worked through, and all their attendant aches and pains, but nothing was ever problematic enough to cause any runs to be missed. And no sickness or illnesses had befallen him either, which can be a tricky feat to pull off when engaged in three to four months of rigorous training amidst the height of cold and flu season.

Denny knew that the best barometer to gauge the feasibility of hitting the target time would be during the sections of the training plan when there would be several long runs with goal pace miles, the bulk of which would fall in the months of February and March. For now, it was a lot of threshold miles, some with small sets of 400s mixed in, and longer intervals, like the last one about to be laid down today. And once again, it got pretty tough right quick; Denny had to dig deep almost from the onset, telling himself to simply focus on the next stretch of towpath, and to keep counting off the fenceposts on the right-hand side, that separated the strip of land from a sharp drop towards the river. Grind, grind, grind, Denny said to himself. He flew by an older couple walking a dog, without even so much as indicating that he even saw them. Block everything out; cover ground. A tenth of a mile at a time. But even that got to be too long. Get to the next lock just up ahead. By then it would have to less than a quarter mile to go. A peek at the watch confirmed the estimate. Denny was in the breach. The only way out was straight through it. Emerson said something like that. It flashed into his mind for an instant, then vanished. Ten meters at a time. Five. Each step. Right. Left. Right. Left.

And then it was done. Denny took his gloved hands and dug them into the flesh at his sides right above the hips, as he staggered forward, trying to suck precious air in to his burning lungs. He stared over at the Lehigh; the water glistened with speckles where the light of the sun danced upon its ripples. The town of Lehighton began to fully reappear in his line of vision through a gap in the trees; her old wooden houses sprawled like an ink splatter up the sides of the hills. After a short bit, Denny was able to resume a normal form of running, albeit at a slow recovery pace as he crossed back over the river, and headed over to his car, parked in the lot by the trailhead to the D&L, where he had left it almost two hours ago.

~

Two days later he was gone. Somewhere on Interstate 81 near Harrisburg, Denny broke down and started sobbing in the car. Why, he wasn't exactly sure? It felt cathartic once the tears had started to flow. Denny had gone to the farm the night before to be with his uncle, but he wasn't feeling too well, and ended up retiring to bed around dinnertime, without even eating anything. They were able to chat a little; mostly his uncle wanted to hear about the latest runs and what was upcoming in the training plan, which made Denny feel almost guilty discussing, as weird as that may sound. Uncle Mike's face looked gaunt, and paler than it had a few days prior; his breathing also seemed to require a little more effort, as he would practically get out of breath after every few words spoken. Though there was still a flicker of light in the man's eyes, and a gentle smile still managed to make a few appearances. Instead of Denny offering assurances that things would ultimately one way or the other be alright, it was Uncle Mike who was promising his nephew those very same intangibles; he counseled him to continue to follow his heart, to not worry about what most others thought about his pursuits, and to always pay credence to his inner voice, for that was the only one which truly mattered, and was the channel us humans have to our God above.

"And don't forget to send me your runs every day Denny," he added.

"I promise," he replied, before disappearing into the dimly lit hallway, where only the sounds of his footsteps penetrated the heavy silence of the old farmhouse.

Denny had gone over to see Keith and Suzanne as well. Suzanne ended up running a few miles with him on the D&L, after completing a workout with a younger lady she was mentoring into the sport. A little over a mile into the run, they had come upon what looked like an ice sculpture, that was one of the most fascinating, natural things Denny had ever seen. It was like hundreds of giant icicles had been attached together; the whole thing was hanging off of some large rocks protruding out of the side of the Mahoning Mountain. Denny even debated going back to get his cell phone to take pictures.

There was another drive down Fourth Street past Jennifer's house. When to let go of something, or of someone, is one of the toughest decisions any of us ever has to make.

Usually there are no right or wrong answers, at least there weren't for Denny. Not now. Perhaps some of this muddled confusion contributed to the tears shed on the highway? He didn't know. So, he kept driving. Certain bridges weren't meant to be crossed, until it was time to cross them. Denny deliberated about this. It sounded sort of dumb. But perhaps there was wisdom in it? Like something Yogi Berra would have said.

Denny heard the voice of his uncle, who told him to just focus on the road in front him. That made sense, so it was exactly what he did.

Chapter 14

Denny knelt on the sidewalk and double knotted his Saucony running shoes. He closed his eyes and gave thanks for another run about to be embarked upon, and said a brief prayer for those who wouldn't make it out on the roads today. The only sound was the faint humming of electricity passing through the utility wires overhead. The street lights on Lake Park Boulevard threw off just enough light to make the street visible in the early morning darkness. It felt colder in the town of Carolina Beach than it had on his last runs in Pennsylvania, which ironically, he had thought about on one of the final days he had been up there. The wind coming off the waters of the Atlantic Ocean laced the air with a shivery bite; thus, Denny wore long pants, and two long-sleeved shirts, which he tucked into his gloves, trying to cover any exposed skin. Sunglasses rested snugly atop his knit hat; by the time Denny finished the seventeen-mile run, daylight would predominate the skies.

Winter though was Denny's favorite season in the small, sort of off the beaten path beach town, for it meant much less people, and much more open space, which made it easier to appreciate the natural beauty of the island Carolina Beach was located on. The island itself, named Pleasure Island, was about ten miles long from north to south, but only a mile or two wide, and was separated from the mainland of North Carolina by the Atlantic Intracoastal Waterway, and Cape Fear River. Over half the land was undeveloped, and consisted mainly of swampy woodlands mixed with old growth pine forests.

Denny ran on the boardwalk, located directly behind the dune line, which extended a half mile north from the downtown. He listened to the acoustics of the ocean, as waves continued to break upon the shoreline, one after the other. The perpetual motion of the sea was something Denny liked to meditate to, when he would sit cross-legged in the sand at night, while the moon and stars overhead kept him company.

He could see the faint outline of the tops of the waves as they crested, and the foamy white detritus left in their wake after dissipating on the sandy beach. The reeds and cattails that were planted and grew on top of the dunes swayed back and forth in the swirling breezes. Denny ran to the terminus of the boardwalk, then past the canal where all the fishing boats were docked; in the afternoons and evenings, especially during the summertime, the strong smell of fish and marine life would permeate the air, after the vessels returned with their daily catches. This morning all was quiet, except for a couple of gentlemen boarding a smaller boat, perhaps for an early excursion out to sea.

The pace being run was easy and comfortable; Denny planned to average in the mid to high seven-minute range, as the workout did not contain anything harder like threshold or pace miles, nor any intervals. Or nothing fancy in this JD long run, as Denny had begun to refer to such workout segments as. And somehow, he had apparently picked up the habit of referring to Jack Daniels by his initials, as if there was some sort of personal, intimate relationship between the two. So much so, that Jackie had begun to mimic this peculiar trait, and also call her coach by their initials as well. Though in her case she actually knew FS fairly well.

A few miles into the run, and in the center square of the town of Kure Beach, located two and a half miles south of Carolina Beach, Denny consumed one of his gels and took a drink of water from a fountain located outside of some bathrooms, that were next to the entertainment gazebo. It was a chocolate pudding flavored gel, that had come from a box of assorted flavors Uncle Mike had gifted him at Christmas. The two had spoken on the phone the night before, and Denny's uncle had sounded in good spirits, and seemed to be doing better than he had been a week or so ago when they had last been together in person. After he chucked the empty wrapper in a garbage can Denny laughed, remembering the exclamation of, "we never had any of this shit when we trained," uttered by Uncle Mike when the box had been opened.

    A touch of niggling pain again announced its presence in Denny's left calf; he had also talked to his uncle about that on the phone, though in the vein of downplaying the concern, for he knew the advice likely to be proffered would revolve around taking a day or two off. In another conversation they had once, Uncle Mike had opined that it was another negative consequence of the electronics and social media that have permeated the sport; he imagined that runners felt more compelled not to rest and take days off, since they had become a little too preoccupied with keeping up with what others were doing that day or week, instead of paying more heed to the warning signs the body was sending out. Nobody ever saw our running journals he had emphatically stated, for those who even bothered to keep them in the first place, except maybe somebody's significant other accidentality stumbling upon one. Denny somewhat agreed, though he did feel like maybe the guy was a bit off base, or had more of a rosy memory of some idyllic, pure period that never quite existed in the sport? But he could also see validity in the sentiments, though he did protest a little on a personal level, saying that he himself wasn't in it for the public applause or adoration. To Denny it was much more intrinsic, or even existential, what drove him to run. Like many matters in life, the truth fell somewhere between both poles.

Once Denny had embarked on a plan or had set his sights on a performance based goal, he felt it was of the utmost importance to remain disciplined in the daily grind, like those baseball players who played every game, day in and day out, regardless of whatever ailments or aches might be troubling them. For he felt as though he thrived off such a mindset; Denny punched in on time every day and did the work, and prided himself on those attributes. This also included a fair amount on ancillary activities to supplement the running. Mainly core and strength work, that he would do early in the mornings before driving into work, or perhaps in the evenings after runs. Planks, push-ups, sit-ups, legs swings. Some while standing, and others while on the floor. Squats. Calf raises. Denny would play music on his Echo Dot; Nirvana, Soundgarden, Rage, and other hard rock or metal would help motivate him to push through the pain. It also made him feel younger too, harkening back to when many of those bands had first gained mainstream popularity.

And on the days when Denny didn't want to get out the door, or he was tired from a long day at the office, perhaps the weather wasn't what was desired, or enough sleep hadn't occurred the night before, he would remind himself to stay true to the discipline, and worship her like a deity. It was rather simple; to run or not to run. Such was the mentality, though occasional rest days were built in to the schedule, in the dull, drab, dark days of January, when Denny would occasionally battle the schizophrenia of being totally and unabashedly committed to the quest, but yet not wanting to do many of the actual things required to be done to place himself in the best possible position to succeed.

He would also remind himself there was a bib waiting for him in Boston, and that it was important to honor the integrity of the race, by getting to the start line in Hopkinton in the best conditioning that he could. For there were tens of thousands of runners, many just as serious about and as dedicated to the craft as him, who would kill so to speak, for the chance to run in the Boston Marathon. Thousands of said runners had actually qualified for the race, only to be rejected because their marathon times weren't under what the cut-off margin ended up landing on. Denny even knew a few in Wilmington. What any of them wouldn't do to be in his shoes, fretting about a workout because it was too windy out, which might mean more of a strenuous effort would be needed to hit paces during marathon simulation miles? Or that Denny was fatigued from so many consecutive weeks of running over seventy miles? Yes, a lot of folks would like to be facing such challenges. So, it fell on him to do the deal, and to do it all with some verve in his heart, and a little bounce in his step.

~

"I would say this is a similar grade."

"Yes. Though Heartbreak Hill might be a bit steeper. At least right before the top." Denny was sandwiched between Colby and Briana, who alternated answering his question, as they all ran up Snow's Cut Bridge, which was the solitary means to get on and off of Pleasure Island, unless one used a boat or decided to swim. The bridge arched up into a large hump to be tall enough for most boats to be able to pass safely beneath on the Intracoastal Waterway.

The advantage also for runners, was that the pitch of the incline made it ideal to use for hill repeats, being that in the coastal region of southeastern North Carolina, almost all the topography was rather flat. Of course, one had to not be squeamish about heights, since at its apex, the water was a good hundred feet or more below. And there was but a narrow, slightly raised sidewalk to use on foot or on bike to get across, hence the foursome ran in single file, with Jean-Paul, or French-fry as he was known by most, leading the pack on the first interval. Denny could see his tall, waifish and pale, thin frame about fifteen meters ahead; the appearance of which, was part of the derivation of the friendly nickname. And the fact that he had been born and raised in Lyon, France.

Beforehand, close to ten miles had been run on the trails of the Carolina Beach State Park, at an easy pace well above eight minutes per mile. Currently, they were attacking the hill at a much faster speed, well down into the sixes. Controlled, hard running is how Denny would describe it. The group would recover somewhat on the descent on the opposite side, then turn right around and come back hard up the bridge. The distance of the entire bridge and road on either side leading up to it was three quarters of a mile. From the spot where they started, and would end the interval, the total distance would be about a bit under a mile and a half.

After the first of the planned three, and on behind the island's main grocery store and strip mall, Denny shucked his long-sleeved shirt and added it to the growing pile of clothing that had already been shed. It had been much colder when the run had commenced an hour and a half ago, just as the sun was initially beginning to rise above the ocean to the east, and sending the first rays of light into the woods of the state park. By now the temperatures had to have risen into the forties.

On the second sojourn across the bridge, Denny looked out at the waterway and beach houses and condominium buildings that all swept eastward until reaching the immense abyss of the Atlantic, about a mile away. The bright orangish, yellow sun had fully risen above the horizon line, where the deeper cobalt blues of the water, melted into the softer, lighter blue hues of the sky. Some puffy white cumulous clouds hung part way up in the sky, as if they had been painted onto a work of art. There could be much worse places to be beating myself into a pulp, Denny thought, as he strained a little to maintain the fast pace being set by French-fry. Once again Denny was tucked into the three-hole, between Colby and Briana. All of them were running Boston in April.

  Naturally Denny took advantage of the opportunity to pick their brains, especially about the Newton Hills, which is what the workout today was attempting to simulate up on the bridge; basically, it was three times ten minutes at or below marathon pace, with two minutes rest in between. After having already put a solid chunk of work in on the softer surfaces of the trails. Jean-Paul had run in the low 2:50s last year at Boston, which was his first time running the event, and was hoping to break into the 2:40s. Colby had gotten below the coveted three hour mark there last year, his third time running Boston, and was looking at a 2:55 this go around, which would also be a marathon PR for him. Briana was apparently being cajoled into taking a stab at the sub three club too, by more than just those who were out running there in Carolina Beach. And in his unmistakable accent, Jean-Paul had invited her personally to undertake the pursuit, the same one that held Denny under its sway. It would be her second trip to Boston; she had run the marathon in 2015.

  On the third and final interval, French-fry checked out half way up the bridge. In running parlance, this meant that he pulled well ahead of the others, with his effortless looking, long strides. Denny tried desperately to latch on to the backside of Colby, who was built a little thicker, or had a little more in the hips and buttocks as he liked to joke, and stood maybe an inch or two shorter than him. But a gap of about five meters had developed almost before Denny could even process what was happening, and it was proving difficult to close. He reminded himself to relax, and to keep turning over the legs, and to take it one small section of concrete at a time. Steel posts that held the fencing in place above the short cement walls of the bridge, also served as visual marks to measure progress by. Denny sensed that Briana had slipped off the rear of him, as he could no longer hear her footsteps or breathing. On the downside through the three of them regrouped like an amoeba, or a chase pack in pursuit of their European friend. But he proved to be too fast to be caught.

After everyone had returned to the designated rest area, and were either jogging very slowly in place, or standing and taking drinks of water, Denny asked how much one's overall pace gets effected by the hills?

"Last year I may have fallen off by fifteen, maybe twenty seconds per mile," Colby replied. "So, it wasn't all that much. But the first year I ran it really fell off." He took another squirt of water, and added, "but I ran like a damned fool that time."

"It can feel much slower when you're climbing than it likely is," Briana said, as she pulled her long black hair back into a ponytail again. "But you make it up on the downhills and flat stretches between the hills."

"I would just maintain an even effort and let the splits fall as they may," Colby said.

"There are so many varying strategies as to how to run the whole thing too," stated Briana. Running in shorts and a purple sports bra, she had to have less than three to four percent body fat on her five-foot eight-inch frame. She was super toned muscularly too, particularly in the arms, and looked ready to race right then and there.

"Yes, I've been reading up on many of them," Denny replied, with a touch of naïve laughter. It seemed to him to be one of those things whereby the more one knew, the less in reality they actually did know. Of late he had been contemplating the Newton Hills, and what the placement of them might have on an overall pacing strategy. For they seemed to throw a monkey wrench into how Denny normally liked to attack a race, by starting out somewhat slower, and then gradually as the race unfolded, incrementally increasing the pace to where he'd be at top speed say between the ten mile and twenty mile marks, when it came to a marathon. The last few miles would be for holding on, and hopefully not sliding backwards too much. He had recently come upon a race simulator that was housed in an Excel spreadsheet, which also broke down the elevation changes for each mile on the course. There were built in mathematical equations that would populate exact splits for each mile, based upon factors that the user inputted, such as what their goal finish line time was, and what sort of pacing strategy they wanted to employ, such as a fast versus slow start, or an even pace versus an even effort throughout the race. It was oddly fascinating to manipulate the numbers, like some sort of mad math geek playing around at a chalkboard in an empty classroom.

One of Denny's coaching pals, who'd run Boston several times, had forewarned him in the fall that it was a difficult course to PR on, particularly the first time racing there. Not only due to the tough terrain, but also because of the myriad of unique logistics needed to be navigated, such as having to wait at Athlete's Village several hours before racing, the later than usual start times, and the sheer volume of runners on the course with very similar abilities, despite the fact that Boston was separated into four seeded waves. Such advice Denny did not dismiss; but on the other hand, it also served to fuel the fire, and make him even more determined to smash his goal on the world's biggest stage.

But that was then, when most of the slate was still blank.

"Hey you just have to take what the course will give you in certain spots," Briana said to Denny. "Plus, the weather can be totally unpredictable there," she also said, with a sheepish grin.

"That's why I ended up going out way too fast early on the one year," Colby said. "The first few miles roll downhill pretty good. What was the one that you could really fly on? Either at mile three or four?"

"Oh yeah. That downhill is even steeper than at the start," Jean-Paul replied, without specifying which mile was being alluded to.

Some of that went counter to the guidance Denny had been reading of late, which was peppered with cautionary tales from runners who had gotten swept up in the initial adrenaline rush and favorable topography the first part of the race, only to crash and burn in spectacular fashion somewhere in the famous Newton Hills. Or infamous hills, as such runners might think of them as. After which it continued to unravel into a slow, painful crawl into the city of Boston. Denny did not want to become associated with such an unfortunate lot; plus, he had heard locally over the years a few first hand accounts from even veteran, savvy runners who had gone out too fast as well, swept away on the wings of the mystique of Boston. Only to painfully regret later their tragic lack of prudence. But it was always a fine line being trod between aggressively and confidently going after a breakthrough performance, versus being too conservative, and denying one's self the chance to shatter their own glass ceiling.

On the cooldown jog back through the state park, Briana must have sensed some of the interplay at work in Denny's head, for she said to him as they dropped a little behind the other two, "just go up there and have fun man."

Wise words indeed.

Chapter 15

The canvas was mocking her. The colors washed out and lifeless. It was as if one of those sad clown faces had emerged from the swirl of paint, and was staring out at Jennifer. If she moved a few feet to the left, the gaze followed her. If she backed up, the eyes remained locked in on hers; the message being transmitted through the medium was that there was no escape from one's predetermined destiny. Doomed, doomed, doomed, down here in this cold, damp basement in the half-light, consigned to a life bereft of passion; art was no longer the vehicle to salvation. It's one thing to suffer and then to create, it's miserable to suffer purely for the sake of suffering.

Sure, she had her boys, and they were doing okay, and there was no way she'd ever do anything too irrational to jeopardize their emotional and physical well-being, and they had been through enough already. Both were many years away yet from being out of the house on their own. So, there was purpose for her after all, wasn't there? But purpose and passion are two immensely different things.

Jennifer took the paint brush that was in her left hand and dabbed the bristles into a glob of earthen brown color, which had been mixed with a lighter shaded yellow; slowly, almost methodically she brought the brush up to the canvas, and ever so slightly touched the tip to the heavy paper. Simultaneously, the tears which had been welling in her eyes began to trickle out; one tear drop slid almost imperceptibly down her smooth, pinkish tinted left cheek. Yet it felt like a fingernail scratching her skin.

"I'm falling apart," Jennifer told the phantom clown face, as she set the brush down on the tray on the bottom of the easel, and then sat down herself on the floor. She wrapped both her arms around her bent legs, pulling them hard into the rest of her body.

How things can change. Though truth be told, some of it she had seen coming, and willfully chose to ignore, in the hope that eventually there'd be a shift inside of her heart, and the whole matter would line up all nice and neat. Wasn't that the way it was supposed to go? She had waited long enough in life, wasn't it her turn to be happy? But affection is not static, it ebbs and flows, and inevitably follows an ordained, true course. Like with like. Still, we can cling to the hope that with a touch more concentrated effort, a little more empathy and compassion, and some good old-fashioned patience, certain desired destinations within, can finally be reached. But at some point, after the joviality of the holiday season had worn off, it had all become clear to Jennifer. The truth, so lucid and pure, could no longer be dodged and evaded. Whatever being sought, was instead receding into the distance, further and further away. So, on day one of the new year Jennifer broke the chains that bound her to such false ideations; she said goodbye to the man she loved, but was not in love with.

Thus, there was another new beginning, but like with many a new beginning, the momentum at some point usually wanes until it stalls out, and we can be left staring into the vacuum of that which we have manifested. Nature abhors a vacuum; humans can feel as if they have been left to wither and die, with no hope for salvation, and the promise that tomorrow may bear glad tidings, or if nothing else, just some small degree of peace and comfort, has all but faded away.

Jennifer knew she was being dramatic, but she didn't care. It was fun in a twisted way to languish in it; hell hadn't she earned the right to do so? She thought about calling him, several times of late, but wasn't so sure just what that might accomplish. Plus, it was better to instead hold on to the thought that at some point she could call him, instead of actually having to go through with it in the present. And that also prevented a door from opening which might lead to even more heartbreak, on an even higher plain. Or so the somewhat convoluted calculations seemed to indicate, did they not? And it also seemed at times like he was in another galaxy anyway, with all those damned miles and states between them. Stupid states. Jennifer wished she could bend the time-space continuum, despite the fact that she really didn't know what in the hell it was to begin with? But it did bring a smile to her face, through the tears that continued to fall. And memories of that one particular night came rushing back; the two of them in her living room late one winter night with all the lights off watching the television with the volume turned really low so it wouldn't wake her sons who were asleep upstairs. She and Denny laid beneath the heavy afghan blanket on the couch watching reruns of Northern Exposure, and that one long haired guy was on the radio speaking all about physics and stuff that made zero sense to Jennifer. God, what she wouldn't do to be lying there with him watching that stupid show again?

  As if an alien suddenly snatched possession of her body, Jennifer practically leaped up off the ground, went up the wooden staircase leading out of the basement, grabbed a coat and hat, and exited out the side door of the house and into the icy cold chill of the night. The snow made a crunching sound as she walked on the cement pathway that was between her house and the one neighbor's; apparently Micah had forgotten again to shovel it like she had asked. Oh well thought Jennifer, what does it really amount to in the grand scheme of things? He's a good kid. So is his younger brother Tobias. The frigid air invigorated Jennifer, like shots of expresso being pumped into her blood, as she walked along Fourth Street before taking a left onto Iron Street, and heading westward through the slumbering town. The motion itself too felt liberating, almost intoxicating; Jennifer stole glances at many of the houses as she quickly passed by. Most of them were the very same houses on the very same streets which had served as the scenery in the entire narrative of her life, for over forty years now. For she had never lived more than a mile away from the home she had been born and raised in.

In the middle of the Grove Park, was the same swing-set that had been there since Jennifer was in grade school; on some nights after dinner, her Dad would take her by the hand and they'd walk the couple blocks to the tree-filled park, and usually end up over by the swings. Tonight, she sat on one of the swings and pushed off from the snow-covered ground with both feet, and began to glide back and forth through the stillness of the air. When she let her imagination take hold, her father's calloused, yet gentle hands could be felt on her back, as he pushed Jennifer to swing higher and higher into the sky, like a baby bird taking flight. There was no fear, only the pure exhilarating rush of freedom. Back and forth she went like a pendulum, back and forth. The past and present for a few magical moments melted together; that precocious, yet charming little school girl got to come out and play. Free to fly, free to explore; the whole expanse of the universe was just a push of her father's hands away.

Back home, Jennifer brewed a piping hot cup of chamomile tea, which warmed and soothed her insides as she sipped the sweet liquid. She sat at the kitchen table, in the dark, with her hands wrapped around the mug. But the moonlight that streamed through the windows, cast enough pale light for her to be able to observe the steam from the tea wafting up into the room, before vanishing into oblivion. There was a sensual poetic rhythm to the visuals of it all, but which could not be articulated into any language by Jennifer; she knew, however, how to capture the essence with paints and a brush. And she knew who too, would appreciate the sublime moment just as much as she was, sitting there at the table minutes before the clock on the wall would strike midnight. If someone outside were to have peered into the kitchen, they would have witnessed even in the low light, a sparkle flickering in the emerald eyes of the woman seated there, and perhaps the slightest of smiles beginning to form on her face. Life is not be endured, it is to be lived to the utmost capacity inherent in each vibrant soul, in the here and now, and forevermore. In a flash Jennifer was down in the basement again, leaving a half-finished cup of tea still steaming on top of the kitchen table.

Chapter 16

The snow continued to fall and blanket the farmland; the landscape was being transformed minute by minute into a wintry paradise, as the snowfall stuck to the bare branches of all the oak, maple, and birch trees, and laid heavier amongst the pines, and had even started to coat the reeds by the pond in white. The sound was at once like something Uncle Mike had never heard, yet as familiar as it had ever been; the muffled din that thousand upon thousands of snowflakes create when softly landing upon whatever lie beneath their joyous freefall. It was symphonic, ethereal; the snow swallowed up almost all other sounds, with the exception of the occasional squawks that the crows made high up in the trees across the far-side of the pond, and the chatter of a lone blue jay who chose to hang around in the pine tree closest to the front porch where Uncle Mike himself sat, under the dry shelter of the rustic, wooden roof.

He slowly rocked back and forth in the chair; Uncle Mike was bundled in a flannel, a sweatshirt, and a winter coat, all of which miraculously for him, managed to keep the cold air at bay. The last time he had on so much clothing was probably when he was deer hunting in Maine. But he wasn't going to miss having another front row seat to all of this. "You have blessed me mother nature today with another snow storm before I depart your holy grounds," he proclaimed aloud. The blue jay voiced its approval of said declaration, which caused Uncle Mike to chuckle. I'm the luckiest fool alive he thought. It had just snowed a few days ago as well; about four inches had accumulated on the farm. The forecast was predicting close to the same, or a little more this go around, but based on what had already fallen, and how hard it was snowing at the moment, the total could end up being more in the six to eight inch range. At least those were Uncle Mike's prognostications.

A pipe was dug out from one of the shirt pockets, and plugged with some tobacco from the pouch that sat on a small table. Uncle Mike took a lighter out from his pants, and puffed a few times on the stem so it would light, and he could enjoy his afternoon smoke, though he was careful not to inhale. Don't tell the doctor Cecelia he said silently, like he did each and every day. Though his primary doctor did actually know that he liked to occasionally smoke, and understood that advising him on how to live out the remaining days was a fool's errand at best.

And when such a time was about to come, his son Roger would be there; the recent phone conversation relieved Uncle Mike tremendously, for it was one of the last ties that needed to be mended on earth. He had started to look forward to seeing Cecelia again, in heaven, for he truly believed such a reunion would take place; a dream he had the other night of the two of them together served to strengthen such a conviction even more. She appeared to him so real, that when he awoke, he felt like he could almost smell her scent in his clothes. From an intellectual, and of course most importantly from a religious and spiritual standpoint, Uncle Mike was curious to see how the whole death experience would occur, such as what would happen in the immediate aftermath of his passing? Not that he desired to cross over a moment too soon, before he was meant to. But instead of fearing the unavoidable, a more enlightened, and less moribund view of the final act in the natural cycle that all sentient beings go through, had been adopted.

Uncle Mike looked at his watch. It was almost four thirty in the afternoon. He figured Denny would be leaving work soon and getting ready to drive home, before then going out and running the first of the two long workouts listed on the plan this week. Since he hadn't gotten a text from him this morning, Uncle Mike assumed his nephew hadn't arisen super early and knocked the sucker out before sunrise. I bet it was a bit too cold for his liking he surmised, as temperatures even down in Carolina Beach had fallen into the twenties, if the data on his smart phone's weather app could be trusted. He preferred the old-fashioned importance of observation, which had been honed over the decades spent being an amateur meteorologist, though Uncle Mike had retired as an official weather spotter for the National Weather Service's field office in Allentown.

 Mr. Hackenberg came outside and joined him on the porch; for a bit the two of them sat in silence, thoroughly absorbed in their own orbs of thought, as they watched the snow come down. Finally, John asked, "how much are we going to get from her?"

 "About thirty minutes ago I would have told you five to six inches. But now I'm going with a slightly higher figure."

 "Why is that?"

 "Just a hunch based on how the intensity has picked up. I really do think the air that somewhat gets trapped in this hollow has the effect of wringing a little more moisture out of the atmosphere. More so with these storms that approach from a more southerly direction." Uncle Mike leaned forward after speaking and turned his gaze skyward, as if to verify his observation with some additional proof.

 "You're probably right. I've noticed how some of the coldest air can sink in right adjacent to the edge of the woods, near where the new barn is now."

"That's interesting to note as well," Uncle Mike replied. "Perhaps something to do with the air currents coming down off the ridgeline where the woods slope up?"

"Could be," Mr. Hackenberg said, as his eyes scanned the frontside of the property. "Some of the biggest storms we've had around here have come up the coast."

"Yes," Uncle Mike rather animatedly agreed, as he coughed from accidentally inhaling pipe smoke. After regaining his composure, he continued, "what was the huge one we had in the nineties? I think 1993. It was the first year Roger was off at college."

"That sounds about right. Maggie was still alive. Before she had gotten sick. Lou may have already been out of school by then."

"We got a bunch of hum-dingers in the mid to late seventies too. Was like one or two big ones walloped us each winter and really dumped on the area."

"Yes indeed. I had just started planting a lot of the land here with Christmas trees. Lou was big enough to be out and helping me. The trees would get completely covered in snow after some of those storms."

"I used to send in measurements every hour to the weather service. I would stay up all night to do. Drove Cecelia nuts!" Uncle Mike's voice raised up with the last few words. He laughed out loud so much so, that it caused his body to spasm enough, that he dropped his pipe onto the porch.

"Guess it's time to quit again," he added, with less violent laughter. Uncle Mike was really enjoying himself. Not every day was as such, which made it all the sweeter. If nothing else, the bad days help us to all thoroughly appreciate and cherish the good ones. One did not have to tell Uncle Mike this tiny nugget.

"This time it's for good right?" asked Mr. Hackenberg, as he lit up a cigar. "We have earned the freedom to do as we please my friend," he added, before asking him what he would care to eat for dinner.

"I say we pan fry up that hamburger meat. Maybe boil a few potatoes to go with."

"I like it," Mr. Hackenberg said. "And we've got some of that apple pie left in the fridge for desert too."

"I almost ate that for lunch."

"Nurse Mancuso would have sent you to your room."

"That was after she had left. I've learned these last few weeks to be sneaky with her."

"Careful there Mike. She's quite sharp."

Like many conversations, this one ended at the point when one of the participants chose not to respond; in this instance it was Uncle Mike, who instead resumed watching with rapt attention the snow as it dropped out of the low, charcoal grey clouds, which by now had almost enshrouded the entire breadth of the hollow. Big round snowflakes had mixed in with the smaller, finer ones that had been predominately falling; the plumper ones descended from the sky at a slower rate, which created the appearance of two storms overlapping each other. It was a curious phenomenon that Uncle Mike had witnessed several times before. Nonetheless, he was just as fascinated now, as he had ever been in his life. A couple feet away his long-time friend also watched the snow; finally, Mr. Hackenberg stood up without saying anything, put his cigar out on the rusted, tin can by the front door, and walked back inside the house to begin the preparations for dinner.

Chapter 17

Denny was reading the novel *Born to Run* again. By now he had lost count of the number of times he had read the seminal book, which never failed to deliver a shot of adrenaline to his running. It was like a junkie sticking a needle in their arm; Denny mainlined it all, and took the tonic with him out onto the roads and trails, losing himself as he ran through the prism of written words being devoured every evening. The banality of an eight mile run was transformed by the pure animalistic joy felt swishing along a trail right before dusk, as the sun slipped below the tree-line across the Cape Fear River, leaving a pinkish, peach glow in the base of the western sky, as darkness crept over the canopy of trees Denny ran beneath. A narrow trail beside the Intracoastal Waterway would transport the mind to scenes so vividly depicted of remote places such as the Copper Canyons in Mexico, or like those high up in altitude in the wilds of the Rocky Mountains.

Each run became an affirmation of life, a testament to the intrinsic beauty abounding on the planet. Plus, Denny was laying down seventy-five miles per week, sometimes even more; he felt lean, fit, and fast, like a wild animal tracking its prey. For him, the prey was the Boston Marathon, the thoughts of which made his bones tingle even on the coldest of mornings, as the days ticked off towards that special Monday in April. With each passing run, the enterprise became a little more real; any sort of communication from the Boston Athletic Association caused his heart to quiver in anticipation, whether delivered electronically through email, or the actual postal system itself.

Denny was grateful for it all, and saved anything received, including the envelopes. He had gotten more involved with a Facebook group called the Boston Buddies, comprised of several thousand runners. It was a rush to be one amongst so many training for the exact same race; a far-reaching band of athletes who were scattered not only all over the country, but all over the world.

On the second Saturday of February, Denny had a twenty-miler on the schedule that included twelve miles at marathon pace. The workout would be a good benchmark for where his aerobic fitness was at, relative to the goal of breaking three hours. The previous pace miles Denny had run two weeks prior had left him uneasy with the prospects; he had struggled when the pace had dropped into the 6:50 to 6:55 per mile range. Or better stated, maintaining that pace felt like it had required too much effort; by no means was the workout fluid or smooth, indicators that perhaps the body was not ready physiologically to respond how it needed to, and how Denny would have ideally liked it to. That being said, he was still able to average under 6:55 for the ten marathon simulation miles, and it had been a fairly windy morning when the run had taken place. Plus, goal pace miles can feel harder than they should sometimes, leaving the runner to second guess their stated ambitions. It was all part of the process, and a process Denny had been through before. There were always ups and downs.

When dawn broke, the weather was much more agreeable on this particular day; the temperatures were in the mid-thirties, and forecast to rise into the forties, with only the slightest of breezes coming from the north. Cold, but not freezing cold, which was Denny's preference. Like most runners he almost constantly fretted about the weather, especially on long run and workout days. After completing the pre-run warm-up routine of lunges and leg swings, Denny put on his new lime green arm sleeves from Runner's Warehouse, which he pulled down snug to the base of his gloves, put a beanie over his head, and headed out the door. Beyond all that gear, mainly for the extremities, he wore just a pair of shorts and a t-shirt, for there was business to be conducted today.

A mile into the run, Denny entered the trails of the Carolina Beach State Park from the greenway, which was a macadam bike and jogging path that snaked for several miles through the town of Carolina Beach. The trail he ran on was unmarked, and seldom used, since it was separate from the main system of trails in the park. The tops of many of the trees bent or leaned in over the single-track trail, which gave one the impression of running in some sort of tunnel. At least that's what Denny thought, so one day out the blue he decided to name it the "Boston Tunnel," since many of his runs the last several weeks had utilized the trail.

The sun hadn't risen much above the distant horizon yet, hence there wasn't much light in the tunnel; Denny kept his head angled low and his eyes peeled to the ground to avoid tripping over any roots, or slipping on any mud slicks, as it had rained heavily two days before. Some of the standing water in there was prone to freeze into ice, most notably in the sections of the woods that remained in the shadows during the day. He hadn't taken a tumble in quite some time, so perhaps Denny was due to go down? He abruptly dismissed the thought as poppycock.

For the last two weeks or so Denny's right knee had been bothering him. He figured it might be a touch of tendonitis since the discomfort, usually rather slight, was beneath the knee cap and not on the outer part, which would be more indicative of an IT band problem. A friend had given him what initially seemed to be an odd remedy, and that was to stand on one leg for thirty seconds at a time, focusing on keeping balance with the leg that was acting up. And lo and behold, whatever had been bugging him had abated a good bit the last few runs. However, Denny had begun to feel a slight soreness or tightness in his left hamstring; he speculated it could be from the twelve-hundred-meter repeats he had run on Tuesday, which had left him very fatigued afterwards. His grandmother for some odd reason just then popped into his mind, as he cut over to Sugarloaf Trail, for she was fond of saying, "if it's not one thing, it's another." Maybe the woman had been a runner at heart too.

 The trails had a virginal, pristine look and smell to them as Denny ran; he was accompanied by the sound of birds awakening in the woods, and the nasally cackling natter of squirrels that skittered all about. He decided to add some easier paced hills to the workout, by repeating a loop that went up and down several short but steep hills near Sugarloaf Hill, which was also included. The sandy surface of the trails over in that section of the park provided some additional resistance as well. Denny chugged up each hill at a moderate clip, then sort of free floated downward, allowing gravity to assist. Atop Sugarloaf, he would briefly gaze out at the Cape Fear River, as it lazily meandered southward towards the ocean. The surface of the water appeared benign and tranquil, which belied the dangers lurking below the surface of the almost mile wide river. For it was besot with dangerous undercurrents and crosscurrents, that over the centuries of recorded history, gave credence to the word fear contained in its name.

 After close to thirty minutes of hills, Denny headed towards the marina and boat launch, allowing his legs to bound easily on the dirt and pine straw covered double-track trails. He had also been making more of a concerted effort of late to get in more miles off road, and on softer surfaces such as trails. Since the days were now staying lighter longer, and into the early evening hours, Denny was able to get in say four to five miles in the state park before it would become too dark to safely see the ground in front of him, at which point he would head back out onto the roads for the remainder of the run. Sometimes the Fitness Trail would be incorporated into the runs; this was a mile-long track shaped in a spaghetti-like loop situated in a patch of wooded land across the street from the main entrance to the state park. Denny decided to head there today, after taking a drink of water from the fountain up under the overhang of the marina building, and right next to the bathrooms. Flytrap Trail led him then through a dense thicket of woods, and across a boardwalk-like bridge which was raised a few feet above the swampy terrain. It was always murky and gloomy in that part of the park, which was one of his favorite spots to run through.

    Denny crossed Dow Road, which traversed the backside of the island, and entered onto the Fitness Trail loop. He circled it once, then popped out to the road to begin the pace miles. Per the standard modus operandi, Denny vowed not to look at his watch until the ding sounded after each elapsed mile, instead planning to rely on intuition, coupled with sensory data to gauge progress. From the jump, he felt rather strong, picking up the sense that he was smoothly flowing above the surface of the roads, with the legs efficiently propelling the body forward. A welcome contrast from two weeks ago. The first mile split bore out the observations, as Denny went through in 6:53, a hair over the pace needed for three hours. But he was holding back a bit; similar to the beginning of runs, Denny knew that the pace miles would also naturally increase in speed, as the internal mechanisms gradually acclimated to the task. The differences were, and would be miniscule. But they would come. True to form, the second mile clocked in at 6:50, and the third in 6:46.

Sometimes a runner gets an early inclination of how things are going to play themselves out over the duration of a training run or race, whether that be positive or negative. Today, Denny knew he was dialed in, and that it was just a matter of staying cool and sensibly executing the rest of the way. Not that it wasn't going to require one hell of an effort to finish the workout. Nor would it not be somewhat painful, and demand much of Denny physiologically. This was something housed in the intricacy of the endurance athlete's brain; in the specifics germane to the run at hand, it was being able to feel the difference between having to strain to run at a 6:50 pace, versus being able to run at a 6:45 clip while exerting slightly less effort.

Denny ran all through the streets of Kure Beach, and eventually onto the boardwalk, which extended for several hundred meters north from the iconic, cement fishing pier located in the center of the town. The ocean's waves rolled in and out; the noise created kept cadence with the rhythm of his breathing. Denny's shoes practically glided on top of the wooden surface, for they only made a trivial thumping noise with each footfall. The sun had risen well above the horizon, demarcated by where the water met the sky. It cast beams of light that playfully rode up and over the white capped tops of the waves. Denny could smell the saltwater in the air; his senses were finely tuned to the surroundings. The miles clicked off in a machine-like precision, with splits that fell through the 6:40s, before dipping into the high 6:30s. And the kicker was that Denny could have gone faster had he wanted to; the final two cool down miles after the hard twelve he relished, like a delectable desert after an exquisite meal. It had been a good run indeed.

~

That evening Denny bundled up in multiple layers, and walked down the dark side street that led to the beach. He took small sips from a thermos filled with hot green tea, in which he had added two tablespoons of honey. Denny wrapped his gloved hands tight around the container, able to feel some of the warmth being generated. On the beach, he stood by the shoreline, watching each successive wave rise up, then crash into the ocean, sending splays of salt water and sea foam that flowed onto the sand until the momentum was exhausted; the water would then return to its place of origin, leaving a yellow, white foam behind. When the wind gusted, the foam blew away too. And when the wind blew hard from the north and on down the beach, it pretty much cut like a knife right thru the body, despite all the clothes being worn, and felt like an icy slap on Denny's exposed face. A cold front by now had cleared the region, and had delivered a rather pronounced change in weather from the calm, temperate conditions experienced earlier in the daytime.

Denny pulled the hood of his sweatshirt over the top of his already covered head and sat down a little way back up from the water. He crossed his legs in the sand in front of him, and pushed the thermos into the sand far enough so it could stand on its own. Then Denny took his hands and placed them on his thighs, just above the knee caps; he closed his eyes and sat very still, while following each breath as air was gently inhaled through the nose, and then a few seconds later exhaled back on out.

But the legs wanted to rebel; apparently, they were too sore and tired and beat up from the morning's long run to remain in the lotus position. Instead, Denny stretched them out in a 'V' flat on the beach, and noted with a touch of amusement, that each leg was equidistant to the position of the thermos. It was doubtful such practices would ever lead him to becoming a bodhisattva, but it was no matter, as he took another drink; the tea felt warm and soothing as it slid down his throat. There was some worry or mild concern that a head cold was starting to come on, for there was a little irritation and scratchiness in his throat. Hopefully it was nothing, but as a distance runner, extreme vigilance was a necessary price for anything health related, as it seemed at times like one had to be really on the defensive against the enemy. Denny made a mental note to take a thousand milligram packet of vitamin C when he returned home.

He did though return to his attempts at meditation; again, by closing the eyes and attempting to do nothing more than following the natural cycle of breathing, in and out. There were sublime moments when engaged in the ancient practice, that the most revelatory, divine thoughts would sprout, despite the irony that thinking was to be avoided. Like a few days ago, about how life on an elemental level was essentially nothing more than waiting for the next breath; this was the same for all living creatures, not only human beings. If the next breath never came, life itself was extinguished. Take another breath, and life is extended. Though when he contemplated this later on, the idea did seem a trifle silly and elementary.

Denny opened his eyes, and continued the meditation session, while staring out at the Atlantic Ocean. He tried to treat himself with a gentle, loving touch, instead of any harsh rebuke, as such advice he had recently gleaned from a book. "Be kind," he whispered towards the ocean. Just be kind.

But despite such a mindset, and despite the success of the day's run and a pleasant conversation with Uncle Mike over the phone before dinner, a strange sadness kept wanting to bubble up to the surface. It was the same elusive, indefinable, nagging feeling that Denny seemed to be vexed with a little too much of lately. Similar as to what would be done when experiencing any physical discomfort or pain when running, a mental scan was performed to try and diagnose what the root causes might be, that in this case, were perpetuating the somber countenance. On the surface, the basic needs of life were being met, such as food, shelter, finances, and on down the line. But he suspected that this was something originating from much deeper, and was something more biological, as if certain wires in the fundamental circuitry of the soul had become crossed, notably as it related to evolutionary stages in not only human life, but in that of all animal life. That though was as far as Denny could get, or perhaps as far as subconsciously he wanted to get, which probably didn't make a grain's worth of sense to anyone who wasn't inside his own head and heart. Or maybe there was something in the way blocking him from seeing just what it was? Like a failsafe inside, designed for our own protection from ourselves? Denny had his suspicions about that.

He turned to prayer more and more, trying not to seek answers, but to merely be content as Francis de Sales had written, to spend time in God's presence. Allowing the father to lay eyes upon the child. Denny had recently reread sections of a book that contained the collected works of de Sales; something that had really stood out this time was the counsel that we must at times remain in the midst of wintertime, though the spirt longs for the splendor of spring, and the freedom of summer. The soul must be content to choke on the stale, dry bread...

Denny wasn't sure how long he had sat in the cold sand looking out at the unlimited expanse of the sea, and up at the jet-black sky and all its tiny little stars which all stretched to infinity and beyond. He stood and looked around in both directions, up and down the beach; not a single other person was out there tonight, at least as far as the eyes could see through the darkness. Denny was alone. Perhaps ultimately, this is what tugged on the melancholy strings inside, playing a tune unheard, so tragically beautiful, that it could move one to spaces emotionally they never knew existed. But also within was a frightening terror for Denny, that he'd be unable to ever find his way back, to where he just figured he was supposed to be. None of it made sense, really. His legs ached as he started to walk again; that did make sense. Maybe all the other stuff did make sense in the eyes of the only other person Denny could think of who could perhaps understand, but they were so far away, on such a cold winter's night.

Chapter 18

Mondays always gave Denny the blues, same as it gave many folks the blues who were on a traditional Monday to Friday schedule. Once the day had mercifully progressed well into the afternoon and Denny had completed most of the tasks that merited his direct attention, he started to engage in his customary ritual of thinking about where he would run, after he had returned back home from work. It was a real mild day out; temperatures had soared into the seventies, and although it wasn't all that unusual for the latter part of February, it was well above normal, and by far the warmest day of the new year. There was chatter about spring being right around the corner, albeit couched with statements about how it was still too early to consider winter to be over. A co-worker even brought up the fact that it had snowed several inches two year ago on her birthday, which was on the seventh of March.

Some days, like today, Denny couldn't decide where to go to get the miles in, as it wasn't a workout or long run day. He had grown tired for some reason of going back to the state park, though he did want to get part of the mileage in on softer surfaces off-road; almost all the distance laid down over the weekend had been on the asphalt too. It wasn't as if he no longer appreciated the Carolina Beach State Park and its proximity to his residence, or the miles of trails and stunning scenery there, but at times Denny's running was prone to fall into ruts, when he felt like he was doing the same things or following the same routes over and over again. As he was about to log off his computer, the thought hit to run some loops on the Fitness Trail, which he had not visited of late. Well that's settled he thought as he grabbed his lunch bag out of a refrigerator in the breakroom. Upon exiting the building Denny was struck again by how gorgeous it was outside. Most of January, and a solid chunk of February had been rather cold and raw out.

The freedom of busting out the door to go for a run always felt a little extra special after the Monday workday had been slayed. Denny headed up the section of the greenway parallel to Cape Fear Boulevard, and that cut through the center of town, dressed in a pair of shorts and a tank-top. He passed several others out walking or riding bikes, undoubtedly enjoying the early evening weather. The sun appeared to be resting comfortably above the woods located on the backside of the island; the warmth being cast off led Denny to perspire a bit, even though he was moving at a casual pace. Boston was exactly eight weeks away; the thought of which again stirred up a tingling sensation inside the body, and caused his heart figuratively speaking, to skip a beat. With each passing day, and with each passing week, the whole thing was becoming a little more real, and not simply some far off event tucked behind pages and pages of months hanging on a wall calendar.

Denny hopped off the greenway, crossed the street, and headed along Seventh Street towards the front part of the Fitness Trail. He always liked to take this narrow, partially hidden single-track trail to connect to the main trail, which itself was wide enough to drive a vehicle on. But before Denny even arrived at his secret trail, it happened; an almost violent seizing of the muscles around the hamstring, in the middle of the upper half of his left leg. The pain was visceral and immediate, as Denny grabbed for the back of his leg and slowed into a limp of a jog, before stopping altogether on the side of the road. A steady, pulsating pain emanated from the back of the leg, and for several moments Denny just stood there stupefied, unable or unwilling to believe what had just happened. He was dumbfounded, as if trapped inside a bad dream. Unfortunately, it was rather real. Denny took a few deep breaths, and tried to regain his composure. He told himself not to panic. To stay calm. After all it was probably nothing. And nothing that a few good stretches couldn't alleviate. Which is what he did, keeping both legs locked at the knees and straight, as he bent over with arms extended downward, until the tops of his fingers could grasp the front of his shoes. Denny held the pose for ten to fifteen seconds, and then repeated the basic stretch two more times. This appeared to help, as the action served to alleviate the shaper pain, and the nausea inducing feeling like the back of the upper leg was being squeezed into a vice grip.

    Next, Denny began to slowly walk up the side of the road, paying keen attention to what felt like every muscle fiber in the left leg. The first thing to check diagnostically was whether or not his natural gait was compromised, which didn't look to be the case. The next thing to do was to ease into a real relaxed jog. The initial few steps were okay, but then it struck again, as his left leg seized up like something was sinisterly attempting to choke the life out of the hamstring, rendering him incapable of taking normal strides. Denny stopped again off to the side of the road. He advised himself to be cool, as he said a quick little prayer to God asking for the fortitude to handle whatever was happening, and to help guide his subsequent thoughts and actions. And to remain grounded in the moment. Not to project. Try stretching again he told himself, like a coach instructing an athlete. Which Denny did. He started to walk again, slowly, passing the entrance to the little trail. He opted not to take it, for it just didn't seem like the right thing to do. Not under the current circumstances.

Instead, Denny entered the Fitness Trail from a more conventional spot about fifty meters up the road. Perhaps if he got onto the softer surface of the trail, and tried running there, the results would be better? The coach agreed, and suggested to give it a whirl. Which Denny did. And the same thing happened, for a third time. He literally couldn't run, for the first time in many years. Right then, a young woman innocently ran by. Denny watched her run, without what seemed like a care in the world, until she disappeared around a bend. The incident was almost surreal; the juxtaposition of a runner out doing what runners do, with a demeanor suggestive of a complete absorption in the dynamic activity, in stark contrast to the runner who just stood off on the edge of the trail, with perhaps a sullen look of jealousy stamped on their face. It all burned white hot inside of Denny. For in those instances he wished he was her, out there running. Nothing more, nothing less. The sole simple act of running in and of itself; the desire he suddenly felt was almost overwhelming.

Nothing remained to be done except to walk home. And pray. For some serenity in all this, which intuitively Denny knew would be of utmost importance. It was strange, or so Denny thought a block or two later, that in a short span of time he did feel a little measure of peace about the thing. The rational side of his brain then began a deep dive into the task of trying to asses the injury, and how or what may have precipitated its onset. Denny recalled he had felt some minor pain in the same hamstring Sunday morning near the end of his run, somewhere in a residential neighborhood between Kure and Carolina Beach, but it had disappeared almost as fast as it shown up, therefore no further thought or attention had been put into the occurrence. Outside of perhaps another cursory acknowledgement of the multitude of aches and pains that are an inevitability of the sport, when a runner is training as hard as Denny currently was. And wasn't it ironic, in sort of a cruel, twisted way, that the past few workouts had been some of the best of the training cycle? But sometimes that's the just way it all goes.

Or maybe some of those very same workouts had been a little too good, in the sense that perhaps Denny had pushed a little too hard? Denny didn't think so, but the possibility had to be analyzed. As did the accumulation of mileage the last several weeks, though he felt from the beginning of the plan that a fairly intelligent, measured approach had been followed, consisting of an incremental increase in the number of miles run per week, and per month. In retrospect had he been intelligent, or was he only fooling himself with the belief that worshipping at the altar of high mileage was the divine pathway that led to the running promise land? Perhaps there were blind spots, when it came to certain components of the workload. As Denny trudged the mile or so distance back home, it became clear that no concrete answers were imminently forthcoming, at least not tonight. But hopefully it was only something minor, a slight bump in the road; tomorrow was a new day, and he could always change things up and go for an easy run and push the next scheduled workout back to Wednesday, keeping everything right on track. Or an extra day off wouldn't matter all that tremendously much anyhow. It felt weird and almost out of body to be walking on the very same greenway he had been running on less than thirty minutes ago. And what made the situation even more poignant, was again how nice the weather was, and just how splendid of an evening it was along the coast of North Carolina.

The first thing to be done upon entering home was to place a phone call to Uncle Mike. Denny picked up his cell phone and dialed, and listened as the ring tone went through once, twice, three times; there was no answer, and he didn't have the words ready to explain the nature of the call over voice mail, so the connection was terminated, and the phone tossed onto the couch. A fit of anger suddenly rose up inside of Denny; he balled his right hand into a fist and went over to punch the door to the water heater, but fortunately caught himself before landing a right hook. So much for remaining in a healthy spiritual frame Denny deliberated, as a small wave of panic also clutched him. If the clock could only be wound back thirty minutes. Thirty freaking minutes! It was only twenty after six. It felt unnatural to be home at such an hour. Denny should be several miles into say a ten-mile run, out and about somewhere on the island. So, he paced up and down a hallway, and even eased into a light trot, until forced to turn around and head in the opposite direction. Did the hamstring feel alright now? It was a tad sore, but perhaps an overreaction had taken place. Or maybe whatever muscles that had misfired had fixed themselves, and returned to a state of equilibrium? Denny went to the far end of the bedroom, in order to maximize the space, and then ran a bunch of faster steps; nope, the hamstring hadn't miraculously healed, as the same wicked, constricting pain flared, forcing him to have to short step his stride with the left leg. It was no use.

    Maybe icing would help? Denny always instructed his kids when they told him something was sore, or pain was being experienced, to apply ice to the muscles. This would help to take down the microscopic swelling of the tissues around the muscles. A frozen bag of peas was grabbed from out of the freezer; Denny sat on the floor and placed the bag on top of a dish towel, and placed the back of his upper left leg on top of the frozen vegetables. What would've Uncle Mike have said if he had answered the phone? Denny mulled this over. Pray. Pray and ice the bastard. That did make Denny want to laugh, though he didn't. Just then the phone did ring; it was his uncle calling back.

"I'm hurt. Hamstring. Shit took me down," Denny said into the phone.

"What?" was the reply heard on the other end of the line, after a second or two of confused silence.

"Locked up on me. Pretty bad. Had to stop the run and walk back home."

There were another few seconds of silence, followed by Uncle Mike saying, "gosh I'm sorry. Are you alright?"

"Yes. I'm icing it now. With a frozen bag of peas. I'm at home," Denny stammered into the phone. There was no reply, so he continued, "I can't remember the last time I had to abort a run so early. Actually, I can. I just remembered." Denny ceased speaking again. He wanted to, or perhaps needed to hear something from the other person on the call. Anything.

Finally, Uncle Mike spoke. "Well take it easy on yourself. A few days rest won't necessarily be the end of the world Denny. May actually do you some good. I don't have it in front me but I think you ran seventy-seven miles last week."

"Yes."

"And I'm sorry boy. I know how well the training has been going."

"Yeah I know. Rest up a bit. I just needed to hear it from someone else."

"And I do understand how frustrating it can be. I've been there myself. Many times." Actually, the reality of it was Uncle Mike had almost never sustained any injury that would have sidelined him for more than say a few days tops in his entire running career. But neither of them was going to quibble over such a statement. As cliché as it may be, sometimes it is the thoughts that really count.

His uncle asked about what had actually happened, and Denny went on to explain in much detail, even adding in the part about the woman running on the Fitness Trail. He adjusted the bag of peas as he spoke, then apologized for being rude and not asking Uncle Mike how he was doing himself.

"I'm alright. Just sitting here by the fireplace reading a book about the Spanish Civil War. And occasionally falling asleep," he answered, with a slight chuckle.

"Sounds peaceful. The sleep part. Not the war."

They said goodnight, not before Uncle Mike assured him that everything was going to work out fine, and to pray for and work on acceptance. And before he went to sleep that night to read the *Prayer of Saint Francis*. It all sounded like sage advice to Denny, who felt better after the phone conversation. If nothing else, the burden had been shared. He thought too more about the last time being hurt; by now it had to have been five years ago, or maybe six or seven when Denny had an IT band injury. It had been later in the fall, towards wintertime, while in training for the Gator Trail 50k ultra at Lake Waccamaw, which was about an hour's drive inland from the coast. The race was scheduled for that next February.

The pain then was on the outside of his right knee, and had been bothering him off and on for several weeks, until one run the entire knee locked up, just as he was about to enter the trails of the state park. Like tonight, Denny had initially stopped and stretched, walked a bit, and then attempted to run again several times. And like tonight, all the attempts proved to be fruitless; at the time Denny didn't realize that weakness in the IT band was the cause of the problems manifesting in the knee, but eventually a proper diagnosis was made through internet research and conversations with many fellow runners, some of whom had experienced the exact same injury.

With such knowledge, came information about how to correct, what in that instance, was a muscular imbalance. This entailed numerous strengthening exercises for the hamstrings, glutes, and core muscles. Denny also began to wear a Velcro band on his right leg just below the knee, as was suggested by a friend in the Wilmington Road Runner's Club. But it took months of work for the injury to ultimately heal, and for the first few weeks Denny was only able to run once or twice per week. There were many more attempts during that time, especially early on, which ended in failure. A lot of days Denny was unable to even get out the door, or didn't even bother to try. Other tries came to a crashing halt with him walking back home after getting a mile or two into a run, at which point the knee would painfully seize, and lock the whole leg up.

Many evenings after work Denny would go run around the Carolina Beach Lake, located a few blocks away from his home, since there was a section of grass adjacent to the cement pathway which circled the small body of water. Running on softer surfaces would alleviate some of the pain, and prevent the knee and leg from being rendered immobile. Denny had read too that running on grass could help expedite a return to a regular running routine, and there were just enough lights by the lake to be able to see the terrain beneath his feet. During the holidays, there were also all sorts of Christmas decorations placed around the lake; palm trees with neon colored lights, flashing dolphins leaping out the water, blinking reindeer working to pull Santa's sleigh. It was a veritable show, and in some bizarre fashion gave Denny psychological comfort. Pretty soon he knew the location of every light fixture. Eventually he was able to get back to running three, four times a week, and also able to withstand a weekend long run on the trails of the state park, where oft times a group of runners all training for the same ultra would meet up. Each Saturday or Sunday morning another say fifteen, twenty minutes was added to the duration of the run, until Denny had gotten up to doing what equated to sixteen, eighteen miles a pop, with only minimal amounts of pain and stiffness in the right knee.

Denny ended up having a pretty respectable race, finishing the 50k on single track trails in about fours and fifteen minutes, which netted him third place overall in the small field.

He hadn't thought about any of all that in a very long time; it brought some solace though, like the phone call with Uncle Mike. Maybe things weren't so bad after all? Maybe if he stayed calm and stayed upbeat all of this would quickly resolve itself in a favorable way. Denny did decide to take the next day off, and err on the side of caution. Hopefully his running could be resumed the day after. It all seemed sensible and logical to him; in the interim he would ice the hamstring, take Ibuprofen to also alleviate swelling, and continue to stretch the legs out several times a day.

~

Two days later, the work day incessantly dragged; several times Denny got up from his desk and walked around, ostensibly to test out his hamstring, which didn't appear to be giving him any trouble. About mid-way through the afternoon he even stood up purposely quick, and proceeded to fast walk a couple minutes around the parking lot, again to no ill effect. Cautious optimism reigned supreme during the half hour commute home; Denny even entertained the thought that if the leg held up okay during the first few miles, he could just go ahead and jump into the longer run and workout listed on the training plan, the one that would have been tackled on Tuesday. Once again, the weather was delightful. Denny changed into shorts and a tank top almost as soon as he got through the front door. He debated running shirtless, but wasn't confident enough that the hamstring would hold up for such a choice of attire, or in this instance, lack of attire.

Certainly, his legs were ready to fire out and do some work, which could be discerned from the get go. They had been granted essentially two days' rest, which could be classed as a positive by-product of the physical ailment. Up the greenway Denny went again, feeling nothing more than some minor discomfort in the left hamstring area. Cautious optimism were the buzz words bouncing around in the brain; moments later such heady thoughts were shattered, as the same vicious tightening, and cramp-like pains started pulsating in the rear of the upper leg, forcing Denny to cease running, and slow immediately into a walk. He hadn't even made it a mile yet. Denny then stopped and bent over to touch his toes for twenty seconds, keeping both legs straight, while counting in his head. Perhaps he should have stretched like this before beginning the run, instead of just doing his usual leg swings to warm-up? Though he had skipped the lunges. The stretch was repeated three more times; Denny reached his arms and hands as far down as possible, until the top parts of his fingers touched the asphalt. The surface felt warm to the touch. An easy walk followed, without much thought as to what to do next or why, for once again Denny was in a state of partial shock. He transitioned at some point into a slow jog; within thirty to forty meters, the run was over.

It was useless. The leg had flatlined like on Monday evening. There was nothing left to be done except to walk on home. Like some sort of walk of shame. On the greenway. In full display, in the middle of town. This time Denny's spirits really sagged; it took a great deal of restraint, and the fact that a young kid was right up ahead with his parents, for him not to cuss and scream out loud. For tonight he was pissed off, angry, though after walking for a few minutes Denny was able to temper his emotions some. But then fear began to kick in; fear and a plethora of questions. Fear about what was actually going on, and how serious it might be? How long might the thing take to heal? Thus, what was to be done in regards to the training plan? On top of all that, how could Denny ever expect to achieve the goal of breaking three hours if he wasn't able to get all the training in, that surely was a necessity to accomplish such a feat?

    Denny didn't have any answers, just a myriad of questions, that seemed to keep getting fired at him from all angles. The natural inclination was to feel sorry for oneself; after all there can be a familiar comfort when languishing in the throes of self-pity. But he didn't want to go there. He couldn't go there. That was just jaded thinking, self-pity that is. A bottomless pit. Tomorrow is a new day. Tomorrow is a new day. Maybe I should sing the damn pithy phrase. His humor was becoming bleak. But it was no time to panic, at least not yet. Perhaps a few more days off, in the wide scope of things, would ultimately serve as a blessing in disguise? Time would tell. In the meantime, ice and stretch. Take ibuprofen. Repeat. It'll all be okay. Or would it?

Chapter 19

    The ground was soft and mushy but solid enough to run on. Keith picked his way along Prairie Grass Trail, as the narrow single-track trail incrementally wound up the base of the Blue Mountain, and away from the D&L. He predominately ran hunched forward, with his head hung rather low, party to avoid tripping on any rocks or roots. However, about every five minutes, Keith would slow and almost come to a halt, in order to look out back behind him to see how high in elevation he had climbed, relative to the ground below. By now the Lehigh River was almost fully visible, above the trees that lined the nearside bank. After another two hundred feet or thereabouts of climbing, Keith came to Powerline Trail, which cut horizontally with the slope of the mountain, and was much wider and easier to run on, since its surface was mostly dead weeds and grass. From there the western end of the town of Palmerton was visible, as was the vast acreage of barren landscape where the Zinc Company used to be located. Keith's grandfather Richie had worked there for almost his entire adult life, as had so many long since departed citizens of the area.

    He was able to open up his stride and air it out so to speak, running on a narrow shelf about half way up the north face of the mountainside. It had become a Sunday ritual for weeks now to come here and run, while Suzanne and the children attended church as Saint Peter and Paul's. For this is where Keith had begun to establish his own relationship with God, or a conception of a god that had been percolating inside of him for awhile now. It was best not to overly define any attempts at communion; rather, what seemed to be more natural was to simply let the feelings flow. All the doctrinaire, sacraments, and organization of religion were not for him; had he been raised up in the Catholic Church, maybe so, and certainly no qualms were to be had with those who believed in their importance.

No, for Keith it was more the freedom of nature in its infinitude, where he could find himself able to penetrate beyond the temporal world, and catch glimpses into an underlying spiritual realm, that had the power to mystify and almost overwhelm, but in a way absent of any trepidation or tangible concern. Out here he didn't have to hide, or assume a role. He most definitely knew what it was like to be boxed in by the very walls one helped to construct. When the pressures of societal expectations become too much to bear. A person then gets desperate and frantically claws at an escape, or gives in and wishes for the end.

There was something primordial about the simplicity of movement, which was in tune with all of those things that were perhaps beyond any rational explanation, but were so deeply felt inside. Or encoded within the strands of DNA. And that to Keith was the jumping off point where God came into play.

When he came to Devil's Furnace Trail, Keith took a right turn and headed up the mountain, slowly making his way up another single-track trail, but one that was more technical than Prairie Grass. His breath became labored; lactic acid started to eviscerate his legs, rendering each step progressively more difficult, or so it felt. But Keith relished the challenge of the climb. The trail became rockier the higher one went, as did the landscape; certain rocks had orange tick marks painted on them, indicative of the optimal path to take. At times, it was prudent to walk, particularly on the steepest of stretches. Patches of snow began to appear, in areas that were shaded more from the sunlight. Usually it took Keith well over half an hour to reach the summit from where Devil's Furnace began, though not much credence was given to time, and pace was irrelevant. He did always keep his Garmin watch on though, in order to download the data later on to his laptop and pour over the information, especially the elevation maps. Such things fascinated Keith.

He grabbed ahold of a branch attached to a gnarled tree that jutted out from some large rocks, and hoisted himself up over to the other side, where the trail wasn't as vertical near the top of the mountain. Keith jogged the last stretch until he got atop the relatively flat summit, at about sixteen hundred feet in elevation. He bent over for a few needed moments, before straightening up and surveying the lay of the land some thousand feet below. To the left, and behind some rolling hills to the north and west, was Lehighton, and up and beyond, Jim Thorpe. The towns were all so miniature and microscopic looking, almost as if they weren't even real to begin with. Blurs of houses and buildings crammed tight together, nestled between the hillsides which rimmed their perimeters, like fortresses safeguarding the inhabitants. The thin, dark blue band that was the Lehigh River curled through the low lands, and connected all the little towns together, as if they were paperclipped to a string. Keith inhaled the pure, crisp air deep into his lungs, before beginning the descent back to civilization. He gave thanks first to the spirit of the mountain, for another trip skyward in her fold, and then started to bound down the trail. There was joy in his heart as he leapt from rock to rock, recalling something read a long time ago about how it was not possible to fall off a mountain.

Or maybe it was a Zen-like riddle that Denny had once told him; it sounded like something he would speak about. And that reminded Keith to text the guy when he got home, though there had been no response or reply from the last few messages sent, which was a bit odd. Maybe he had grown tired of hearing about my runs, or jealous about the ones like this, up here on so many of the trails he loved and had introduced me too? Who knew, Keith pontificated as he ran; his wayward friend could be very mercurial at times. He could always bore Suzanne with the details, or ask Niki to go for a walk after dinner. It hadn't been that super cold of late, so maybe she'll want to go with me again. And so it went inside Keith's mind for a time, until the thoughts just sort of extinguished themselves, whereupon the silence was shared with the ever-changing landscape, footfall after footfall, until he eventually found himself back on the D&L, less than a mile away from the parking lot where the run had commenced, a good hour and forty-five minutes earlier.

  At the truck, Keith took off his running shoes, stripped off his sweat pants, and slipped into an old pair of beater sneakers kept stashed in the rear cab behind the seats. After a few cursory, light stretches, he leisurely walked over to the small boat launch, and gingerly waded into the gently flowing waters of the Lehigh. The frigid cold water was always an initial shock, but in due course his body somewhat acclimated to the conditions. Somewhat being the operative word. Keith waded further into the river, which was pretty shallow, not even reaching a height much above his knees even thirty, forty feet from the shore. He searched around for a smoother spot on the river bottom to sit down, submerging his legs and backside into the water. It was damn cold, but also felt good.

  The sun shone high enough overhead, to cast an ample amount of light onto the river; the iron grip of winter had been loosened of late, as the month turned over to March. Keith tried to get a fifteen-minute soak in after these long, rambling Sunday runs, for he had read an article in *Runner's World* magazine about the benefits of doing so. Plus, it was meditative, once the cold was partially overcome.

A red-tailed hawk circled overhead near the edge of the river, above a thicket of trees near where Keith had entered the water. The mighty bird appeared to be gliding on the air currents with no apparent effort; it would swoop downward, then suddenly fly parallel to the ground, before lifting skyward again, as if propelled by an unseen force. He watched intently as the hawk gradually made its way downriver, until disappearing around the bend. Something inside of Keith shifted; perhaps the word grace would be the only way such a sensation could be verbalized, if one were to even attempt to do so. When the holy, white light is so blindingly bright, that it becomes impossible to actually see. This can occur in an instantaneous flash, and be gone before we even have the chance to think about grasping ahold of it.

Keith's legs were numb by now; he used his arms to help raise his body up and out of the river, then walked ashore. He scurried back to the truck and toweled himself off for the short ride on home.

Chapter 20

Day twelve. Like the twelve days of Christmas. But that was perverse, since there was no mirth or merriment in any of this; the best that could be done the past twelve days was a five mile run, gutted out in pain, which in hindsight was pretty stupid to being with, since Denny couldn't fool himself into thinking that his natural gait wasn't being compromised. He should have stopped, but what could be viewed as a borderline maniacal stubbornness had prevailed. Other attempts were made too; a couple of minutes running with minimal pain would buoy Denny's spirits, only to have them be summarily crushed once more, when the hamstring seized yet again. So, he'd take another day off, stretch, ice, eat ibuprofen. Deep down, Denny knew the cocktail wasn't working; the desired effects remained elusive. He reached out to runners, soliciting whatever advice they might be in position to volunteer, of which there was a fair amount. Including a variety of stretches and stretching techniques new to him. Jackie even emailed pictures. Other friends sent sympathetic messages. Word had traveled; Denny was now on the unofficial list of local endurance athletes on the shelf. A most dubious place to be.

Aerobic fitness was being lost, or so Denny assumed. For by now it had to be, if one believed in the reliability of decades worth of scientific research. A marathon runner like him couldn't cut two weeks out of the middle of a training plan and not expect negative consequences; or phrasing it in more succinct and personal terms, Denny was becoming more and more doubtful that he would have a plausible shot at breaking three hours. The kicker was that just prior to the injury, he was feeling as good as he had running wise in a long time. But now Denny was left kicking and moaning, unable to let go of the notion of wanting to wind the hands of time backwards, to three some weeks ago when that twenty-miler with all the pace miles had been killed out on the roads of Pleasure Island.

His entire daily routine was askew; there seemed to be an inordinate amount of free time. Denny would get home from work at five thirty and not know what the hell he should do with himself? And then there was the whole eating thing. That was all off kilter now as well, as meals and food always seemed to be tied into the training and calories being burned and calories that needed to be replaced, and treating oneself say after a hard workout or a long run. The harmonious interplay was broken. The lunch and dinner hours had fallen into becoming a monotonous function, a necessary means to sustain life, like animals in the wild. Denny continued to pray, and pray often, that much could be said. And he did try to remain somewhat upbeat, and for the most part succeeded at maintaining a relatively half-decent disposition in the company of others; but a multitude of fears continued to gnaw at his running psyche, and they were becoming a little more troublesome and pronounced with each passing day. Denny could also look in the mirror, and see behind any exterior façade; what was underneath was an obsessive, melodramatic, insecure, neurotic exercise junkie, left flailing around like a drowning man, desperately grasping for a life preserver.

The last few weeks it seemed as if things had begun to spiral even lower, but Denny himself, on a conscious level, was mostly oblivious to such changes. Perhaps there is a reason why we can be partially blind to our own souls? At some point on a particular Friday evening the door to the refrigerator had innocuously been opened. Inside, amongst many other items, was a bottle of beer; the same bottle of beer that had sat in the exact same spot far back on a shelf for well over two months. Rather tangentially, it would have been noticed by Denny dozens upon dozens of times. After all, he was the one who had placed it in there, as the bottle had been a holiday gift from a co-worker whom happened to brew their own beer at home. At the time, Denny didn't have the heart nor the inclination to tell this woman that he did not drink; after all it was much easier, and also more polite to graciously accept the kind gesture, and simply take the bottle home with him. Which is precisely what he had done, giving the matter nary a thought afterwards.

  Denny took the label-less dark green twenty-two-ounce bottle out of the refrigerator and set the gift on the kitchen counter top; it was cold to the touch, as he ran his hands up and down the smooth exterior glass. He recalled the half sheet of paper that had been included in the box with the bottle; on it were typed instructions about how to pour the contents into a glass for optimal enjoyment, that had something to do with how the sediments used in the brew process would settle, after being opened. Some kind of vintage number or batch number and bottle number indicative of when the beer had been made and bottled was also on this paper. Denny remembered now that it was a pumpkin ale; ironically, he had never cared for the taste of pumpkin too much, though he would eat a piece of pumpkin roll if offered. Never a piece of pumpkin pie. Lauren had unfortunately found that out last Thanksgiving. She was a nice gal too, and there were many other reasons it hadn't worked out. None of that, however, was actually going through Denny's mind; instead he merely stared at the bottle setting in front of him, like thousands had in his lifetime. And he had learned through bitter experience, it ultimately wasn't the thousandth bottle that would be his undoing, rather it was a single, solitary drink that had the power to destroy Denny, and to destroy anything and everything around him that he gave a damn about. Still he thought about it. He pondered the taste. And the effects, if they be much, the contents would have on him. For it had been such a long, long time.

Denny placed his right hand on top of the bottle and tried to twist the cap off, just to see if it would open, or if a bottle opener would be the requisite tool for the task. It became readily apparent that one would be needed, since the cap didn't want to budge. That didn't surprise him, since it made logical sense that a home brewed beer should not have a twist off cap, though extrapolated further, Denny had to conclude, if he was being honest with himself, that he knew precious little about the home brewing process, and what difference, if any, that the type of bottle cap would have on the bottle and the contents therein. What was obvious, in contrast, was that one needed a bottle opener to open this bottle, or a real strong set of teeth to rip the cap off. But there was no real desire anyway on Denny's behalf to even open it up; the whole thing after all was a rhetorical exercise.

Perhaps though, if he did open the bottle, a whiff of smell could be taken? Nothing more than that. Like a sommelier would do with wine. Denny opened the drawer in the kitchen where all the utensils were kept, just to see if he even had a bottle opener in the first place. He could also pour the beer into a glass, simply to watch and see how the sediments would actually settle. Denny thought he recalled the instructions specified a waiting period after the pour, for the beer to be in optimal consuming condition. Or was the wait period for after opening the bottle, before the pour?

Maybe they were lying around somewhere, the directions that is. Denny looked in the cupboards where there were glasses and mugs, and plates and dishes too. Then he realized it wasn't logical to have placed the paper in there, so the question begged, what were the logical places such instructions would have been stored at? On top of the refrigerator flashed inside his mind as a likely location; a check though revealed no such luck. Perhaps they would have been stashed inside a desk drawer in the den, but after some quick digging through various drawers and compartments, it became painfully clear that the elusive half-sheet of paper was not housed there either. Could it be in a dresser in the bedroom? That notion was dismissed as making no rational sense. But, Denny thought, there was another solution yet to be considered, which could potentially solve the dilemma. He had Piper's cell phone number, so he could just text or call and ask her what to do, right? This idea was rejected forthwith, for it was a road Denny did not want to begin to travel down, for more than one reason. Something to do with the law of unintended consequences.

Then another thought hit him. Can openers. Since he didn't have a bottle opener, he could use the back of the handle of a manual can opener. Most people probably didn't even know this. Denny took one of the two that he had, and clamped the handle on top of the beer, careful though not to actually pop the cap off itself, for this was all still in the theoretical stages. Instead, he remained frozen in a pose with his right hand holding the can opener, with his left hand wrapped around the body of the bottle. As he stood there, motionless, Denny took notice of how quiet it was. There was no television or radio on. The windows to the outside were all shut, as was the sliding glass door to the back patio. An occasional vehicle on the road below could be heard, but that sound was muffled, and seemed far off. Inside there was silence; an intensely penetrating, powerful silence. Only one light was turned on; the elongated, cylindrical bulb under the hood of the stove.

Moisture had begun to form on the glass bottle; small droplets of condensation could be felt, and a few even began to slide downward, forming tiny rivulets of water that eventually disappeared into oblivion, once the surface of the countertop was found. Denny removed his left hand from the bottle, which he realized he had been squeezing rather hard. He took the palm of his hand and placed it on his forehead, feeling the clammy, dampness of his skin; Denny also hadn't realized how flushed and warm he felt, despite the fact that the thermostat was set at its usual temperature of seventy degrees.

"What the hell am I doing?" he asked out loud, in part to shatter the eerie silence. A wave of fear coursed through him, so powerful that it felt like his legs were going to get taken out from under him. Denny released the can opener from his right hand, allowing it to fall to the counter with a metallic clang, as he lowered himself onto the linoleum tiles of the kitchen floor.

Denny also noticed his hands were trembling a little, and perspiration could be felt on other parts of the body too. Maybe God hears our silent pleas at those crucial moments when he's truly needed; maybe the rational side of our brain has just enough fortitude to be able to muster the quintessential thoughts desperately needed at life's pivotal crossroads? Or perhaps those theories bled into each another, at least for the lucky ones? For Denny knew what he had to do was to pick up the phone and make a call, to the person who could best be able to assist him right then and there.

"Hello," came the voice on the other end of the line; it sounded way off, yet so close in Denny's ear.

"Hi," was all he could meekly muster in response. A few interminable seconds of silence ensued, so much so that Denny was able to clearly hear Uncle Mike breathing.

Finally, his uncle, who could sense the disposition of the caller, cut the silence with his voice when he asked, "what's wrong?"

Denny wanted to blurt out that everything was wrong; it hit him like an oncoming freight train barreling through the pitch-black darkness of a tunnel. And he was frozen, standing on the tracks, his feet glued in place by all that was in fact wrong, and had been wrong for some time now. For suddenly Denny felt overwhelmed, not by the thought of taking a drink, for that had vanished the instant he had decided to make the phone call. He felt overwhelmed by the multiplicity of negative feelings that had been bubbling inside, buried at unfathomable depths within his soul; only occasional electric-like impulses were sent out though, which would give Denny the queer sense he was off-kilter, in some entirely imperceptible way. Like the thought of having certain thoughts with the power to wake him up in a sheer panic in the middle of the night. Any attempts to penetrate deeper into the abyss only led to more confusion, or muddled half-truths.

And thus, they talked. Openly. Honestly. Denny unloaded and unburdened himself, holding back tears at times. The subject of running barely came up in what would end up being an almost hour-long phone conversation; for two people who didn't particularly care much for chatting on the phone, it was a lengthy call indeed. At some point, Uncle Mike steered the talk to himself, and to specific events from the past not many people had known about, including his nephew. To say it was revelatory and poignant would not be hyperbole; the phone call answered some things Denny and others had wondered about and sensed throughout the years, the details of which were not known. And it also allowed Denny to powerfully see the humanness and fallibility, of a man whom he had admired and emulated in many sides of his own life for so long.

"At first it was only a few shots of bourbon here and there," Uncle Mike had begun, in a steady, but emotionally laden tenor. "But before long I was licking half a bottle after work. More on the weekends." He explained how this was right around the time his son and daughter-in-law were expecting their first baby.

"I recall thinking to myself that Olivia was going to go into labor in about a week to ten days." Uncle Mike paused for several seconds; once again Denny could hear him breathing. All the talking by now had drained almost every last ounce of energy from him, but the guy knew he had to forge ahead, like the endurance runner he once was, pushing through the pain and exhaustion until that finish line was crossed.

"It's okay Uncle," Denny almost whispered into the phone. Both of them, in their respective ways, were hanging by a thread.

"Anyhow. I had it all planned out to quit again. Give myself a few days to straighten up and dry out before it. They were counting on me for a whole bunch of important things." The strain in Uncle Mike's voice was palpable and visceral, even as heard from six hundred miles away. This was bringing him close to his own edge.

"Yes, I see," Denny said, almost involuntarily.

"Anyhow I couldn't stop. Absolutely couldn't. Everything just kept getting worse. Much worse." It sounded like he was gently weeping as he spoke.

"I understand," Denny interjected sympathetically, when the silence became a bit too much to bear. And he most certainly did understand, through his own losing battles with an unbeatable foe. All of it now with his uncle and cousin was clicking into place, as unfortunate as it was.

"I missed the entire thing. Seeing our granddaughter being born. All of it. When I came out of a blackout it was a week later. Some friend of your Aunt Cecelia found me wading in a lake with no shirt or shoes on."

"Jesus. You were on one hell of a bender."

"Yep." Uncle Mike sounded weak and raspy by now, but he soldiered on, determined that the recipient fully received the message on this given night.

He began speaking again, and stated, "I didn't get to see Eva until she was almost four years old. And me and Roger were never the same. I don't blame him. I don't."

"I had no idea," Denny replied. It was true. No one had ever told him any of this. But then again, they didn't necessarily have the closest of extended families; many years at best, it was an exchange of Christmas cards sent through the mail.

"That's the reason Denny I wanted you to think about some of your history. Like I had you do before driving up." Uncle Mike paused, and coughed once. "Don't ever, ever forget the misery. And all the heartache it caused."

"No sir. I won't." Denny was emotionally drained himself, and could hear the cracks in his own voice.

And so, the two had said goodnight, and the phone call had come to a close.

Denny did feel a tad guilty for the ordeal he had just put his uncle through, but Uncle Mike had assured him like he had in so many instances before, that everything happens for a reason; us humans just don't always have the capacity to discern what those reasons are at the time the events are occurring. That's the sovereign province of God.

Uncle Mike had lived his penance, but perhaps he had also found a way to transform some of it into something beneficial, beyond whatever might lie ahead with him and his own flesh and blood. He prayed often, and believed with every fiber of his being in forgiveness, and in the inherent good which can flower from the dirt of our own worst experiences.

Miles and miles away from where he sat in his reclining chair, a man crossed a dark parking lot to a dumpster next to the road. A bottle was tossed into it, which landed with a dull thud atop the trash that was piled up inside.

Chapter 21

    Finally, some of the intense stretches a fellow coach had given Denny began to have a positive effect on the hamstring. The amped up core work which had been suggested to him as well, also may have been paying dividends. For he had been able to run the last two days, with not much noticeable discomfort, and little in the way of lingering after effects. And for the first time since shortly after the injury's onset, Denny was beginning to feel a budding optimism building inside. The time had arrived, or so the ardent hope was, to start to climb back on the horse, especially if there was any chance of having a solid showing in Boston. He assumed there was close to zero margin for error from here forward, as the race was a little under five weeks away.

    Keith had enthusiastically jumped into the fray as well, once Denny had finally let on as to what was up with him. He didn't have much to offer training wise, but was instrumental in helping to boost Denny's flagging spirits; though the suggestion was made that he try yoga, as it was an activity Keith himself had taken up a couple months after being released from his lengthy stay in the psych ward. The virtues of which were also very much mental and spiritual, helping to clear the mind and sharpen one's focus. But in lieu of the muscular injury, the ancient activity could be of much benefit physically as well. Denny told him he'd consider giving it a whirl, knowing full well that it more than likely was not going to happen. Still he appreciated the thoughts, and appreciated the attention his friend was bestowing upon him from afar in aiding a return to the straight and narrow, running and life wise. Denny even discussed with Keith about some of the bouts of sadness, and the general "fuckedupedness" he had once seen it written as, that he had been feeling of late. The unexpected and unwanted challenge too of finding equilibrium while barely running. For better or worse, it was about all Denny knew.

"You were there throughout it all for me. It's the least I can do to repay the favor," Keith had texted the other evening. "We are all pulling for you from up here you crazy bastard," the message had concluded.

"Thanks! It means more than I can express," Denny had replied back to his buddy, as a smile appeared upon his face. And it did mean the world to him. The pall of sadness that sometimes wrapped itself around him did not necessarily vanish into thin air; but it also didn't threaten to suffocate Denny as much as it had been persistently attempting to do. There were other ways to cope and manage and feel okay without having to go out and bash his body into pieces on a run. Though Denny did suspect he was becoming just clever enough at duping himself into such a belief.

The beast inside stirred. The open roads beckoned, like the doors being thrown open to the holy tabernacle. There was work to be done, and Denny craved to get back at it. He wanted to be serious again; that kind of seriousness he had once seen defined as the ultimate state of freedom and happiness.

Because this is where Denny felt whole, complete. It was simultaneously an escape, and a home. He flourished within the dichotomy; an hour or two a day Denny got to be the best version of himself, where he felt entirely comfortable in his own skin, and didn't have to shade his true identity by even the slightest granule to the outer world around him. The incessant rattle inside the brain subsided; usually the thoughts that came were congruent with the actions of the body. There was a fluid harmony, something that could be at times a rarity in Denny's life, when not out voyaging on the roads or trails. The complex web of vicissitudes experienced as a member of the human race relaxed its grip when a pair of running shoes were strapped to the feet.

Each evening Denny would head to the Fitness Trail on foot, after vigorously stretching his hamstrings in the living room, and for good measure, after adding a few more quick stretches on the sidewalks out front. As he would head up the macadam greenway, Denny would nervously wait for any pain or tightness to invade the left hamstring; it was like running on eggshells, figuratively speaking.

Tonight, like he had done the previous few nights, Denny checked his watch at the quarter mile mark. No signs of distress. Then again at the half mile mark. All good. Which was good, but prudence, was to be strictly enforced. Such a mindset also helped to keep Denny grounded in the immediate moments. He had even invented his own mantra; stay present, stay positive. He liked it, and clung to it, like a child holding its parent's hand. Over and over again he would repeat those words to himself. Denny tried to stay humble, very humble, and remind himself continually that every step was a gift. And he wasn't out of the woods, from the standpoint of the injury. Not by a long-shot. But with each day, and with each run, more and more sunlight began to filter through the clouds, which did wonders for Denny's disposition. As the watch beeped at the mile mark, he reminded himself again to stay present, and to find gratitude with each subsequent mile. The time spent away from the cherished sport may have been relatively brief, but it was enough to beget a brand-new appreciation for the simple joys running brought forth.

Like the feel of shoelaces in Denny's hands as he double-knotted his running shoes. Hanging sweaty, wet clothes on a rack to dry off on the porch. Downloading the data of a run from his Garmin watch to the Strava app, and checking out what others had run as well. Being an active member of the running community on a daily basis. Writing down the details in a running journal. Texting Uncle Mike the details. Passing others out running, walking, or cycling. Lending an encouraging word or two, or a simple hello or wave. Recalling the young lady, he had seen running the evening he had first gotten injured; the vision of this stranger loping along the trail, gliding through the trees, and disappearing into her own future. Thinking about where to run, and what to run while sitting at his desk at work. Exchanging information about runs with friends in Pennsylvania like Keith, Trent, and Suzanne. Messages from friends in Wilmington asking if he wanted to run. We are all so blessed, Denny contemplated, as he ducked onto the single-track trail leading to the Fitness Trail. For we get to do, what we love to do.

~

By about the third mile repeat, Denny wasn't thinking about how blessed he was, or how fortunate he was to be out there running on this precise evening. True, such an attitude still very much formed the core of his running persona, but tonight the focus was on the work, and grinding out a tough workout in the darkness of a cool March evening, on the blacktop streets of Kure Beach. There was a loop there, like a rounded off rectangle measuring almost exactly one mile, which traversed some quiet residential neighborhoods close to the more primitive, backside of the island. And since the training plan called for six times one mile, it was an ideal location for the effort. Denny figured if he could push this one hard tonight and stay on his feet, he'd be back close to where he wanted to be. Maybe not completely form a pure fitness metric, but more so mentally and spiritually, as he continued forward along the winding road towards Boston. Or so was the hope. If no other lesson had been learned the past several weeks, it was that there were no guarantees in this, or anything for that matter.

Halfway through the set of milers, Denny's performance was in line or even exceeding what he had hoped would be the case; each one had been completed in slightly under six minutes. After two minutes of very slow jogging he was off again, running down the fairly dark street, careful as always to not go out too fast at the start, though the Garmin watch was not utilized to gauge pace. Perceived effort was again the catch phrase, and the training tool being employed. The skill had been refined over many years, and more meticulously in relation to the marathon, during the present training cycle. Tweaked and adjusted too, post hamstring. The geographic lay of the loop lent specific markers that could be rather accurately used to measure elapsed distance. The two worked in concert with each other, that is perceived effort and distance, though the former was subject to an amount of variability as the evening unfolded and progressed.

Denny wore shorts and a t-shirt, and a backwards baseball cap on his head, along with a pair of gloves to prevent his hands from getting cold. He could feel a slight trace of perspiration on his head, even though temperatures had likely dipped into the upper forties by now. But the toil of the work kept his body temperature raised; for him, these were about the perfect conditions to be doing a workout in, as there was also almost no wind blowing at all. Denny flew by the pool and tennis courts, part of the neighborhood community center, and roughly halfway into the mile, and just before the left turn onto the second of the two long straightaways. It was the point in the interval where an uptick in exertion or output became a necessity, as did a heightened awareness to remain focused on maintaining the speed needed to finish another mile south of the six-minute mark. All of this was subtle, yet acute. Denny took it street by cross street; calculations whirred inside the brain, helping him retain the ability to accurately guess within a few hundredths of a mile what had been run, and what remained to be run. Countless signals within the body provided a continual stream of sensory feedback. He knew when he took the final left turn, about two hundred meters were left, without having to articulate the idea. It was half a lap on a track. The legs continued to churn; the arms continued to pump in precise cadence. The mind went blank. Nirvana was briefly attained, on a physically demanding precipice.

Five minutes and fifty-four seconds. Number four was done. Denny was pleased again. Perchance, not as much fitness had been lost as had been feared; the last week, aerobic strength could almost be felt to be increasing by the day. And he was able to get some runs in while injured, though they had hurt like heck, and might not have been the smartest thing to do. But what was done was done, and may have served to stem some fitness loss. Though how much did all of that matter at this point? What mattered right now was the next mile, and the next rep in the workout. Stay present he told himself, for the ten millionth time. And then Denny was off again, plunging madly, headlong into the chasm of darkness, accompanied by the soft rapping of sneakers, as they briefly made contact with the road.

On the backside of the loop, Denny's lungs began their silent scream; his heart threatened to constrict into a mangled blob inside his chest, as the lactic acid that corroded the legs, forced the cardiopulmonary circuitry to nearly redline. Stay present. Stay positive. He was on the periphery, somewhere in the margins between life and death, where all the greats of the sport have the innate ability to not only withstand, but to thrive. The beauty of running though, is that it doles out opportunities for each of its loyal participants to spend time inside that very same realm; anyone can thrive just as poetically as the Olympians of yesteryears have done. We can all be heroes too, even if it is only for one night, on some beach town's poorly lit secondary streets. For in the grand scheme of things, does it really matter all that much where our victories occur?

Five minutes and fifty-three seconds. A second faster than the previous mile. Denny was getting stronger as the night unwound. His legs were about thrashed, but his mind and spirit were as sharp as they had been in a long while. A certain coolness prevailed; Denny took off for the final time with the confidence of an athlete who knew they'd successfully be able to complete the task. The pain which would arrive could be handled, and dealt with an equanimity born from the depths of suffering. Denny was on a higher plain, able to function within the turbulence by staying true to the internal compass within, which helped guide him through the fog of the workout. It hurt. It hurt like hell again. But again, the pain was run straight through, not around. Denny dry heaved in the last hundred meters, yet kept grinding the legs through cycle after cycle until the Garmin beeped. When he was able to regain composure, Denny looked at the watch; it read 5:51.

On the much slower paced run home, Denny periodically glanced up at the immense sky above, which stretched out over the ocean, and eastward into oblivion. It could have been his imagination playing tricks, or he was a bit woozy still from the milers, but some of the stars appeared to be actually twinkling, like written about in the time-worn nursery rhyme. He was able to find the Big Dipper. As he causally ran, Denny remembered all those nights from his childhood that him and his friend Blaine, who lived a few houses away, would sit outside for hours intently watching the sky for shooting stars, that would mysteriously streak across the horizons. It was a serene memory, from an idyllic, peaceful time, that Denny carried with him until he got to the end of the run and on back home, as if being enraptured in one long prayer, without actually praying.

Chapter 22

When he pulled the green envelope out of the mailbox and saw the familiar hand writing and return address, Denny's heart skipped a beat. In actuality, his heart rate did increase, and pulse began to race. It was almost comical to rapidly recall many of the instances that something like this precise moment had been wished for, in a variety of variations. Some of the fantasies did entail physical mail, while other were centered around a phone call. The real outlandish one was a surprise visit in person; such as Denny would return home from work, or say from a run, and there Jennifer would be, sitting outside his front door, perhaps reading a book or magazine as she patiently awaited his arrival.

He must have stood there a short time by the row of mailboxes; one of his neighbors said hello, with a slightly amused look on their face. Denny took all of his mail and walked up the four flights of stairs and into his condominium, wanting to prolong the anticipation of opening and seeing whatever contents were contained within the one particular envelope, which from the look and feel of, probably was some type of greeting card. However, it must be noted that Denny did catch himself somewhere on the stairwell with the thoughts that it could all be much ado about nothing, and that it might be in his best interest therefore to temper the enthusiasm downward a peg or two. But it wasn't a holiday, nor anywhere near being his birthday?

From what Trent had mentioned over the course of the last few months, Jennifer had been attending wrestling matches sans boyfriend. Of course, that might mean nothing at all; the guy's schedule could have changed, or perhaps he had had his fill of attending scholastic sporting events? Or maybe there was a solid reason Jennifer didn't want him there, like it was affecting how her son was wrestling? Though Trent had also mentioned that Micah was having a good year, and was seeded fourth or fifth heading into Districts. Ah, the suspense of it all. Denny decided to go for a run first, and open the thing when he returned, for after all it was probably not much of anything life shattering anyhow. Don't be a darned fool, he lightly admonished himself, while changing into running gear.

    Denny headed towards the state park, entering as usual through the Boston Tunnel. His pace was steady, his cadence smooth, as the ground virtually whooshed by beneath his shoes. The epic race was under a month away; talk of tapering was now beginning to appear on the airwaves. There was still some minor pain and touches of tightness in the left hamstring, most noticeably during a workout and longer run, or after running hills harder on the bridge or in the park. Overall, Denny felt like he had escaped the worst of it, and gotten through the ordeal relatively unscathed, despite some missed training time. He no longer worried about not being able to run the marathon, and had been focused more on getting quality miles in and completing the twice weekly workouts, some of which Denny would scale back the volume of a bit, opting to err on the side of caution. The weekly mileage had ramped up, but not to the levels sustained before the injury. This week Denny hoped to and planned to lay down close to fifty miles. All of this bounced around in his head as the run made its way to Sugarloaf Trail, and towards the small, rolling, sandy hills where Denny would once again spend some quality time.

    About three miles managed to elapse before the envelope and Jennifer tried to steal the show. Denny heard the voice of his uncle loud and clear cautioning against expectations, and their potential effect upon one's peace of mind. The man's conviction could sway even the most skeptical. Stay present. Stay positive. Denny's own voice intervened in the dialogue, as he picked up the pace a quarter to a half click going up the first hill, before taking a hairpin turn onto Yellow Blaze Trail, where the steepest of all the hills was located. His legs would become a little wobbly when cresting the frontside of that hill, despite only taking about twenty seconds to get to the top. By now he seemingly knew every inch of the climb, and assessed progress with each step. The devilish ascent served to divert his thoughts; on the winding, less pitched far side of the hill Denny's mind was freed up to ponder what the future might hold, and if said future might include a certain fair-haired girl back up in his hometown in the state of Pennsylvania.

It's nothing man, it's nothing. This new voice was stern, and adamant, and seemed to be emanating from an exalted position of authority. Like many, Denny had a healthy distrust and skepticism towards figures of authority. And it was fun to speculate, wasn't it? Why shouldn't he be allowed the indulgence, and some latitude? Plus, intuition, or one's gut feeling shouldn't be stifled or ignored, and Denny's gut had a strong sense of where things might be heading. If he set himself up for a little fall so be it; the choice was his to make. At least there was a chance. What some people wouldn't do for just one more chance, one more roll of the dice? Like the Journey song. And that was ironic, and some kind of sign too, that such a song would pop into his head right then and there, since Jennifer was a big fan of the band herself.

The friendly argument bandied about while Denny zipped up and down the hills; before he knew it, thirty minutes had elapsed on the homemade circuit, and he began to head the long way out of the park, running a trail that paralleled the

Cape Fear River. The presence of the river provided a steadying influence on Denny; the wide expanse of water slowly flowed southward towards the Atlantic Ocean, in an almost identical fashion as it had done yesterday, the day before, and the day before that. There was something divine and wise in its constancy.

When Denny returned home, he performed the post run strength and stretches with an almost militaristic precision, before picking up the envelope off of the kitchen counter top and tearing it open without any more deliberation. He pulled out the contents, which was a card in the form of an invitation; momentarily Denny's heart froze, as he thought shit, is she getting married? But he regained his composure forthwith. The card was an invite to an art show at a gallery in Jim Thorpe next Friday night, featuring several local artists, one of whom would be Jennifer. There was also a folded piece of paper in the shape of a triangle wedged inside the card; its effects were quite the opposite upon Denny's heart, causing it again to beat a bit more rapidly in nervous anticipation. For it was a silly thing they had shared a few years ago, writing love notes to each other and then folding the paper up into triangles, like girls and boys used to do when the two of them were in school together. He pulled the meticulously folded note carefully apart and read the words hand written by Jennifer.

"Hey buster. I know its been awhile but I really want you to be here for this show. It would mean the world to me, as there is no one else on this mighty planet who sees things like I do, and knows me like you do. I miss you so, so much Denny and the little wet spot on the notebook paper is from where a tear drop fell from my eyes as I was writing these words. Love you always, Jennifer. PS. It occurred to me by the time you may be reading this that the little wet spot on the page will have dried, so I circled it, and took a picture to show you as proof when you get here. Which I so hope you can and will. Bye."

There was a cute, goofy smiley face drawn beside the circle too. Denny re-read the note, slowly, savoring the words, as he imagined them being spoken by her. And he studied the invite and information about the art show. Then he folded the note back into a triangle, using the creases in the paper as a guide.

"Looks like we are going to Pennsylvania," Denny announced out loud, and began making a mental checklist of things that would have to be done or taken care of beforehand, including what to tell his boss at work. But he had been granted leeway before to work remotely, and didn't see why it should be much of a problem for a day or two; I can always travel at night if need be, he told himself. Just don't mess it up. From the perspective of Jennifer. That's what the priority is here. I have to phone Uncle Mike too, he thought. I can see him as well which will make him happy. An effervescent energy thumped inside of him, as he also mulled over options of where to stay there, and thought about the whole idea of Jennifer apparently about to have some of her paintings on display in public for the first time ever, and how that was such a huge, tremendous deal for her. It was all so wonderfully wild; Denny couldn't wait to jump on the road again.

Chapter 23

Denny sat on a chair inside the screened-in porch and sipped on a mug of coffee. There was a frosty bite to the early morning air; little patches of snow lie scattered about the front yard, like markings on the side of a big, brown animal. Some light from the sun did manage to trickle through the trees to the east and south of the cabin, and Bear Mountain was partially visible to the north, between some of the trees that grew on that part of the property. Denny's longtime pal Ed had been gracious enough to let him stay at his hunting cabin in Franklin Township, about five miles to the east of Lehighton.

He set the mug down on the concrete foundation, and massaged his left hamstring area with his hand; the elongated muscle was a bit sore and tender from the nine-hour drive last night. Perhaps Denny had favored it a bit while in the car, without realizing he had done so? Of course, it would have been worse had it been his right leg, the one used to step on the pedals. But he wasn't sure just why it was acting bothersome; what Denny did know was that it was a fine morning to head out the door and to go for a run, so he finished most of the coffee and went inside the small, rather spartan cabin, to change into running gear.

"Aye captain," Denny said to the mounted head of an eleven-point buck, who kept watch of the home from above the fireplace. A bear skin rug was in front of the couch Denny had slept on for a few hours late last night. Ed had told him he was welcome to stay for as long as he wanted, and his lovely wife Theresa had even stocked the refrigerator with some groceries, including a big plastic jar of homemade hot bologna, a local staple of the area that could be found in most grocery stores.

    The dirt road the cabin was situated off of, wound back to a country road that Denny followed on foot up and over a moderate sized hill into the woods; the road then dropped rather precipitously into the valley where Beltzville Lake was, which was created in the 1970s by the Army Corp of Engineers, by constructing a large dam on the Pohopoco Creek. The orangish, brown edifice at the head of the lake was several hundred feet in length, and was visible for a brief stretch where Denny ran, before he hung a left, and began to proceed eastward towards the sun, which by now had climbed part way up the morning sky. It was still cold, around thirty degrees, but the warmth of the sunlight could already be felt, and temperatures were expected to rise pretty rapidly and top out in the low to mid fifties in the afternoon.

    The hilly landscape was a pleasant reminder of the life once lived, at least through the prism of running. And Denny felt fairly strong, plus the hamstring had apparently loosened up; a few miles in and he wasn't even thinking about his left leg anymore. The distances covered slipped almost indiscernibly by. Before he knew it, Denny was in front of the main entrance to Beltzville State Park. He decided to follow the road in, which eventually made its way to the lake itself. Very few people were there, in stark contrast to what the scene would look like in the summer, when scores of people would arrive to hang out on the beach and swim in the designated areas of the large body of water. Something of which Denny did often when growing up, many times riding to the lake on his bicycle. Most of the same buildings remained; the concession stand that a guy who lived in their neighborhood used to manage, the bathroom and change houses, and the nature center that the Cub Scouts would go to for wildlife presentations conducted by the park rangers. Today by the shoreline, a lone man walked his dog.

Denny exited back out of the park, the first time he had been there in many years, and continued in an easterly direction, over a bridge which spanned one of the numerous inlets off the lake, and past the marina building and boat launch ramps. He had no notion of where he was headed, nor any distance or time frame in mind as to how far or long the run might go or last. Not this morning. Besides, the whole hamstring injury and subsequent period of recovery had thrown the overall training philosophy into an adjusted, somewhat new perspective; the discomfort earlier was a poignant reminder of what the past several weeks had entailed. Hopefully some lessons had been absorbed and internalized. And through it all, Denny had found an unexpected appreciation, a queer sense of freedom, in not strictly adhering to a plan. Though he did for the most part stay true to the workouts, but not nearly as rigidly. Maybe he was contradicting himself a little, he had to concede? But Denny dismissed that as bunk, and dismissed much of it as frankly too much analyzation, and too much pontification. It felt damn good to be running at that very moment, and that's what mattered the most.

As the hills rolled by, with the lake keeping pleasant company off to the right side of the road, Denny kept hearing the word further being whispered inside of him. He had been reading Thomas Wolfe's novel *The Electric Kool-Aid Acid Test*; Ken Kesey had named the bus he and the Merry Pranksters traveled around the country on "Furthur." The word connoted pursuing a deep exploration of the human psyche, and pushing beyond whatever boundaries might lie in its wake. So, Denny ran further and further out Beltzville Road, past the scattered houses and barns and semi-barren farmlands and expanses of woods which comprised the land. Time and distance receded further into his consciousness; Denny hadn't looked at the watch since shortly after leaving the state park, and had blissfully lost track of the number of times it had beeped since then.

When he got to the dirt parking lot of the Wildcreek Trails, Denny made his way to the single-track trail which plunged downward into the dense woods that swept towards the lake. The old growth forest consisted primarily of tall pine trees, that lent a fragrant, sappy odor to the primitive environment. There was much brush of briars and thickets and smaller deciduous trees that were mostly still bare of leaves at this time of year. Still it was rather dark and gloomy in the woods, and noticeably chillier and damp too. The trail briefly exited the woods and crossed a much wider, grassy trail, before diving down into a steep ravine, that sloped all the way to the shoreline of the lake. Here the surface of the trail was a little rockier, and also full of roots; Denny slowed the pace considerably, and carefully stepped his way towards the water, part of an isolated cove that cut back away from the main body of the lake. Beltzville Lake itself was not nearly as wide several miles to the east of the dam, and was surrounded by woods on both sides.

Denny crouched on the shoreline and took his gloves off. He cupped his hands in the ice cold, clear water and had himself a quenching drink. The surface was placid, especially in the undisturbed cove, though he could see the larger expanse of water off to the right was just as tranquil. Only the tiniest of ripples travelled along the top. Denny had been exactly where he was many times before; the spot, and many others in the vicinity, were some of the most beautiful and peaceful places he had ever come across and were etched inside his soul, forever reminding him of his ancestral home. The only sounds present emanated from the natural contours of the land, and from the creatures who made the surroundings their home. Denny soaked it all in, embedding another mental snapshot in his mind, before putting his gloves back on and making his way on up the trail and up and out of the ravine.

~

When the steak was placed on the hot grill, a distinct sizzling sound came from the meat, as its natural juices sprang forth and leaped all about. After a few seconds Denny closed the lid and walked back inside the cabin to the tiny kitchen, where a pot of red beans was simmering atop one of the two burners on the stove. The smell of jalapeno peppers and red onion blended together with the beans, all of which had been slowly cooking for over two hours. Denny was famished as he walked outside onto the screened-in porch; he flipped a switch which turned on a light that was affixed to one of the corners right beneath the roof, for darkness was about to prevail. In the sky to the north, the faintest trace of a crimson and purple hue was visible on top of Bear Mountain. Denny blew on his hands to warm them, as once the sun had begun to set, temperatures had rapidly fallen off. There was even a rumor about some snow that could arrive on Saturday, though nothing too noteworthy was being forecasted.

Denny ate his dinner at a table positioned by the front windows of the living room. He watched one of the local newscasts, WNEP out of Scranton, and the national news, as he ate by himself, enjoying the serene setting. The steak was succulent, with enough charred grill marks to trap most of the moisture inside the meat, that had been cooked to medium-well. Denny used tiny pinches of salt to add a touch of flavoring. The red beans practically melted in his mouth; the heat from the jalapenos and the sharp, yet sweet taste of the onions fused into a delectable medley with the natural flavor of the beans. He ate slowly and with purpose; the kind of purpose that is earned by spending a couple of hours on the roads and trails.

Tomorrow he would see Jennifer. For the most part Denny tried not to think about it all too much, or think about her, or her and himself. Stay present he told himself. He also knew she was understandably apprehensive for the art show, and the numerous attendant details of which she was a novice, and learning about on the fly. Denny could hear it in her voice when they talked on the phone earlier. He assured her that it was all going to work out, though not before adding, what the hell did he know? The sound of Jennifer's laughter, even if only coming through the speaker of a cell phone, was music to Denny's ears.

He called Uncle Mike after dinner, to make sure he was still set to come to the art show as well; he insisted again on riding up there with Mr. Hackenberg, instead of allowing Denny to pick him up and drive him to Jim Thorpe, which he didn't mind in the least doing.

"It'll give us senior citizens something adventurous to do together," he had said rather adamantly, though with a noticeable strain in the vocal cords. But as usual, his uncle didn't want to discuss much at all about the cancer or his health. From what Mr. Hackenberg had informed Denny a few days ago, it was looking at best that only a couple more weeks of life were likely left. Evidently the man was not about to go gently into the good night; those around could only step back and admire the tenacity and joie de vivre being exuded, until seemingly the last drop of living had been drained from the physical body.

After washing his plate and utensils, cleaning off the grill, and putting the pot of beans in the refrigerator, Denny grabbed his car keys and headed out to meet Trent at Pappy's Schoolhouse Tavern. The country bar was only a five-minute drive from where he was staying, and had been a favorite of Denny's and many of his friends' after turning twenty-one and becoming of legal drinking age, and before he and some of them had migrated out of the area. Back then the place was called Frank's, and had arguably the best wings around, including their signature suicide ones, which were the hottest Denny had ever eaten in his life. Even the medium flavored were pretty darned hot, but also plump and tasty too. It seemed in the present day and age, good quality wings were hard to come by, and were always over-priced.

Denny walked in the front door and found his buddy seated on a stool at the bar and talking to someone. The Flyers game was playing on the television set which hung on the back wall, above all the bottles of liquor. He slapped Trent on the back, and saddled up to the empty stool on his right.

"Hey man," a somewhat startled Trent said, as he turned to face his friend. "You always do make the most notable entrances."

The gal behind the bar came over and asked Denny what she could get him. The place wasn't too filled up, though most of the seats at the bar were occupied, and a few small parties sat at tables on the floor. It appeared to Denny to be a typical night in these parts. "Can I get a club soda with a lime please," he responded to the barkeep, and added, "I'm responsible for this guy here."

"Sure thing darling," she replied.

"I've become reformed too," Trent said, with a grin on his face. "But it's a work in progress," he continued, as he took a drink from a mug of beer. "Hey you remember Mr. Claypool? From high school?"

"Yes." Denny leaned over the bar and looked to the man seated to the left of Trent and drinking a bottle of Heineken beer, who was in fact Mr. Claypool, one of their former teachers. Oddly enough he didn't look all that different from the last time Denny might have seen him, some twenty-five years ago.

"How are you sir?" Denny asked enthusiastically as he got up to shake his hand.

"Not as well as you I dare reckon," he replied. "I hear you're running all over the place down in the Carolinas."

"Gotta stay one step ahead of the man."

The three of them chatted amicably at the bar. Mr. Claypool had always been one of the so-called cool teachers, as he had a keen sense of humor and a fond appreciation for the absurd underbelly of life, which Denny had always taken an affinity towards as well. No wonder they had gotten along. They all recalled that he had once lent out an old beat up station wagon, whose floor was partially rusted out, to Denny and Trent and a few others to drive around on some dirt roads on a big farm just outside of town.

"These days they would have fired me and jailed me if I did something like that," Mr. Claypool said. "Thankfully I've been retired for a few years now."

"He shoots a mean game of darts," said Trent. "I don't think we knew that."

"It's one of the perks of having too much time on my hands gents," the former teacher stated. It was sort of amusing in a light-hearted way after all the years having a conversation, where it seemed as if the roles hadn't changed all that much. A few minutes later, Trent and Denny excused themselves and went over to the shuffle board machine, a short board version of the game that is set up conceptually like bowling, with ten mechanical pins to knock down at the one end of the table. The game was a ubiquitous sight inside of small town and rural bars in Pennsylvania. There was even a competitive league here, Trent reminded Denny, comprised of bars in and around Lehighton.

Trent sprinkled white powder on the surface of the board out of a plastic container that had been sitting on top of the machine, above the pins and in front of the electronic scoreboard. He stated that it would assist in the integrity of the match, since the alleyway at Pappy's tended to have more friction, and therefore a slower surface compared to the one at the American Legion, or the one at Cousin's Bar way out in Mahoning Township. His mannerisms left nothing in the way to suggest that he didn't know exactly what he spoke of. Trent took the first shot, and opened the first frame with a strike.

"Good start hoss," Denny remarked.

"I shot a 254 last week," he replied, without any air of braggadocio.

Denny slid the metallic puck and knocked down nine pins. He picked up the spare on the next roll. It had been a long while since he had played; perhaps his last game would have been on this very same machine.

"Wow I just remembered watching Kenny Smith shoot a 299 here," Denny exclaimed. He took a drink of the club soda. It tasted terrible. Or more accurately, had little taste at all; he wondered why he had even ordered the drink to begin with.

"He shot a 299?" Trent asked. "That's insane."

"Yes, a couple of us were here. I think Tiny Faust. Maybe Slappy? Wendy? I don't quite recall all of that part of it. Anyhow he had a perfect game going. And like in baseball, I think we made a concerted effort not to speak about it once he got into the seventh or eighth frame. Same superstitious principle."

"I can see that."

"And the guy had it. Until the very last shot. We were all pretty much holding our breath. Missed one damn pin."

"Heartbreaking," Trent laughed.

"I may have shed a tear," Denny said, "I may or may have not seen Schmitty since that fateful night."

"Heard he's serving time in a Malaysian prison on weapons charges."

"That figures."

The first game was won handily by Trent. Not a surprise, as Denny had difficulty throwing strikes, despite slowing the speed at which he slid the cylinder along the board, as suggested by his friend. They took a break and sat down at a table. Trent was eager to know more about what was up with Denny's unplanned trip northward, and what was going on with him and Jennifer again. He always wished that the two of them could somehow, someway get it right and stay together, though the obstacles in place were duly noted. Then again sometimes Trent wished Denny would just simply commit to her, and commit to doing whatever it took for them to find some kind of lasting relationship. For the most part he had held such thoughts in reserve, but he knew how fleeting such opportunities could be.

"I'm going to wing it I guess," Denny began. He pulled the lime out of the cocktail glass of club soda and sucked on it for a moment. It was sweet, with a real pungent kick. "Her show, or the art show is tomorrow night. We'll hang out then and this weekend." He always had the inclination to play things like this close to the vest, though he wasn't exactly sure why? Denny took another sip of the drink and added, "her boys are at their dad's this weekend too. So, it works out nicely."

"She's super talented. I didn't realize it was her who designed the cover and did some of the other art work for the wrestling handbook this year. And these posters used for a bake sale during the holidays back in December."

"Oh? I don't think I saw any of them."

"I might have a few extra copies laying around the home. Jill helped hang them up all over town."

"Funny I was up here then but didn't see any. Or maybe I did and didn't pay any attention to." Denny sucked on the lime again, and squeezed some of the juice into the drink. He looked up at Trent and smiled. "Perhaps I wasn't meant to see such things at the time, don't you think?"

Trent looked Denny square in the eyes and quickly responded, "I think she is really cool. Don't let her get away again."

"Point taken," responded Denny, as he was a bit surprised, though appreciated the candor. The two of them got up to shoot another game of shuffle. And it was a point most definitely taken by Denny, for it was something that had gnawed at a part of him for the better part of two years now. But how to solve the seemingly intractable differences that formed a huge gulf between them; what could change this time around? He was getting ahead of himself, way ahead. Denny needed to remind himself over and over again to stay grounded and remain in the now, and to trust in that which wasn't readily apparent, and to trust in the idea of life being dynamic and fluid, ever-changing. No one could be certain of what the next day may bring. And this was a good thing. He needed to likewise remind himself to be grateful. Grateful to be in the position he currently found himself in. How many times would he have lived and died just to be right where he was, holding the dice in his hands?

"I'm not sure why Journey gets such a bad rap," Trent said, in response to some of what Denny had made verbal to him. "I'll jam out to their older stuff any day of the week," he added, before sliding the puck down the wooden board, and executing another flawless strike.

"I hear you cowboy."

Chapter 24

"Come on," Jennifer pleaded with her youngest son Tobias, who apparently was intent on taking his sweet time coming downstairs with his school backpack and weekend bag to take to his father's house. His brother Micah waited in the car, taking advantage of the situation to sneak in some cell phone use, which had been prohibited for the next two weeks, except to contact family members. The punishment from his mother was the result of making a lower grade on his latest Biology exam.

Finally, Toby made his way down just in time to be shepherded into the back seat of the car for the short ride to school; once the boys were dropped off, Jennifer drove a couple more blocks to the hospital in order to begin her last shift of the week. Her mind, to say the least, resembled one of those gyrating pinball machines; thoughts bounced from the growing lack of obedience in her sons as they were getting older, to how to convince her own mother to go see the doctor again about her worsening arthritis, to her first ever art show at a gallery in Jim Thorpe tonight, before landing squarely on the one thing that always seemed to shake everything up and down and side to side and turn it all inside out. And that was the fact that Denny was currently in town, literally within a few miles of her very location this fine Friday morning. A quick glance at her watch revealed it was 6:57.

"Good morning Doris," Jennifer said to the head nurse at the third-floor station, as she picked up her clipboard out of the marked shelves on the wall.

"It surely is," Doris replied. "It's Friday and it's a payday. All is well in the world now isn't it?" She was a short, somewhat plump woman in her mid-sixties, who wore glasses and always had her dark brown hair pulled into a bun. A real no-nonsense lady too. About the exact person you would expect to find in such a position, or at least that is what Jennifer always thought.

"Yes ma'am," Jennifer managed to squeeze out, before turning down a hallway and heading to the first patient's room listed on her rounds. She hated to be late, and hated to feel like she was in any kind of a rush, for then it may have an adverse, unintended effect on those whom were in her care. Most had already suffered enough, and deserved doses of undivided attention.

Doris had known Jennifer for twenty years. Actually, much more. She was still good friends with her mother, who also used to be a nurse at Gnadden Huetten Memorial Hospital. Doris knew the details of Jennifer's life almost as well as Jennifer did, and understood it was natural for her to be a bit fritzed in the brain today, as she would term such a countenance. Therefore, she hadn't said anything more, instead letting Jennifer go right about her duties. "If they could all be so diligent," Doris said aloud. An orderly who was standing nearby nodded their approval.

For the next few hours Jennifer stayed pleasantly engaged in her work, until she paused and rested for a few minutes in Mrs. Steigerwalt's room. She was an elderly woman in her nineties who had been a patient there now for a short time. The two had developed a warm friendship, and looked forward to seeing each other most every day. Jennifer enjoyed hearing stories about her late husband of sixty-two years, and all the whereabouts of their children, grandchildren, and even three great-grandchildren, some of whom she had met there in the hospital.

"How are you today?" asked Jennifer, with genuine affection in her voice, which was one of the reasons she was so good at what she did for a living. She took Mrs. Steigerwalt's right hand and gently rubbed the upper part with her fingers. The patient smiled, though the pain in her eyes could not be masked.

"I'm fine dear," she replied, in what amounted to nothing more than a loud whisper. The frail, delicate woman closed her eyes for a few moments, then reopened them, and asked, "tonight is the big night, yes?"

"It is indeed. The big one."

"It's going to be wonderful dear," Mrs. Steigerwalt said, while even managing to lightly squeeze Jennifer's hand. "And your Denny will be there too?"

Jennifer instantly felt a flush feeling on her face. "Well he's not my Denny," she stammered, then said, "but yes, I believe so."

"You are so pretty. And talented," Mrs. Steigerwalt said, while looking deep into Jennifer's eyes, before closing her own again.

The acts of caring and kindness exhibited were almost too much to bear; for a brief spell tears began welling up inside. Jennifer hadn't realized until then how truly raw her emotions must be. "Thank you. You are very kind to say that," she managed to say, before excusing herself from the bedside, and from the room.

She almost walked into a doctor in the hallway, before ducking into a bathroom and wiping the tears away that had formed in her eyes. Jennifer splashed cold water on her face, then looked at her own self in one of the mirrors. She instructed her reflection to pull it together, for pete's sake, and momentarily debated calling Denny, but decided against it. Instead she took a break and walked downstairs to the cafeteria on the first floor, and purchased a raisin bagel with cream cheese, and a cranberry juice. For a short while Jennifer allowed her mind to go blank, a trick she had been taught in therapy several years ago. She stared out across the parking lot and towards the woods, which climbed up and over the hill towards the section of Lehighton known as Meadowcrest, and northward towards the Orioles Club and recreational grounds that sat atop the ridgeline. Jennifer did wonder if it was going to snow Saturday, as it looked like the sun was no longer shining outside.

  Meanwhile, a little over a mile away and just beyond the opposite end of town, Denny was pulling into the parking lot at the trailhead of the Lehigh Canal Towpath, next to Weissport. He had decided to sleep much later than he was accustomed to, which felt good and much needed coming off of the long drive and long run. Plus, he had stayed out with Trent well into the evening, even stopping off at Ruby's Saloon on Bridge Street to shoot pool with Joe Solt. Normally Denny was an early riser.

  There was much familiarity with the towpath, and the canal; as Denny began to run, it was as if he had never left. Never left a few months ago, or a few years ago, or had never left twenty some years ago to go live in another part of the country. Time itself seemed to stand still here, at least as measured through Denny's running, which had an uncanny way of bridging the breaches between past and present. But he imagined the same could be said for many a place; this happened to be one of those that he was most intimately acquainted with.

  Once again, there was no specific idea in mind as to what to run today, though Denny figured he'd shoot to get about ten miles in, and mix in some up-tempo stuff into the fray as well. He had finished reading *Running with the Buffaloes* again, but had forgotten to give the copy to Trent last night. Nonetheless, he thought about one of the training tenets stressed by Coach Whetmore, which had originated from the philosophies of the legendary Arthur Lydiard; the runner has an almost unlimited capacity to develop their aerobic capabilities, and can best accomplish this through longer, steady runs like the one Denny had taken yesterday, and planned to do today, though of a lesser duration and distance.

He also figured while in Pennsylvania, even if for only a few days, it would behoove him to run as many hills as possible; thus Denny decided to run to where the wide part of the towpath ended and do an out and back from there, which would net close to five miles. After, he'd head into town, and hit a bunch of the bigger hills there; good additional training for what would be encountered in Boston. The window to develop muscularly in the legs what would aid in the marathon's hilly terrain was coming to a close as well. These thoughts caused Denny to shake his head, figuratively, in disbelief, since it didn't seem like it was all too long ago that the Boston Marathon existed as this ungraspable thing way, way off in the future, too far out to even fathom what it might actually be like to be there in person. My had the times changed.

Denny ran and stayed for the most part comfortably preoccupied with thoughts about running and training, and the upcoming marathon. He imagined what it would be like to arrive at Athlete's Village, and what he might do to kill the necessary time before his wave would be called to head to the famous start line, painted across some street in Hopkinton. Or what the bus ride might be like, sitting there amongst all these fleet-footed runners, getting ready to run the oldest, most famous marathon in the world? Would people be chatty and excited? Or nervous, focused, and rather subdued?

And Denny tried to imagine various parts of the course, such as the places and landmarks he had seen before on television, and had read about in books or on websites. Like the Wellesley Scream Tunnel, Heartbreak Hill, the Newton Firehouse. What would it feel like to turn right on Hereford, then left on Boylston? To be running towards the finish line with all those raucous, screaming, cheering fans mobbing downtown Boston? Such thoughts produced goosebumps, despite the clouded over skies and raw, chillier air temps today.

After blasting the steep, fiendish hill that began at the base of Fourth Street on Bridge Street, Denny's legs felt mushy and jelly-like, while he waited for his breathing to return to a more normal baseline. By now close to ten miles had been laid down, including several other big hills on the north and east sides of town. Since he found himself a few blocks from Keith's house, Denny decided to head over there and pop in, and see if the guy was home. The gradual downhill on South Second Street was welcomed, and allowed his pretty thrashed legs some much needed recovery. Denny hit the stop button on his Garmin, and walked up the cement walkway leading to the sunroom of the house; the sound of barking dogs inside could be heard. He rang the bell and peered through the door at the two dogs, who never were able to recall who he was, or maybe just never liked him to begin with. Denny was unsure. A few seconds later Keith appeared in the room, and came over and opened the side door.

"Hey a surprise visit from running man," Keith said, while keeping the dogs back with his legs and one arm. "Don't mind them," was added as well, as he caught Denny's wayward look behind him.

"Just laid down a robust ten miles. First five on the towpath," Denny announced, as he walked inside.

"Nice. I've laid down two conference calls and an eight-page report," replied Keith, with unmistakable deadpan.

"Hard to say who's been more productive to this point."

"Toss up," Keith said, with a chuckle. "Take a load off. As soon as this phone rings I've got another meeting I need to be in on." He held the cell phone that was in his other hand up into the air, as if to additionally accentuate the statement.

"No worries. Only dropping in for a second." The dogs had relaxed, and retreated into the far confines of the dimly lit room. "Busy day?" Denny asked.

"Yeah. So, what's the deal with tonight? It's tonight right?" Keith's tone and mannerisms gave away that in a good natured, yet mischievous way, he was intrigued with the raison d'etre of his friend's sojourn.

"Yes it is. I'm going to enter the world of art and fashion. Of which I have little experience."

"Jim Thorpe I'll have you know is known for its haute culture and high society. Oh, and grab yourself a drink. You look thirsty."

"Thanks." Denny walked through the open partition in the wall and up the solitary step that led into the kitchen. He rummaged around in the well-stocked refrigerator, before pulling out a cherry flavored Gatorade Zero.

"Actually, in all seriousness there are a lot of cool things going on in Thorpe. We just don't get up there that much."

"You guys must go through a ton of Gatorade."

"Yes." Keith had sat down and was typing on a laptop computer at a desk in the sunroom. After a few moments, he asked, "How's Jennifer? You see her yet?"

"No. Not yet. She's good I hope." Denny took a long swig of the electrolyte rich drink; it tasted really good too, and really hit the spot. He hadn't realized how thirsty he was.

Keith continued to work on the laptop and speak into the monitor, which was facing a window and away from Denny. "Suzanne has twenty bucks on the two of you getting back together."

"Only twenty?"

"I have my doubts. But I've become a little too conservative perhaps as I age," Keith stated, as he typed.

"Hopefully not politically. "

"On some things. Economically for sure."

A cell phone rang, which was Keith's. "Hey I've got to get this. Sorry bud," he said before answering the call.

Denny put his knit hat and gloves back on and headed towards the door. The two exchanged a rather meek fist bump, as Denny mouthed that he would talk to him later. Keith took the phone to his chest and said," let's get out tomorrow," before sitting down at his desk again.

"Sure thing dog," replied Denny, as he exited out into the cold, and started running towards his car, parked over at the towpath. The nippiness of the air was a sudden contrast to the warmth of the Druckenmiller house, but there was only about a mile and a half left to be run. And as he ran along Second Street, thoughts of Jennifer and the art show tonight and Uncle Mike and Mr. Hackenberg started to pop into his mind; Denny had purposely shielded himself from this avenue of mental activity this morning, as he was prone to dwell upon all kinds of mundane details, and imagine all kinds of contrived scenarios, most of which would likely never come to pass. No, he wanted to go with the flow, and exist in the now as much as possible, and be there and be supportive of Jennifer.

"It's in your hands big fella," Denny whispered to the clouds, as he cut down a side street and picked up the pace. He was hungry now too, and was eager to also get indoors again.

Chapter 25

"I can't even stand to go in there and look! Is that crazy? Am I crazy? Don't answer." Jennifer whacked Denny in the chest with the back of her hand. It was just like old times, save for the detail that they found themselves outside of an art gallery nestled on a narrow street in the historic section of the town of Jim Thorpe.

"Let's get some coffee," Denny suggested.

"Goodness no. My hands are already shaking."

Denny took one of Jennifer's hands from her coat pocket and held it in his. It wasn't shaking, but it was a little moist from perspiration; wow, she must really be nervous he thought, as it's pretty cold out here on the sidewalks. But he wisely kept the observation to himself. Heck, he'd be super nervous too. So, he tried to think of something to alleviate the tension, even if only momentarily.

"I have a funny feeling everything is going to work out fine tonight. Trust me." Denny winked at her, beneath the pale, yellow glow of a street light. Jennifer reciprocated with a smile, just before she leaned in and kissed him.

"I know," she said softly.

Just then they heard someone holler from up the street something about getting a room at a hotel; Denny didn't have to turn around and look to recognize the voice of Mr. Hackenberg. When he did, he saw the man walking down the street; Uncle Mike was beside him, using some sort of a walker on wheels to move forward, while still though using his own legs. Jennifer and Denny went to greet them and to inquire if any assistance could be used.

"Hello young man," Uncle Mike said, as Denny came over and kind of grabbed ahold of one of his arms, while wrapping the other around his backside in a makeshift hug. His voice sounded gravelly and strained such as it had over the phone. His complexion was even more wan in the face than it had been, plus it looked like he had lost another ten or fifteen pounds, if that was even possible? But Denny did not want to appear to be the least bit troubled by any of all that in the company of his beloved uncle, as Jennifer came around to the other side, and gave him a kiss on the cheek.

"That's more like it sweetheart," Uncle Mike said, with a smile.

"Oh Uncle Mike thanks so much for coming," she replied. Her eyes were visibly gleaming, even in the half-light.

They introduced her to Mr. Hackenberg as well, who insisted she call him John. Once in front of the gallery, Uncle Mike was carefully helped up the three steps which led into the entranceway. Several people were milling about, going in and out of the front doors. There certainly seemed to be a buzz in the air, or an intangible feeling like this was going to be a happening spot to be, which pleased Denny immensely for Jennifer's sake. She had informed him how there were a half a dozen artists who had been selected to exhibit and sell their artwork tonight.

Inside, a nice sized crowd was gathered in the front room, which also contained a makeshift bar off to the one side. Denny asked Uncle Mike if he wanted a shot of whiskey to warm up.

"Make it a high ball," he replied.

"I didn't realize it was a 1920s themed event."

"What?" Jennifer asked. It was pretty noisy inside as well, as people moved about chatting and shaking hands and exchanging hugs, while others made their way to the bar and ordered drinks. Jennifer said all the artwork, and her paintings, were in a series of smaller rooms through the doorway and just past where the bar was, so the four of them attempted to make their way through the crowd, which wasn't the easiest thing to do, especially for Uncle Mike. Denny was eager to see what works of art Jennifer had selected for the show. Usually she liked to paint in a style that would be considered along the lines of abstract; most of the paintings Denny had been privy to in the past consisted of intricate shapes and geometric patterns, with contrasting colors meant to evoke emotions in the viewer. Though Denny had such a limited understanding of art, that any explanation he might try to formulate would sound simplistic, or be well off the mark. Fortunately for him, Jennifer was very patient with her detailed descriptions of what it was she was trying to convey.

She took ahold of his hand as they snaked their way through the arched doorway and out of the main room, past a large mural that to Denny, looked like something from a Disney cartoon. He turned and said this to Uncle Mike, only to find he was no longer right behind them. Instead his thoughts were conveyed to a hipster looking young lady with pink streaks in her black hair, who much to Denny's surprise and amusement, agreed emphatically with his causal take. They did finally reform their group, and helped maneuver Uncle Mike into the room which contained Jennifer's paintings, all of which were tastefully displayed on a white wall, and lit by small lamps hanging above each individual work of art.

What immediately struck Denny was the raw explosion of colors, that looked as if they wanted to leap off of the canvas. Jennifer talked to them about how hard it was for her to only choose five paintings to bring here out of the hundreds she still had left in her house. Over the years she had given dozens away as gifts or thank-yous, including a few to Denny the last time they were together. The one exception, or the one painting Jennifer knew belonged in the show and would serve as the centerpiece, was a painting that no one but her had ever laid eyes upon before, and was in a much different medium and style than she normally created in. It was an oil painting of two young children, sitting together and gazing off into the distance at a body of water like a lake, partially obscured by the trees and landscape in the foreground. Denny instantly knew the origins, and for a moment felt like he couldn't breathe, for he was so moved at an almost unfathomable depth by what his eyes were beholding.

Yes. That's what it was. Jennifer locked eyes with him from a few feet away, confirming what Denny knew to be true. She had captured artistically, the time two summers ago the two of them had hiked Wildcreek Trails at Beltzville Lake, and had stopped to rest for a while in the middle of the forest. And it had been after the most heart-breaking of talks, finalizing verbally what was known by both at the time, that the complications in their relationship were too insurmountable to be overcome. So, after walking some more, they had decided to sit down and have a snack and simply gaze out at the aqua-blue lake, up ahead in the near distance through the piney woods. Not by any conscious intent, Jennifer and Denny succeeded for the next hour at forgetting the big sloppy real-world mess surrounding them; instead, the holiness of each and every passing moment was cherished in a reverence forsaking any and all thoughts about the past, or the future. The present had been discovered.

The innocence of childhood, the simplicity of being viscerally alive was evoked so provocatively in Jennifer's painting. This almost brought tears to Denny's eyes, as he continued to be mesmerized by the canvas hanging on the wall. Mr. Hackenberg also appeared to be fixated by the artistic rendering himself; he stood motionless by Denny, not saying a word. Finally, he did look at him, and merely said, "amazing," before meandering slowly away to look at more artwork.

A golden silence washed down upon Denny, drowning out the cacophonous noise contained within the gallery's walls. Everything appeared to be moving in slow motion, but he was super sensitive though to the nuances of any kinetic actions, able to glimpse the root origins on some kind of sub-atomic level. Denny witnessed Jennifer and Uncle Mike off in one corner of the room; it looked like they were engaged in a meaningful conversation, and she kept leaning in closer and closer, in order to hear him. A young, well-dressed couple stood in front of another painting, talking enthusiastically about the contents. But then in an instant, sight and sound returned to their normal properties. Did I have an out of body experience Denny wondered? He eased away from the oil painting, and on out of the room. A sudden thirst was evident; Denny returned to the main room in the front, to see if there might be any bottled water at the bar.

He laid his hands on the wooden counter and waited for the bartender to approach. Denny stretched his quadricep muscles, alternating between grabbing one leg, while keeping the opposite hand on the bar. No one seemed to notice, or care. As Denny waited to be served, he caught sight of an old friend seated a few stools away. He made his way around some folks, and walked up behind Kurt and rapped him on the back.

"What the... I'll be damned. Denny Defilippis. What the hell are you doing here?"

"Dabbling in the local art scene. I heard this was the place to be tonight."

"It definitely is," Kurt replied, as he stood up to shake hands. "It sure has been a bit. How's life down south treating you amongst the plantations and cotton fields?"

"Hot as blazes for six months of the year. But I've learned to adapt, and appreciate the value of a quality air conditioner."

Kurt laughed. He looked like he was in good health and spirits, and had kept himself relatively fit over the years, though Denny didn't ask him if he still biked. His wavy black hair was much shorter than it used to be, and he no longer sported a thick goatee.

"I hear you. Quite the opposite from around here some years," Kurt said. "But seriously, what brings you up to these environs?"

"A girl. And a dying uncle. Both of whom are in the building right now."

"Come again?" The noise in the front room had reached a fever pitch, and more people kept trying to enter the gallery. Denny wondered if there was even a fire code, but also knew it was a real positive sign for all the artists who had their work on display like Jennifer. He glanced about, but didn't see her. It was remarkable how quick the two had become attached again, and Denny could already feel that fuzzy feeling a person gets when physically near someone, contrasted with a proximate separation like now, when Jennifer was apparently in another part of the building. All of which flashed inside of him in less than a half of a second.

"Do you remember Jennifer Merluzzi? She was in the same grade as me. She's one of the featured artists."

"Okay. The name sounds vaguely familiar. You used to go out with her way back in the day?"

"Yes. One and the same." Denny realized of course by any count, she and he were embarking on their third go around. Perhaps this time would prove to be the charm.

"I'm sure her name had to have come up on the great expedition," Kurt stated. Both of them laughed. "One day I am going to have to tell my children about that, but I think they may still be much too young."

"Yes, I'm positive it did. The nature of our relationship helped carry us back over the Mahoning Mountain." Denny paused, and then asked, "so how are your kids? Anna and Dominic, right?"

"Doing well thanks." Kurt took a couple of sips from the cocktail he was drinking. "They are actually over at my parent's house in Franklin Township as we speak. Anna turned twelve three days ago."

"Cool. Wow. Time flies doesn't it? Hey I'm staying out in Franklin myself for a few days. At a cabin Ed has off Green Street."

"Nice! Nothing beats a little visit to the old homeland. We try and get up here a couple times a month." Kurt and his wife Adrienne lived in Nazareth, about a forty-five-minute drive to the south and east. Denny knew he was a journalist for an on-line news magazine based out of the Lehigh Valley, but couldn't recall the name of it off the top of his head.

He was however, finally able to obtain a bottle of water; high quality too as he joked with Kurt, before excusing himself to find the rest of his party. He had to also laugh internally at the mention of the great expedition, of which he had not thought of in forever. And it would had to have gone down around the timeframe that he and Jennifer had first been a couple, planning out their lives together with the insouciance that only the young possess. Denny was still trying to finish college, and Jennifer had finished Nursing School and was working at a clinic in Allentown. He couldn't quite specifically sort it all out, though the actual night itself was a wild tale to be told, and would forever bond him and Kurt together.

It all began when they decided to split a bag of mushrooms, mixing them in with plates of gravy fries at the Bowmanstown Diner. Somehow it came about that it might be a stimulating, novel idea to travel to an equestrian farm located somewhere out in Mahoning Township, or so they thought. For it was rumored that a very rare, albino colt had been birthed there recently, and this animal was a progenitor to a fourth dimension, where universal secrets that had stymied generations of great thinkers, could perhaps be unlocked. Where this information originated from, neither could attest. But it was just the sort of heady thing to blow open the doors of perception in such malleable minds.

The only thing that perhaps in retrospect could be considered sane or be of any meritorious consideration, was that the vehicle being used for travel up to that point, was summarily ditched, in favor of setting out on foot, shortly after the summer sun had fallen behind the hills to the west. Denny and Kurt thus set out on a quixotic search, with nothing more than the curious thirst for answers to certain existential questions, prevalent in those who fall under the sway of hallucinogens, and heavy doses of marijuana. Though years later Denny had been able to connect some of the mental abstractions from that point in his life with intellectual and spiritual pursuits discovered completely sober, through activities like meditation and prayer, and within the sport of endurance running.

On this given night, the horse stables sought turned out to be much further away than either had realized or planned for; it ended up taking them many hours to locate, and involved a series of difficulties along the way, the greatest of which ended up being that this albino colt slept in an inaccessible barn, located behind a fence of electrical wire that encircled the entire property. After some debate, the decision was reached that it would not only be potentially dangerous to try and breach the fence, but it would be bad karma to trespass onto the farm. And it was also noted that it could be potentially problematic if caught while under the influence and possession of illegal narcotics.

So, there was nothing left to do but to trudge on home. An idyllic stream down the road was first sought though as a place to rest and recoup, and to quench their thirst from. Up and down the very same hills and mountain, and on back through the sleepy valley the two wearily trekked. By the time the outskirts of Lehighton were reached, the sun had already reappeared, and risen across the banks of the Lehigh River. Denny and Kurt stopped off at the Beacon Diner and drank coffee and ate a hearty breakfast; at some point while watching the morning unfold, the name the great expedition was proffered forth to capture the spirit of the night. By whom, neither could recall. Or wanted to take credit for. But the legend of the walk, and its newly coined moniker, quickly spread to the farthest corners of the small town, and throughout the surrounding countryside. Or at least it did in their grandiose vision of the halcyon night.

Denny found Jennifer talking to a distinguished looking woman, who looked to be in her sixties, in front of one of her displayed paintings. He did not want to interrupt, but when Jennifer caught sight of Denny, she motioned for him to come over and join them.

"This is Carolyn Freidman. The owner of Vintage," Jennifer said, as Denny smiled and shook hands with the woman. He couldn't help notice the sparkling glimmer in Jennifer's emerald green eyes. In general, he had never seen her look so stunning; her curly blond hair fell down upon the long-sleeved black dress she was wearing, which couldn't have been more than a size six, and extended to the top of her knees. With brown leather boots on, Jennifer stood maybe only two inches shorter than Denny. But it was something much deeper than superficial looks that he was attuned to and attracted to; her very being exuded an effervescent, omnipresent glow, that is naturally radiated by a person when they are right where they are meant to be, at a given moment in their life.

"Such a pleasure to meet you," Denny did respond.

"The pleasure is all mine," she replied. There was an underlying warmth to the proprietor of the gallery, who looked quite elegant too, in a long turquoise dress, with a white sweater wrapped around her neck and shoulders. She wore a string of pearls as well and was about the same height as Jennifer. The two could have easily been mistaken as mother and daughter.

"I've informed Miss Jennifer of some very good news," Mrs. Freidman continued. "Several offers have been made for her paintings."

"That's wonderful," Denny replied, as he exchanged a quick smile with Jennifer. "I am not surprised in the least."

"I'm delightfully captivated once again myself. There is an indelible complexity to Jennifer's painting style that I cannot put my finger on." The gallery owner then lowered her voice, and looked right at Denny as if to share some forbidden secret with him. "And that I dare say, is often the hallmark of quality art."

Jennifer, who had heard every word, did reply. "Thank you. Your opinion is of supreme value to me."

"This is all so very exciting. And what a lovely gallery you have here," Denny added, as he bounced his gaze between the two women. Jennifer looked like she was about to burst, though she was performing a yeomen's task maintaining her decorum. Denny knew what this meant to her; not necessarily from a financial standpoint, though the extra income would be much welcomed and certainly could be used, but from the idea that the world-at-large appreciated the beauty and intrinsic value of something that she had poured her heart and soul into creating. He couldn't wait to hear more after the show about what she was thinking and feeling. And he knew from the look in her eyes that she couldn't wait to share her emotions on this most momentous of nights with him. Denny politely excused himself, as Mrs. Freidman was introducing Jennifer to a gentleman who had walked into the room.

Denny moseyed in and out of the other rooms in the gallery, causally looking at some of the other paintings and even a few sculptures that were on display, while half-heartedly trying to find where Uncle Mike and Mr. Hackenberg had drifted off to. Though after a bit, he did become somewhat worried since he couldn't find the guys anywhere in the building, so he made his way out to the main room in the front, and then on out the front door. As he stepped onto the sidewalks, Denny saw Mr. Hackenberg walking towards him, with a look of concern on his face. This can't be good Denny surmised.

"He almost collapsed so we had to do some fancy footwork to get him out of there," Mr. Hackenberg said, before Denny could even open his mouth to speak. "Thankfully there are some kind and understanding patrons in the art world who lent a hand."

It was cause for worry, but nothing too dramatic. Uncle Mike was in capable hands, and nights like this pushed the limits of what he could be expected to handle. Undoubtedly, he understood this himself, better than any of the rest possibly could. He was stubborn to a fault, like most people Denny knew, and had been adamantly insistent that such a night not be missed, for Uncle Mike knew what it meant to Jennifer, whom he had always adored and liked from way back when she and Denny were wild-eyed idealistic punks barely into their twenties. And he knew what it meant to Denny, and what Jennifer meant to Denny, who walked to the car and checked on his uncle. When he looked into the passenger's side, Uncle Mike was found asleep, with his head resting on an arm that was propped up on the vehicle's console. Denny was going to just walk away, but his uncle must have sensed the presence of someone outside for he jerked awake and sheepishly grinned, then rolled down the window to speak.

"I'm only resting for a few minutes my boy," he said.

"Yes, I see. These artsy types can sure wear us lay people out right?"

"Something to that effect," he replied. Uncle Mike pushed his glasses up his nose and face. "How did it go for Jennifer?"

"Very good so far," Denny told him, without delving into any specifics. He had learned to pick his spots with his uncle, plus there was something else he was curious about, and wanted to query him on. "If I may ask, what was it the two of you were intently discussing in there?"

Uncle Mike attempted to shift his weight a little in the seat; he looked extremely uncomfortable, and when he did move, a pained expression washed across his haggard face. His whole body bore the indicators of someone who was not well, which was evident to all who crossed his path.

"I asked her if she had studied Cezanne. I thought maybe he was an influence on her work." Another weak, but loving smile appeared. This damn disease could never steal his mind, nor rob him of his wit.

Denny didn't bother to press the issue. He had to smile too at being one-upped again by one of the best. Perhaps Jennifer would tell him later, though he had a pretty good inclination as to the subject matter. Instead he rubbed his uncle's right arm; Mr. Hackenberg had climbed inside and started up the engine.

"Go home and get some rest big fella," Denny said.

"I will Denny. I will." And with that, the two men pulled out and headed back home to Slatington, as Denny turned and headed back down the street towards the gallery. He had the urge to whistle out loud, despite the fact that he didn't know how to. For he knew that for better or worse, life would never be exactly the same ever again.

Chapter 26

"Burrr. I'm freezing."

"Me too. But I am loathe to get up from under this or I'll really be cold." Denny pulled the heavy blanket even tighter around him and Jennifer. The couch was so soft and roomy too that getting up from it seemed like it might require a herculean effort, certainly more than either of them was willing to make at such an early hour.

"I wonder if it's snowing yet?" Jennifer asked. She managed to sort of half sit up in an attempt to see out the front windows of the cabin, but it was still dark outside.

"It's not going to start until later this morning," Denny replied, with an air of confidence, as he sat up as well, and debated the merits of crossing the living room to put more logs on the fire.

"You big meteorologist man," chided Jennifer with unmistakable sarcasm, as she rubbed his shoulders. He had mentioned some soreness before, which was probably from an increase in the number of pushups and planks done during the week, partly so he could look as fit as possible when he saw her. The looking fit part he withheld, instead dropping references to the upcoming marathon in Boston, and how such exercises were an aid in preparation. To which Jennifer just nodded.

Denny did roust himself up from the couch and added firewood in the fireplace; one of the bigger logs let out a pretty loud crackling noise as it settled into the flames.

"Oh my," Jennifer exclaimed, as she laid back down. She was joined by her companion a few seconds later.

"So, I've been meaning to ask. What made you change your mind about us?" Denny wrapped his arms tight around her as he put forth the question.

"What do you mean?"

"I'm not sure what I mean," he swiftly replied, somewhat regretting that he had brought it up. But he carried on, nonetheless. "I was merely curious about the details. If there were any?"

"Oh, there always are Denny. You know that." The fire was now rekindled and roaring in the background; small waves of heat could be felt across the room and on the couch. Soon the first hints of the day's light would begin to filter through the trees, and into the cabin.

"Of course, it all comes down to being in tune with and following the universe's signs."

"Hey don't mock me." Jennifer managed to free her right arm just enough to elbow him in the stomach. Denny grunted, though it felt more playful than painful.

"I assure you I am not," Denny said. "I have begun to become much more attuned to the mysteries of the cosmos. You know I've always found such things quite fascinating."

"Yes. And now you're seeing it more on a personal level." Jennifer paused, and stretched her slender body out like a house cat. "Well. There was this one evening I was coming home from my Mom's house. It was a little after I had called it off with Barry. But I was still sort of waffling at times on it all. Not that I did not know I hadn't made the right call. But you know how it goes." Jennifer shifted again on the couch. Denny moved a little in order to accommodate.

"Sometimes these things are hard to explain. I was getting out of my car and sort of mulling some of this over and not really paying attention to things in the dark, and something my mom had said about you was also very much on my mind at the moment. I had to park on the other side of the street because my stupid neighbor on the left side daughter's boyfriend had parked where I always park in front of my house. And so, I got out of my car and started to cross the street and someone running almost ran right into me and knocked me over! I was like what the hell? Scared the living crap out of me too!"

"Dang. That's crazy."

"Yes. But I quickly regained my composure and started to walk inside the house when I realized that it was a sign from the universe that I had completely made the correct decision, because my heart of hearts belonged to you. I mean why else would someone like that cross my exact path in that exact way at that exact moment? Is it possible they weren't even real to begin with?" Jennifer's voice raised to match the excitement of the words spoken; the conviction of which was not lost on Denny.

"Wow. That's wild. And yes, it is a sign. Or was a sign." Whatever it actually was, Denny was happy that the incident had occurred, and had been interpreted as such. He had to admit as far as signs go, there was a fair of amount of symbolism in the thing too. Like if he had gotten hit over the head with a painting.

"And so... here we are," Jennifer concluded, feeling sublimely happy herself, and content lying in the arms of Denny in some cabin out in the wilderness of Franklin Township. She recalled too those years back when she used to listen to him and his friends incessantly extoll the virtues and natural charm of Franklin; I guess they were on to something she thought, before drifting off to sleep again.

~

"I don't know man." There was a slight edge to Denny's tone, though he caught himself almost immediately, realizing that any traces of negative energy could end up being detrimental. Old habits die hard, especially the bad ones. One of which for Denny was being a little too prickly or sensitive when questioned about certain personal matters in life. And his friend had his genuine best interests in mind, and was only wondering where things might stand.

"Well I do know, and apologize. Actually, I'm trying to be comfortable with the idea that I don't need to know everything." Denny laughed out loud at some of his own absurdity. "These things are never easy, are they?"

"Try being married," Keith replied, with a laugh of his own, as the two ran on Second Street. The hills and small mountains that rolled up and away from the Lehigh River basin to the north and east were visible ahead, just below a thick bank of ashen, white clouds. It had always been one of Denny's favorite views when running in the town of Lehighton.

"I'm better suited to run seventy miles a week."

"Whatever keeps the motor humming." The cold air seemed to cut through the runners, even though both were wearing long pants, multiple layers of clothing, as well as gloves and beanies. It felt like it could start snowing at any moment; when the wind swirled about, it was downright raw.

Denny clapped his gloved hands together and let out a rather loud "WOOOO"

"Yeah dude," Keith replied in response.

They proceeded out Coal Street, then commenced the climb into the heights north and west of town. Denny did fill Keith in on a bunch about the art show, the whole scene at the gallery, and how he had bumped into Kurt. And how his uncle had to be rescued. And of course, much about Jennifer. He did realize too how appreciative he was to have someone to talk to the next day while everything was still fresh. Though Denny didn't particularly care to leave her behind at the cabin for an hour or two when their time together was limited, but Jennifer said she wanted to go shopping anyhow and stock up on food and supplies for the rest of the weekend, in case they became snowbound. Which Denny didn't mind in the least, should that end up happening. For he did love snow, and snowstorms. It was one of the tradeoffs made by moving well to the south, where it rarely snowed along the coastline. Then again it was nice not to have to endure lengthy, harsh winters, particularly from a runner's point of view. On the flipside, the summers the last few years never wanted to end, and tended to beat one into a pulp, regardless if you were an outdoors person or not. Denny continued to ramble on, like one big stream of consciousness out of a Hemmingway novel, as the runners crested the tough climb, then turned westward, where the topography on top of the ridgeline was a little more forgiving in its elevation changes. He was feeling some fatigue in the legs, no doubt a product of the past two day's efforts.

Keith predominately listened, as he was struggling to run the hills without adverse and noticeable effects upon his breathing, though he was in decently better shape since the last time Denny was in Pennsylvania. "I get going for a good bit and then fall off," he explained, in response to being asked. "Winters. As you alluded to earlier. In your dissertation."

"No excuses. Got to stay disciplined my friend. Hit the treadmill. Biggest key to sustained improvement."

"Well it's not easy to do with kids. And the job as such."

Throughout the years, there always seemed to be some sort of a contentious wedge in the friendship, that extended into numerous facets of life, including and perhaps most frequently, the sport of running. The root of which was the fact that Keith had two kids of his own, and a third stepson in college, whereas Denny did not have any children. Therefore, Denny couldn't comprehend the demands on time, resources, and energy having kids elicited, thus his accomplishments, again to circle back to running, were to be viewed through the prism of not having a family to care for, thereby diminishing them by some unquantified degree. Or to flip it around somewhat, people like Denny had more time, energy, and resources to devote to their athletic pursuits

Denny could also see the merits in the postulation, and had to agree to an extent that it was true. But there were perhaps innumerable intangibles that people like Denny missed out on, by not having much of an immediate family, when it came to competitive activities like running. And again, he had to acknowledge, if being honest with himself, that he was being too sensitive in all of it to begin with, and shouldn't regard such comments personally, or take as an alleged dig. What Keith said, and had alluded to many times in the past in similar contexts, were merely reflective of the framework of his life, in regards to extra-circular pursuits. Denny knew many people with extremely busy and fulfilling lives that included children and challenging jobs, who did manage to train at very high, demanding levels. Such thoughts though, he kept to himself. He was happy for the company, as the two longtime running buds rolled up and down several smaller hills above the Mahoning Valley. Sometimes the more things changed, the more they stayed the same. Denny wondered if in ten, twenty, thirty years from now they'd still be running these very runs?

"I suspect you'll be out here at some point doing the Ukes run solo," Keith surmised. "And filling me in on it in detailed depth at my retirement villa."

"I can organize the senior citizen turkey trots." But Denny, like most people, had natural trepidations when it came to growing older, or getting old. He was living as a witness to it currently with his uncle. It was impossible to fathom all that he must be going through, yet the man looked to be doing it with an amazing display of dignity and grace. And with his own running, Denny knew at some point it was inevitable he'd slow down. Or was it? Could one tie up and bind the hands of father time? No. It was not going to happen. Denny was being foolish. Uncle Mike would preach acceptance, and gratitude for what was being granted on any given day.

"You never know what's going on inside of someone though," Keith said, in response to more of Denny's musings.

"True. So true my friend." Denny knew this without a shadow of a doubt, as evidenced by all that he himself was fond of keeping buried and hidden at times. The ugly, unvarnished truths he tried like hell to evade. Perhaps he was developing a little more humility, and with it, the ability to embrace his humanness, and all of its glorious imperfections.

"You're in a philosophical mood today," Keith observed.

"All the artwork last night must be spurring on these dalliances into the unknown."

"Or a certain blond."

After they had surmounted another lengthy hill, the terrain leveled briefly at the frontal lip of the ridgeline. The clouds had sunk far enough, that the top of the Mahoning Mountain to the south of town was now veiled in a greyish, white misty fog. As Keith and Denny plunged down Beaver Run Road back into Lehighton, the first flakes of snow began to delicately drop from the sky, almost as if in slow motion. Denny reached out and tried to grab some snow out of the air; a smile crept across his half-frozen face.

Where Denny liked to be, or needed to be was on the periphery, not only in running but in life. Out on the edges, perpetually searching. Maybe that's why for so many years he sought answers to metaphysical questions in bottles and pipes, in backroom bars and dimly lit drug dens; but the closer he came to feeling connected to the ungraspable and undefinable, the farther it all fell away from him. Over time the gap grew larger, until the chasm opened so wide it almost swallowed him whole.

"Since long ago I wandered way out on a cliff with the brilliance of an angel." Denny quoted the lyrics, instead of butchering them by singing. He used to sign off on letters written while in college with those words. For they represented a proverb he was living by, and could live by. Until he realized he couldn't.

"I saw them at the Allentown Fairgrounds," Keith said. "Right after I got back from the Persian Gulf."

"A returning war hero."

"Yes. Something like that." A light snow was falling; the snowflakes had become smaller, much finer in size, but the precipitation had also become a little steadier as they approached Keith's house, and the end of the six-mile run.

"You heading right out to the cabin?" he asked.

"Yes. Jennifer should be there soon."

Keith smiled. "A nice romantic weekend in the woods."

"Let's hope." Denny was feeling pretty positive about the whole thing, but he didn't want to get carried away or too caught up in all of it just yet.

"Roll with the tide my brother. And enjoy the moments." Keith paused for a few seconds as they crossed Coal Street and cut down Third Street, and passed in front of Saint Peter and Paul's. "With these things too much philosophizing tends to muddle it. Trust me on this."

"I do," Denny replied. "And thanks for all the advice."

"You bet."

~

Jennifer brought the groceries in from the car; she lingered briefly on the stone driveway to watch the snow that had just started. She always thought there was something magical when snow first began to fall, like opening a new book to page one and reading the first few words and sentences. The thrill of a new adventure, and the uncertainty of where it all may lead. But she wasn't sure if that made much sense. Oh well, the snow made her happy, and the thought of spending another day with Denny made her happy.

She unpacked what had been purchased at the supermarket in the kitchen, then went over to the fireplace and put another log on the fire, though she wasn't sure if it needed another one yet, as it still felt kind of warm inside. Jennifer noticed the pile of wood next to the hearth had only a few logs left; she debated going out to the porch to bring some more in from the big pile, but figured she'd leave that for Denny to do, since he seemed to derive a real sense of pleasure from performing chores like that.

About fifteen minutes later Jennifer heard the sound of another vehicle coming up the driveway, and the double toot of a horn, so she walked outside to check and see if it was Denny, or whom it might be. But it was Denny who hopped out of his car, clutching something behind him. Why the heck did he honk the horn, Jennifer wondered? Then again it was foolish to try and make a lot of sense out of some of the things the guy had a penchant for doing.

"Hello darling," Denny said as he walked over the small patch of yard from the driveway to the screened-in porch; a light dusting of snow had already accumulated on the ground. It was cold enough for whatever fell to stick to any surface, as temperatures were in the upper twenties. Currently the forecast was predicting three to five inches, as the snow was expected to last well into the evening hours, though at light to moderate intensities.

"Close your eyes," he requested, which Jennifer obliged by doing. She felt Denny take her right hand and wrap it around something wet and a bit rough feeling which she instantly recognized as the stems to flowers.

When she opened her eyes, the optics of the red roses against the drab browns and olive greens of the wooded front yard, speckled with white from the nascent snowfall, presented a striking contrast, like something Jennifer would be inclined to create artistically. "Oh Denny these are so beautiful. But you didn't have to."

"I know," he replied, giving her a hug while she held the flowers to the side. "But I wanted to."

"Maybe we can dig up a vase somewhere inside. Come on it's freezing out here." The two headed through the door to the porch and then through the door into the cabin. The smell of a wood burning fire was so earthy and homey; if Denny could have bottled it and taken it with him, he would have.

Later in the afternoon Jennifer began preparations for the lasagna she was planning to make; all sorts of fresh vegetables were arrayed on the table in the living room, as there wasn't enough room in the kitchen. She did manage to find a cutting board and a set of sharp knives. Denny offered his assistance, but was politely shooed away from the means of production. His grandmother used to do the same thing to him. It amused Denny to watch Jennifer wash produce in the sink, then carry into the living room, using whatever mismatched bowls and plates that could be scrounged from the cupboards, not before first thoroughly cleaning any silverware or dining ware being used.

"I work in a hospital," she reminded Denny. "Cleanliness is an absolute necessity," she added, while unintentionally waving a sharp knife in his direction. All he could do was laugh, and vow to keep at a safe distance.

So, he decided to bundle up and go adventuring in the snow, and perhaps get a good old-fashioned country walk in. Denny headed out the driveway and down the now snow-covered dirt road to Green Street, and towards the little church that was about a half a mile away, and had stood there ever since he could recall as a kid. He walked up the entrance way to Grace Lutheran Church and on back around through the parking lot, which was entirely vacant. There was a long driveway or road, that per its outline beneath the snow, headed up the hill and into the woods. Denny decided to follow. The snow continued to come down at a light but steady rate; by now he guessed about two inches had fallen. He stopped in a grove of trees to watch and listen to the holy symphony being conducted by mother nature, nearly slipping into a trance as he did.

    He heard the words of the poet Rainer Marie Rilke, "staying is nowhere," so he continued up the incline. The road or pathway narrowed into a trail, which climbed rather abruptly into the woods. After hiking uphill for several minutes, he came upon a clearing in the woods and a vista across the valley towards Beltzville Lake, barely visible through the low ceiling of clouds and snowfall. The hills and woods on the far side of the lake had been blotted out by the elements, as visibility had been reduced to no more than a mile or so. Denny stood and watched for a few minutes the wintry scene as it continued to unfold moment by moment, before turning around and beginning the short trek back to the warmth and dryness of the cabin.

    Once inside the screened-in porch, Denny brushed the snow off his clothes. As soon as he opened the door to the cabin, he was greeted by the heavenly aroma of food being cooked, the result of Jennifer's laborious work since he'd been gone. "My goodness it smells divine," he exclaimed, while stripping off his sweatshirt and flannel.

    "Really? I guess I need to walk outside and come back in," Jennifer replied. And then she walked outside and came back in, and agreed with Denny's observation.

Dinner that evening was wonderfully delightful. Jennifer also managed to find some candles in the back bedroom to set on the table, as the two of them feasted by the window, and watched the snow continue to fall outside. On the menu was lasagna stuffed with Italian sausage and green peppers, a tossed salad with all the usual vegetables, plus raisins and pecans, and garlic bread covered in butter that melted right into it. They took their time eating, savoring all the scrumptious food, and savoring the time spent with each other, chatting about all sorts of things. It all felt quite comfortable, and ordained. A bond existed between the two; a resilient bond that had withstood all the years, all the comings and goings, the partings and the reunions. Would it all become permanent this go around? Who knew; such matters could be navigated later. They had pledged fidelity to each other, and for now, it was all either wanted or needed.

Jennifer asked Denny about Boston, and how he thought the training was unfolding of late. He was always a tad reluctant to go into his running all that in depth with her, as far as the nuts and bolts details were concerned, for fear perhaps that much of it would bore her. Or maybe it was more of a deep-seated fear that it would reveal a major flaw in his personality, in that he put too much stock into what most of society might deem a causal hobby. Of course, the irony was that for one, Jennifer already knew this, and two, it was one of the primary reasons that she was enamored with him. She lovingly reminded him of this, and reminded him that she could also relate to such a viewpoint, in light of her own personal feelings towards art and painting, which admittedly might skirt the line of what could be deemed obsessive. And how that sometimes, our biggest discoveries are found while we are out on the periphery.

"That is so uncanny," Denny said, while wiping his chin with a napkin. "I was just talking with Keith today on our run about being out on the periphery."

"It's where all the action is right?" Jennifer asked rhetorically, as they both laughed. "So, what's your goal for the marathon? I know you must have one. And you keep evading direct answers mister."

"Yes, I can be rather devious at doing that. Such as answering a question with another question. Isn't that what all the great spiritual masters do?"

"Or they extend out tangents in the hope that the questioner will forget what in the heck they had even asked to begin with?"

"Indeed," Denny replied. He took a drink of water, and set the plastic cup down in a somewhat deliberate fashion in front of himself. "I want to break three hours. At Boston. You see it's one of those magical numbers in the sport of running, at least from the perspective of us mortal amateurs. Like a benchmark. That signifies one is a really solid marathon runner, if they can run it in under the three-hour mark."

"I bet you will," Jennifer stated. "I know how you are when you set your mind on accomplishing something."

"I was feeling much more confident in the earlier part of winter before I hurt my hamstring. Also, that served to reconfigure my priorities some. Though I could simply be employing the line of thought as a crutch. Or as an out if I don't think I can do it."

"Well I don't think you are. And there is nothing wrong with seeing things in a new light when circumstances change. To me it's a measure of growth."

"Yes. Thanks. I never looked at it in those terms. Three hours will be right near the cusp of my ability. Physiologically. And the Boston Marathon is not the easiest course around."

"Because of the Newton Hills?"

Denny was touched. He smiled and responded, "apparently someone has been studying the course?"

"Yes. I may have stumbled upon some information," Jennifer replied. "And hey, if a goal doesn't intimidate you some, then it's not a big enough goal."

"That's a great way of looking at it. Puts a perspective on it I hadn't considered," Denny said. "I need to fire Uncle Mike and hire you as my coach." It felt good too, to be verbalizing much of what he had initially sought to do when the training cycle had started in December. For it stirred the beast even more that lived and breathed inside, and had been poking its head out of late. Some of this caution had seeped in, which was an anathema to what was encoded in Denny's running DNA. For he much preferred to go all in; if he crashed and burned out there on the roads so be it, at least he couldn't be accused of not taking a chance.

Jennifer was apparently operating on the same wavelength, for she stated, "it's better to throw your hat in the ring and fail then to just sit on the sidelines. My Dad used to say that."

"Sage advice."

"Maybe you needed some time to not be as outcome focused? Get back to enjoying the aesthetics of it, or the root causes of why you love running so much. Then combine the two."

"Yes!" Denny agreed. "Think you may have hit the nail on the head there. Purity and love, and goals. They don't have to be mutually exclusive."

"I found myself in a similar predicament with my painting. Having to reorient, if you will."

"Because you hurt your hamstring too?"

Jennifer threw a piece of garlic bread at Denny, which somehow missed his head from four feet away. "As I was attempting to say. I got a little too caught up in the impending art show, and trying to see what else it might open up doors to. Before I knew it, I was totally freaked out because I hadn't even come up with the concept for my paintings that were going to be displayed at my gallery debut in New York City. You know the show that purely existed as a figment of my over active imagination."

"One day though," Denny said.

"I had to get back to the bare basics and get back to why I do all of it in the first place you see." Jennifer broke off another piece of bread; this time she didn't chuck it across the table. "And why I paint so much is to prevent me from going insane and sending the boys off to boarding school. While I rest comfortably in the asylum, catching up on a year's worth of daytime soaps."

"I'd come visit. I used to like General Hospital. My sister got me into."

"You're such a prince, aren't you?"

"A well fed and stuffed prince right now. God that was all so delicious." Denny was full. The last couple of days he always seemed to be famished, a result no doubt of the increased training load. This week he had actually topped out at sixty-four miles, a big jump. Plus, he was making a real concerted effort again to curb sugar consumption. Just then Jennifer's cell phone rang.

"Ah ah ah. It's Carolyn Freidman again," she announced, before answering and saying hello.

From the one side of the conversation Denny was privy to, it sounded like much good news was being conveyed to Jennifer. She stood and smiled, and then came over and shook one of Denny's arms excitedly, while continuing to speak with the gallery owner.

"Yes. Thanks again. For sure. You too," Jennifer concluded her side of the conversation into the phone, before setting the device down on the table, and emitting a high-pitched yelp.

There was a second or two of silence as both of them looked at each other. "And?" Denny asked.

"All the paintings have sold and she wants me to do another show next month. Also, it's going to be a solo show. Just little ol me. Oh my goodness Denny!" Jennifer literally started to jump up and down in the living room.

Denny was blown away too by the fantastic news. "This is so amazing!" he blurted out. "Yowser!"

"It is. It is." Jennifer stopped jumping and lowered her voice as the news began to settle in. For someone who had spent the bulk of her adult life primarily engaged in the care and service of others, carving out whatever time she could to pursue her own calling and craft her own talents in the obscurity of a dimly lit, dank basement, this was beyond good news. To state that it was a tremendous validation in much of what she believed in would fail to capture the entire essence of the occasion. It was a step. A leap.

"I'm so happy for you," Denny said, as he pulled her in real close. "So happy."

"And you're here," she whispered in his ear. "My lucky charm."

Chapter 27

Uncle Mike laid in bed quietly snoring; there was a plastic tube attached to his nose, split in two and held in place with a Velcro strap around his forehead, all of which came from out of an oxygen tank held in place on the opposite side of the bed. Denny himself sat on the wooden rocking chair beside the bed, and watched his uncle beneath the light cast out by a small desk lamp behind him. Occasionally the wind would rattle the one window in the room, a grim reminder of the cold reality the scene set forth.

Denny sat there for a time and watched Uncle Mike. Mr. Hackenberg was downstairs brewing a pot of coffee, and cleaning up some things in the kitchen. He had filled him in on all the latest medical news from the doctor's appointment the day before, and the nurse's checkup a few hours ago. A change in medication was necessary; a net side effect would be a reduction in energy levels for a couple of days, hence he had been mostly asleep the past twenty-four hours, and would be fairly out of it for the short-term. The oxygen was more of a precautionary measure however. All of this was precipitated by a drastic drop in the white cell count in the bloodstream, or something along those lines. After stabilization, the prognosis wasn't much better. Realistically he could be looking at a few more days, or a few more weeks. A bit of good news though was that one of the drugs now being prescribed should alleviate the more debilitating pains Uncle Mike had been experiencing in the extremities of late, that in turn led to the walker being used. Much of this Denny was unaware of, except what he had witnessed Friday night. The guy was a fighter no doubt; at some point though don't we all go down for one last ten count?

Ostensibly just to get up and out of the rocking chair and move about, Denny began haphazardly rummaging around the bedroom. He came across a calendar tucked beneath a notebook, and copy of the Bible, all stacked neatly on top of a clothes dresser. For some reason he opened the calendar; what he found inside was that his uncle had written down how many miles Denny had run each day, along with annotations about where some of the runs had taken place at, or what the workout was on specific days. Each run's information was printed inside the day's corresponding box.

"I'll be damned Uncle Mike," Denny said, as he took his hand and slowly traced through the weeks that were in the month of January. He read the distances and times, and if applicable, the details of many of the individual runs, and also any notes that were jotted in fine print in the margins; snippets of memories and mental images of places popped into Denny's mind as he pored through the data. There were also weekly mileage totals tabulated at the end of every row, and a monthly total written at the bottom of the page. He flipped to February; there were a lot of white, blank boxes from all the days the injury had prevented him from getting outside to run.

There was a guttural grunt from the bed, and a rustling of sheets and blankets; Uncle Mike had apparently heard someone in the room, as he opened his eyes and shifted some of his weight onto his one side so he could try and see what was taking place.

"John is that you?" he weakly asked. His voice sounded very hoarse, as if he had a bad head cold.

"No. It's Elvis." Denny sat back down on the rocking chair, and slid it over to right beside the bed. "How are you? Can I get you anything?"

Denny looked out the window. Some of the last vestiges of daylight were visible; bright, reddish orange and pinkish hues in the sky just above where the sun must have been, hidden now behind the hills to the west of the farm. The landscape could still be discerned, all covered in a blanket of fresh snow that had fallen the day before. It was one of the most idyllic, tranquil displays of the natural world Denny had ever seen; a transcendent moment, heightened as a result of his acute emotional state internally, even if it wasn't fully graspable on the conscious level.

"Yes. Another blanket. Please." The sound of his uncle's softy spoken words could have been originating from the embers of a dream.

Uncle Mike's frail body, the same body that had run tens of thousands of miles, and helped him accomplish a hell of a lot of other things as well in life, was already covered in multiple sheets, blankets, and a comforter. The internal organs could no longer produce much if any heat at all. There simply wasn't enough energy anymore, at least not tonight. Denny got up and looked about the room, but couldn't find anything else to lay on top of the bed.

"It's in. Look..."

Denny walked over beside his bed and leaned in so he could hear what Uncle Mike was trying to say, which was that there was another blanket inside the closet in the room. Denny did find it, and placed it gently on top of the bed and his body, carefully draping it over the sides and bottom.

"Much better," his uncle said. He even managed a weak smile.

There was a silence in the room, and a silence in the house as far as Denny could hear, which for some reason he found awkward, or disconcerting, so he started to tell Uncle Mike about a book he had recently finished reading, one that his uncle had given him years ago about the imperfections of spirituality. Denny had also read the book then, but hadn't gotten much out of it. This time he had, particularly all the allusions to the confusion and angst all humans are destined to sometimes feel, or this conception that something is off, but we can't ever seem to be able to understand or articulate what's distressing us from deep inside.

"Yes," Uncle Mike said. "Let me say. The key is…," he began, but the effort presently was a little too much, so he ceased speaking mid-sentence and closed his eyes. Denny flashed to a scene from the movie *Ocean's Eleven*, where Brad Pitt's character gets interrupted, and never finishes instructing Matt Damon's about the one thing he should never under any circumstances do, so as to not blow the con.

"Come on man I need this info," Denny whispered aloud, with a slight smirk on his face. Much to his surprise, his uncle heard him.

"Well there isn't any info," he said. Uncle Mike pushed the top blanket down off his chest, and attempted to adjust his body again as if to try and sit up; Denny reached over and grabbed one of the pillows and stood it vertically by the head of the bed, which helped his uncle to re-position himself, and presumably be able to converse easier with him.

"I'll say this. I spent much time earlier in life. Staring into the abyss. Challenging a god if one was there. To show his face." He tapped Denny on the back of his hand, that was resting on the bed. "I wanted answers. As to why? Why any of this? Because I felt askew. Adrift. Or not complete. Unless I could obtain some confirmation there was an objective. Or a point to all of this."

"And that would make you feel better then?"

"I don't know what I had hoped to gain." Uncle Mike's voice raised when he spoke the last few words. It also looked like a touch of color had returned to his face. His greyish, white, scraggly beard gave him an air of gravitas, like an old-time prophet. "But," he carried forth, like someone heavily measuring the weight of each word, "we must all arrive at the realization, that it's the nature of our human condition. To feel torn asunder. But," he tapped Denny again on the back of the hand, "when we commence to accept this belief, instead of fighting it, we are able to walk into the light of God."

Uncle Mike smiled when he finished speaking; a smile brimming with seventy some years of having lived life to the fullest, pushing up against many of his own edges, and slamming headlong into many a brick wall along the journey. Time and time again he had picked himself up, arisen, and strode with dignity into the dawn of a new day.

The two talked some more about the book and spirituality, about Jennifer and her art and the successful show she had in Jim Thorpe, and how her and Denny's relationship was and might be. Uncle Mike asked for an update on his running, and how the final ramp up to Boston was progressing. Denny discussed in detail a few of the last harder runs he had done, and how he was trying to strike a balance between letting go of attachments to precise time goals, yet still pushing himself to the brink in order to position himself to succeed at the highest possible levels. All while staying grounded and humble, or at least trying his best to do so. Uncle Mike said he understood, and told Denny how proud he was of him, for all the stuff he was doing off the roads as well.

He had Denny fetch his cell phone, so that he could download for him the Boston Athletic Association's app, which would allow Uncle Mike to not only stay abreast of any marathon news, but more importantly it would provide the means to track Denny in real time during the race itself. There was a continuously ticking countdown to the start of the race when the app first opened every time. Denny assured him he'd show John how it worked as well, and also send both of them his bib number and corral and wave assignments as soon they were issued. What was left unspoken, was the fervent hope that come race day, Uncle Mike would still be there, and be able to share in the experience and grandeur of the most historical of foot races with his nephew.

Before Denny took leave and left the upstairs bedroom, his uncle motioned him over by his bedside; he leaned in as close as he could to Uncle Mike, who whispered in his ear, "don't let her go again." And with that, the two bade each other farewell. Denny slowly walked out of the room; he stopped for a brief moment in the doorway, and thought about turning around for one last glance. Instead he smiled and rapped the wooden beam atop the door frame two times, then disappeared into the hallway and on back down the staircase of the farmhouse. He said goodnight to Mr. Hackenberg, and got into his car to begin the drive south yet again.

Chapter 28

North Carolina was awash in springtime; temperatures many a day climbed into the seventies by the afternoon, beneath a majestic light blue sky that seemed to stretch endlessly from the ocean in the east, across the coastal plain and Cape Fear River and beyond to the west. Puffy white clouds floated like giant marshmallows, occasionally producing rain showers that continued to quench the soil beneath. Everywhere yellowish green buds continued to awaken and open into leaves, and the first brightly colorful blooms on the azalea bushes started to appear in their stunning arrays of whites, pinks, violets, reds, and numerous shades between. Of course, with spring came all the chalky, dusty, yellow powdery pollen, but a well-timed gully washer or thunderstorm could wash most of the nuisance away. The days stayed light much longer; this allowed Denny to be able to complete runs in the evening before the sun completely slipped away. Or if he did opt to rise and run early, perhaps only a lightweight long-sleeve shirt, or a lone pair of gloves was needed to be worn.

After an unexceptional, yet rather enjoyable nine-mile run, most of which was completed on the trails in the state park, Denny found a square shaped envelope from the Boston Athletic Association waiting for him in his mailbox. And once again, such correspondence caused his heart to flutter; by now Denny was most unequivocally in love with the Boston Marathon, cementing the crush first experienced almost a year and half ago when the requisite qualifying time had been run. He knew the contents within were most likely the bib and start line info; instead of ripping it open, he brought the mail inside, choosing to perform the post run strength and stretching routines first, similar to what had been done the evening he had received the card from Jennifer.

Ten minutes later Denny opened up the envelope, carefully running his fingers along the top edge as to not rip any of what was contained within. He pulled out a thick piece of paper, similar to the feel of construction paper used in children's art classes, that had on one side a miniature replica of a race bib with the number 6794 in white, set against a red backdrop. There was also a number seven printed on the left corner of the bib. On the back was an explanation of what the numbers and red color meant; in Denny's case, he was assigned to the first wave, and seventh corral, which was right around where some of his experienced Boston-running friends predicted he would start. The information also contained all the details about picking up the actual bib at the expo, as well as the precise clock times each of the waves would be starting the marathon.

It was all becoming more and more real; again, Denny could feel goosebumps, as he laid the paper down and began to text the details to Uncle Mike and a few friends as well. Social media was abuzz with runners sharing their race day assignments; the collective energy continued to slowly build, and Denny only assumed it would only intensify exponentially form here on out. He wanted to lap up every last drop.

The next morning, he was up super early, not by design. Unable to apparently sleep much more, and feeling pretty wide awake at a little past four thirty a.m., Denny decided to just get out of bed, strap a pair of shoes on, and blast out some mileage in the mild, dewy dark. On the pavement, Denny looked up at the sky and stars, and felt intensely grateful to be exactly where he was at that precise moment. To the extent that it almost choked him up a touch. Denny hit the start button on his watch and started running towards the ocean; he could hear the surf crashing onto the beach from a few hundred meters away.

Denny ran the length of the boardwalk; the sound of shoe leather repeatedly striking wood added to the pre-dawn musical performance, and he had the best seat in the theatre. The moon was vividly yellow, and almost full, hovering well out over the mighty sea. He headed out Canal Street and towards the north end of the island. The pace was frisky, especially for how early it was, not only in the morning, but in the duration of the run. But he felt good, and thought what the heck, let's just roll with it, formulating a plan on the move to run a ninety-minute time box; the objective being to see how far one could run distance wise in a pre-set allotted amount of time. His friend Natalie, who was also running Boston, had turned Denny onto the workout idea when they had done a long run two weekends ago, that included a lot of hills in downtown Wilmington, and the inclines on the bridges spanning the Cape Fear River. The effort had beat him up pretty good, and caused a fair amount of pain on the top of his left foot again. But the last few runs his foot had felt alright for the most part, and the only thing causing a bother of late was just some minor twinges and tenderness in the left hamstring.

The light thrown off by the moon helped guide the way, though Denny was so familiar with most of the island, he could almost go on auto-pilot when running. He caught sight of Snow's Cut Bridge, about a mile away across the waterway. A larger fishing vessel lazily idled well off the shoreline, with a bright light affixed to the top of the mast, which illuminated netting that hung down over the boat's sides. Denny thought about some Jack London novel he had read long ago, before losing sight of the boat and the water behind a series of houses and condo buildings.

A little way up the road the watch beeped and the face lit up, displaying a mile split of 7:03. Three miles in, Denny decided to jump the pace a hair faster, partly out of curiosity to see how it might feel. He hadn't come up with an estimated distance that might conceivably be laid down in an hour and a half this morning. Nor did he care to. He just ran. After coming back through the center of Carolina Beach, Denny headed out the greenway towards the darker, more remote parts of the island. A woman passed by walking her dog and exchanged a hello. The next two miles were clipped off in the 6:40s; across from the basketball court at Chappell Park, Denny took a left onto the newly completed section of the greenway, which weaved behind the backsides of several residential neighborhoods. He felt strong, composed, in control, as he cruised along one of the large drainage ponds the pathway went by. The tall, thin pines next to the water were silhouetted against the black sky.

A few miles later Denny found himself on the Kure Beach boardwalk. The first traces of dawn were visible above the horizon where the ocean met the sky; hues of peach, orange, and pink melted together, creating colors perhaps unseen, at least to Denny, who allowed his mind to go blank, in deference to the mystical, raw beauty displayed from the delicate brush of mother nature. Once again, the sounds he heard were that of his running shoes hitting the wooden boards, and the ocean's surf churning away on past the partially visible swath of sandy beach. There were lessons hidden within the infinite motion of the salty seas; such truths, however, usually lived just beyond the comprehension of her eager students. If nothing else, the ocean stretched the bounds of Denny's imagination.

From an athletic standpoint, he was dialed in. The last mile had been run in 6:33, and the ability was there to turn the screw even further, with a little over fifteen minutes left to go. It was tough, focused running, but Denny remained in control as he headed northward now on Lake Park Boulevard, back towards Carolina Beach. Turn the legs over, he reminded himself. Just turn the legs over. Eat up ground. Knock the minutes off. The watch will beep again. When it does, you'll have less than ten minutes. Probably closer to eight. Take it a block at a time. A minute at a time. Trust your fitness. Trust the process. Think about Boston. In less than three weeks you'll be boarding a plane. It'll be here before you know it. The watch beeped. The numbers read 6:20.

Someone honked and waved from a vehicle. A big black suburban. Or a range rover. Denny wasn't sure. And he had no idea who it was. No matter. Someone would tell him about it later. Happens often. Yeah, I remember seeing you Denny would lie. I remember I was dropping sub 6:30 miles at the time. In the twelfth mile of a run. Killing it. But he quickly stifled his ego. Told it to shut-up. A fuzzy haze appeared in front of Denny; he wasn't sure if it had something to do with fatigue, or a problem with his vision? Or was it sea fog rolling up from the beach? Whatever it was, he blasted through it. Had to be less than five minutes left now. Break it down into thirty second segments. Ten of them. Maybe nine by now. Run through the pain in your right calf. It's nothing. Can't do a run like this and not expect something to flare up. I'm about to redline. Losing the ability to process oxygen. Denny felt like he was floating alongside himself while he ran, making diagnostic commentary about the body beside him. Suddenly it was comical. He felt himself smile. Like he would tell others who ran or were thinking about running, if you can't have fun with this shit, find something else to do.

The watch beeped again. Sweet music to the ears. He flicked his wrist. 6:06. Flying. Just over a minute and a half left to run. Denny passed by the lake. He noticed a bunch of geese in the water, probably taking a rest from migrating north. Denny wondered why flocks of geese were not observed when they fly north in the spring, in the same vein that we all seem to make note of when we see them flying south in the fall? A glance at his watch revealed fifty-three seconds and counting left to be run. He thanked the geese for the brief distraction. At this point he was moving about as fast as he physically could. Denny checked his watch again. The pace read 5:55. And then it all came to an end, just like that.

    Denny sort of stumbled into a cool down walk, and found himself right near the beach access point by his home, so he decided to walk onto the beach and slip his running shoes and socks off. The sand felt soothing to his feet. Denny meandered to where the water from the waves was rolling up the beach, and waded on in. The ocean temps were a bit of an initial shock, but as he walked out farther into the water, his lower body adjusted. He got out to where the sea level came up to near his knees; the motion of the waves also felt soothing to the legs, like being in a whirlpool. If his right calf had the ability to speak, surely it would have thanked him.

    The sun was beginning to appear above the horizon; the upper part of the fiery, deep orangish colored disk projected its light outward across the sky. Some of the beams speckled on the water like tiny yellow diamonds that rode the waves towards the shoreline, before dissipating in a million directions. Until the next wave arose from the depths, and the light show began anew. Denny stood in the ocean, hypnotized by what he saw, like one enraptured in the throes of a religious experience that defied logic, existing in the spaces independent of time or place.

Chapter 29

Denny was at the point where the biomechanical motion of running had practically become a state of homeostasis. On days when his legs felt creaky, heavy, or fatigued, once he got going for several minutes, it was as if the body physically recognized being in its natural element, and dropped any notion there might be to fight the process. Not that any of the aforementioned problems vanished; rather, they did not impede the objectives being sought on the roads and trails. Denny could simply be imagining aspects of this, but even if so, it was a useful mental trick to get him moving most every day. These thoughts lingered, on an early morning run in Carolina Beach, twelve days out from the marathon.

After looping the north end of the island under the cloak of darkness, Denny proceeded over to Snow's Cut Bridge for some faster paced hill repeats, being convinced that the more hills he could continue to run before leaving for Boston, the better his performance might be on race day. Though he figured it would be best to cut the hills out next week, and keep the legs as fresh as could be.

At the top of the bridge on the first trip across, some tightness began to creep into the left hamstring. Denny maintained the rather brisk pace, not wanting to give any credence to the signal his leg was sending him, hoping that it was just some minor stress that would flare occasionally since his return from injury. Plus, the mindset was that there was a job to be done; fuck it he rationalized, now is the time to run through it, plenty of rest and rehab will be forthcoming shortly.

And that is just what he did. Fortunately, the low-grade pain never got any worse, and Denny was able to complete successfully what he had set forth to do.

But not before a rather random and bizarre occurrence took place, though not altogether arbitrary, based on the pedigree of the persons involved and their concurrent racing plans. On Denny's third trip across Snow's Cut, he spotted a small light up in the distance coming from somewhere near the top of the bridge. The light was moving towards him too, and once Denny got closer, he realized that what he was seeing must be a headlamp being worn by someone, also running. And as they were about to intersect, Denny correctly guessed that the fellow runner was a guy named Bernie Holcombe from the Wilmington Road Runners, who was also racing Boston. They had never actually met in person, but were connected through some mutual friends, and followed each other on Strava.

After introducing themselves, the two stopped and chatted for a few minutes about their training, the upcoming marathon, travel arrangements, and what hotels were being stayed at in Boston.

"Only another Boston Marathoner would be up here doing this in the dark," Bernie said, as the runners bid farewell for now. "What a crazy little universe we exist in, right?"

"Indeed. Sometimes it's nice to know we are not alone," Denny replied, as he turned to continue across the remainder of the bridge.

"See you in Beantown amigo," Bernie hollered over his shoulder, above the sound of a truck driving by.

Denny picked the pace up rather rapidly, and blasted up and over the top of Snow's Cut, and on back down onto the island again. At some point the watch beeped, indicating a 6:28 mile. Adrenaline can be a powerful stimulant.

Fifteen minutes later he was home. The first indications of daylight had become visible to the east, out over the Atlantic Ocean. Some puffy, grey cumulous clouds were slung low across the peach colored light of the lower portion of the sky; a palpable amount of moisture was in the atmosphere the last few days. Humidity levels were slowly on the rise, a sure signpost that spring was well underway in the south. It was a far cry from the cold and snow Denny had recently encountered in Pennsylvania. And it was getting to be the time that Denny, and scores of others, many of whom might be loath to admit, would begin feverishly checking the long-range weather forecast for Boston. For weather and running tend to find themselves inextricably intertwined.

~

It was difficult some days for Uncle Mike to hold a cup of coffee anymore, so a thermos was made with a specialized straw coming out of the lid, that allowed him to indulge in his morning routine. Occasionally he would have the strength to get out of bed, with the assistance of Mr. Hackenberg and the attending nurse. But it had become too much of a trial for Uncle Mike to get up and down the stairs; the solution to this though, was to move a bed and his personal affects into the living room. That way he could look out the front window towards the pond, and also have the ability to watch television and take meals in the same room. Lately though he wasn't eating much. His son Roger was flying in, followed shortly by his wife and children. The final days were at hand.

But in regards to Denny, that did not stop Uncle Mike from continuing to keep track of the running and training; the boxes on the calendar were assiduously filled almost daily, but the actual writing now had to be done by Mr. Hackenberg. He could still manage to use his cell phone, albeit not without a fair amount of fumbling around at times. Uncle Mike had developed a predilection for opening up the Boston Athletic Association app and looking at the countdown clock, as well as checking the tracking information for Denny, which would always show him standing at the start line in Hopkinton.

On one occasion Mr. Hackenberg came up from behind and remarked, "he still hasn't moved yet?"

"Maybe if I shake it, he'll start running," Uncle Mike replied. When he laughed, it caused him to nearly choke. The man may have been knocking on death's door and losing appreciable strength daily, but his sense of humor stayed resolutely intact. Whether or not he'd ever get to see the blue stick figure actually move was in the hands of God.

~

There were a hundred and one things to do, or thus it seemed. I need to start making lists, Jennifer thought, as she yanked on a large suitcase that was wedged on a shelf in her bedroom closet; it finally came free and crashed to the floor on top of a pile of clothes that laid at her feet. The thing was too darned big anyhow, so Jennifer crawled under the bed and pulled out a soft-sided suitcase and backpack that had probably been there since she had moved into the house after the divorce. She looked at the backpack for a second, then remembered that Micah had forgotten the books now several days overdue at the public library, since she recalled seeing them sitting beside the toaster oven in the kitchen.

The phone rang. It was Doris returning her call. Jennifer took a deep breath and answered.

"So, Monday and Tuesday. But you might come in during the afternoon?" Doris asked again.

"Yes ma'am."

"Okay. Let me switch a few people around. And if no one can cover Tuesday I'll take your morning rounds."

"Thank you thank you thank you," Jennifer repeated into the phone, while she opened the backpack with a free hand and pulled out a notebook and sketchpad that was inside.

"Oh, geez kiddo it's the least I can do," Doris said. She knew how important this was to Jennifer, and also secretly wished that despite how crazy some of the things sounded that her younger colleague did, that she could sometimes swap places with her. "You're really going to go watch an entire marathon? How long do these things take anyhow? And for goodness sakes dress warm."

"I will Doris. Promise. See you in a few." Jennifer hung up the phone and stood up, then did a little dance in front of the full-length mirror on the back of the bathroom door. Next on the agenda was to purchase airline tickets. Jennifer sat down again and opened up a laptop computer and went on-line, giddy with excitement that her plan to fly up and surprise Denny before his race was fully in motion now. In another couple of days, she'd be in route to Boston as well.

Chapter 30

The flame of the candle swayed in a cosmic dance. The light emitted moved in perfect choreography, climbing up the wall, then abruptly fading out again, only to cast a faint glow elsewhere. Denny sat cross-legged on the living room floor in front of the candle, which was encased in a glass cylinder, and had a painted picture of Our Lady of Guadalupe on the outside. He had picked it up in the Mexican section of a grocery store last fall, in case he lost power during the hurricane. But he had ended up evacuating anyway, and hadn't lit the candle until tonight.

Denny closed his eyes, and moved his hands above the candle to feel the heat being generated by the flame. He counseled the mind to relax, and attempted to mediate. But thoughts kept occurring. Instead of indulging in or becoming agitated at the intrusions, Denny tried his best to ignore, while lovingly requesting such interruptions to leave him be. His proclivity for undue worry and dwelling on minute details had kicked into overdrive, in anticipation of all the logistics to be navigated the upcoming weekend in Boston. Just get me on the airplane, get me my bib, and get me to the start line, became his petition to the running gods; hopefully the unorthodox request would help alleviate some of the stress.

With candle in hand Denny stood up and walked over to the far wall of the living room; he held the candle and watched the movements of light and shadow as they spread across the painting, briefly bringing parts into a dim focus, such as the surface of Beltzville Lake, or the face of the young girl who was sitting on the forest floor. He peered very close at the face, so that the flickering of the candle's light had the effect of making the girl's eyes gleam or glitter, almost identical to the sparkle in Jennifer's eyes at times. A warm tranquility washed over Denny as he stood there, enthralled by the visual he had helped to create.

For what good comes from worry; some verse from the Bible came into his mind, and his heart. "Sufficient unto the day is the evil thereof." Or something to that effect. Uncle Mike would probably know.

Denny called him the next evening. His uncle was in decent spirits, or so it sounded over the telephone. He was happy that his son was with him, and had even decided to stay there at the farmhouse. Uncle Mike asked Denny how he was handling the taper, and if he felt like he was ready to race. Denny said that a part of him was climbing the walls, and his mind seemed to be in overdrive as well most of the time, though he had been through it all before, and wasn't necessarily perturbed by it.

"Well we get accustomed to expending high levels of energy, that perhaps on a molecular level, it all needs somewhere now to go," Uncle Mike said. "I'm like you. Believing in the whole mind body connection." There was a long pause, and Denny could audibly hear his uncle breathing. Finally, he asked, "how's the hamstring?"

"Okay of late. Hasn't really been a problem since that last run on the bridge."

"Good. That's good." Again, there was a lengthy pause, and Denny could hear heavier, almost disjointed breathing. After several more seconds, he wondered if his uncle had fallen asleep on the phone, which had happened before.

"When do you fly up?" Apparently, Uncle Mike was not asleep, or had woken back up.

"Tomorrow. After work."

There was no response. Silence.

Then the voice of Denny's cousin Roger came on the connection. "He's exhausted himself for the evening," he said. "I'm going to hang up the call."

"Okay. Good night," Denny said.

He and Roger had never been all that tight, even when growing up, though they were close in age. But Denny was glad he was there, and didn't really want to get involved in anything between his cousin and his father. For Denny knew what it was like to have strained relationships in one's immediate family. Mr. Hackenberg sent him a text message later in the evening, with a brief update. Uncle Mike's health was declining even more down the inevitable slope, and he would likely pass within the next few days.

Meanwhile, the countdown to the gun at Boston continued to wind down.

Chapter 31

When he first caught sight of Jennifer amongst the throngs of travelers at Logan Airport, Denny broke into almost a full sprint, nearly knocking a few people over, as he zig zagged through the baggage claim area. She happened to glance up and in his direction about a half of a second before being lifted off the ground and into a giant hug.

"Welcome to Boston," Denny said. The exhilaration of the extended weekend kept getting ratchetted up even more, and the whole escapade had felt like a mad crazy rush from the get go. It was almost hard for Denny to wrap his mind around the idea that the actual race was now less than forty-eight hours away.

The two of them got a ride downtown from French-fry and his wife who had arrived at the airport about an hour before Jennifer, and were staying just a few blocks away on Beacon Street. After dropping her bags off, Denny and Jennifer headed out on foot and subway train to the Seaport Convention Center, where the marathon expo was being held all weekend. The streets were crowded; most everyone looked like a runner, or someone who was there to support a runner. It was mild out, at least by New England standards, but the weather gods were perhaps plotting a cruel twist of fate, for the forecast kept getting more and more ominous for race day Monday. Heavy rain and wind were being predicted, with temperatures in the thirties. Jennifer told Denny on the T, the name used for Boston's public transportation system, that at the last minute she had packed a bunch of winter clothes, though she did suggest that it perhaps would be best if he'd stop checking the weather app on his cell phone for the time being, and worry about all of that later.

"Good advice," he concurred.

A few minutes later they entered the lobby of a large building, not before encountering a rather elaborate security protocol. "After the bombings a lot of things changed here," Denny said to Jennifer, after they were both through the metal detectors.

Inside the main ballroom, runners from all over the world were gathered, many dressed in previous year's celebration jackets of various colors, with the iconic unicorn emblazoned on the back. Denny's father had shipped him this year's jacket as a present. But he dared to not even so much as take the jacket out of its plastic wrap, for he had been forewarned by Sylvester Reynolds in the Wilmington Road Runners, that to do so was to invite a terrible curse to be cast upon one's race. And to assuage any skepticism Denny or anyone else might have as to the merits of such advice, a story was told of a runner from the club who did not heed such a warning a few years prior; this tale ended in terrible tragedy, with the offending runner reduced to walking the last several miles of the marathon in abject misery, finally crossing the finish line around the five hour mark.

Even Jennifer took this to be very serious; she offered to take possession of the jacket until after the race. "I'll stash it in my backpack," she said, as they climbed the stairs to the room that contained the bibs. "And give it to you after you've finished. Then you can put the sucker on." Her conviction sold him on the idea, not that he had to be.

"I might need a water proof parka by then." It seemed like just about every conversation amongst the running masses revolved around the topic of the weather forecast. Some even began to speculate whether the race would be cancelled if snow and ice mixed in with all the cold, drenching rains that were expected from what was now being called a nor'easter. But a look at the Boston Marathon's history indicated that the race went on, regardless of the conditions. It was embedded in the lore of the event. On the flights up, Denny had read the book *Duel in the Sun*, about the 1982 race that came down to Alberto Salazar and Dick Beardsley battling it out almost right to the finish line on Boylston Street, on a day with almost intolerably warm weather for a marathon. And a few years ago, some friends from Wilmington who had run said it was so hot that the race actually offered entrants the option of a deferment into the next year's edition, but the race itself proceeded that day as scheduled.

"Well at least you won't have to worry about it being too hot on Monday," Jennifer stated, while not batting an eye.

He leaned in and kissed her on the cheek as they entered another large room. "You always manage to put a positive slant on things."

Denny found the correct line that corresponded to his bib number; there had to be a dozen tables or more being utilized just to hand out all the race packets to the marathoners. He tried to soak in the significance of the moment, which from an emotional frame of reference was almost overwhelming. It was another step in the process, and literally only a few more steps in the journey, but momentous ones at that. For it was something Denny had mentally pictured countless times, stemming back many years ago when he first had the inkling to try to qualify for Boston.

A gentleman dressed in official volunteer garb, greeted Denny with a hello and smile when he got to the front of the line. Denny reciprocated, and showed him his driver's license, and the requisite card that contained all his personal race information. Upon being handed the bib, which was wrapped in plastic, Denny was wished good luck on Monday, and told to enjoy the experience.

"Thank you sir," he replied in kind. Denny walked back through the room to find Jennifer; hundreds of runners were standing in lines, awaiting their own magical moments.

"You have to get in that line over there," Jennifer said, as she pointed. "Then I can take a picture of you in front of the giant mural of the course."

"Yes indeed. We can send it to Uncle Mike."

"He would love that," agreed Jennifer.

After the photo op, the two of them headed downstairs to walk around the expo, by far the biggest one Denny had ever attended. It was as if the entire running world had descended upon downtown Boston, which in many ways, it had. Denny wanted to find a pair of waterproof gloves, and was also debating purchasing some type of headwear, but he wasn't sure what, if anything, would actually do any good. Cheap, pullover ponchos were also suggested not only for Denny, but for Jennifer too, by members of the Wilmington contingent. Though it seemed like such items were being sought by just about everybody, rapidly diminishing the availability of such gear.

However, Denny did find a vendor who still had waterproof gloves for sale, but all that remained were smaller sizes. He tried a pair on that fit tight, and had to be stretched to cover his wrists.

"What do you think?" he asked Jennifer

"Purple looks good on your hands."

Denny did appreciate the degree of levity Jennifer continued to supply during the day; it was just enough to keep his mind from wandering too far into any corners, of which little good would derive. From a performance standpoint, the past few days Denny had shifted from thinking about what it would take to break three hours, to what measures would have to be taken just to survive the thing. For another mitigating factor was that he, along with most everyone else who wasn't an elite, would also have to wait outside for a good chunk of time at Athlete's Village, before anyone's race would even begin. The buzz too, was that the location would more than likely be transformed into something like the mud fields at Woodstock, if the forecast came to fruition.

Jennifer and Denny weaved up and down the long rows of merchandise for sale, and the many display stands and vendor booths offering free samples of all types of foods and beverages. They tasted organic energy bars, ate some delicious yogurt made on a chemical free farm in Vermont, and discovered a store that produced and sold all kinds of beef, bison, and deer jerky. Denny washed the salty jerky down with an electrolyte sports drink, the cups of which were being handed out on trays, like waitstaff would do at a black-tie cocktail party.

"Take it easy champ," Jennifer remarked to him. "Save some room for dinner tonight."

"You know I'm a sucker for free food."

"Me too."

"Plus, this is my day to pack it in. Sunday I'll start to cut back."

Eventually the pair made their way through the masses of people towards the exits. Denny spotted Scott Jurek signing books; a line of people snaked around the corner. He pointed him out to Jennifer, and told her a little of whom Jurek was as a runner and a writer. She leaned in and said into his ear, "maybe that will be you one day."

~

"Oh man I don't want to look. I'm scared."

"Just pretend like you're in the movies. None of this is real."

"That's your advice for everything. It's a bit surrealistic for me mister." Jennifer kept her hands firmly over her eyes and stood several paces away from the windows.

Denny wanted to go outside and on to the observation deck of the Prudential Building, but he figured it would be a prudent course of action to take it one step at a time. From the floor to ceiling windows, he could see the metropolis of Boston laid out in front of him, all stately and proud and important looking as it sprawled out towards the open waters leading to the Atlantic Ocean. To the left, there was a view into Fenway Park, where the Red Sox were currently playing the Orioles. The players on the field looked like ants at work outside their colony.

Denny took both of Jennifer's hands and grasped them in his, and told her on the count of three to open her eyes. "I've got you. You aren't going anywhere."

"I know Denny," she said. When she did finally open her eyes, Jennifer was awestruck by all that could be seen. Her fear of heights almost dissolved on the spot.

"Now do you remember being here in Junior High?"

"Okay. I think so. It was dark out?"

"Yes. We were here on that Friday night. Most everyone went into a show at the planetarium, but Ed and I ducked out so we could watch the Red Sox game. Roger Clemens was pitching." Denny, to be honest, had a vague recollection of being up there, after all it was a class field trip taken almost thirty years ago, but small fragments were still lodged in his mind. Such as hitting his head on purpose on the low hanging eaves in the House of Seven Gables. And eating lunch in Quincy Market one afternoon.

"You boys were just rebels then," Jennifer said.

"Yes. We thought very highly of ourselves."

Later that evening the couple stumbled upon an authentic Italian restaurant situated in an older, genteel neighborhood in the Brookline section of Boston. The tiny eatery was on the first floor of a three-story townhouse, on a tree-lined street a few blocks off of Beacon Street. The smell of food wafted out to the sidewalks before they even ducked inside. Upon entering, it was like stepping into a kitchen in Sicily. The food was delectable; Jennifer had ravioli stuffed with lobster, while Denny feasted on seafood linguine with roasted red peppers. Before leaving, Jennifer raised her glass for a toast; it had been one of the best days in a long time she announced, as the two glasses clinked above the small, wooden table.

Denny wholeheartedly agreed, and as they walked outside into the dark and now much colder and windier evening, he was also thankful for the fact that he hadn't thought much about the race for the past several hours. But as he zipped his jacket tight, he knew all of that was most certainly bound to change.

Chapter 32

Don't get nervous in the pack. The words kept repeating inside Trent's head, as he careened down Flagstaff Mountain. It was from a book he had read a long time ago, *Once a Runner*. How appropriate he thought, as the pack Trent was in today was barreling along at speeds that were borderline nuts. It was definitely a crazy way to begin a half marathon, but he figured once the field hit the base of the mountain, and entered the trails, the runners would start to get strung out fairly quickly. In the meantime, he held on, as did those around him.

Somewhere in the second mile of the race, once the course got on the Switchback Trails, Trent was able to settle into a groove, and find what felt like a more suitable running rhythm. He had gone through the first mile in 6:22, but knew there was no way anything near that fast of a pace could be sustained for thirteen miles. Not that he wasn't feeling strong or confident, having strung together several solid months of training, a good bit of which was done on the treadmill in the garage. March saw him achieve a record monthly mileage total of 177 miles, shattering the previous best by almost twenty miles. All of that continued to contribute to bringing his weight down; Jill remarked the other day the difference she could see in the contours of his face, and how he was even beginning to look younger, if somehow that was possible? It had inspired her to start back up running herself.

Once the course spilled back on to the roads, and into the historic section of Jim Thorpe, Trent felt like he was able to increase the pace, as he'd been forced to slow some on parts of the rather technical, single track trails. But it had also helped him to conserve energy, though admittedly Trent wasn't all that sure how to appropriately pace himself in a half, especially one varying so widely in terrain. There was a timing mat laying on one side of the road, and an electronic clock on a stand at the ten kilometer mark, but out of a nascent superstition, Trent chose not to look at the clock as he passed by, though he was relieved when he heard a shrill, high pitched noise, indicative that the timing chip on the back of his bib had been read. Such technology wasn't in wide use the last time he would have entered a local road race. And for whatever reason, Trent didn't trust the thing.

Around mile eight, and after the course had crossed over the newly constructed pedestrian bridge that spanned the Lehigh River near the old train station, Trent noticed the first real signs of fatigue settling into his legs, and general soreness in the arms, and neck and shoulders. He shook his hands a few times and attempted to self-massage the shoulder blades, but didn't think it did much good. Thirst too was now an issue; Trent hadn't taken any fluids yet at the aid stations passed, and was not carrying any. Fortunately, it wasn't that warm out. Temperatures likely wouldn't make it out of the forties by the time he finished.

Trent thought over what Denny had talked to him on the phone about, concerning the middle to latter miles; try to race the thing hard to around mile ten or eleven, and then hold on and gut it out the remainder of the way. He had turned the app on his phone on silent after the third mile, but all the miles were marked with signs, so Trent always knew the approximate distance remaining. Plus, the course map had been pored over a good bit, so he had a pretty solid indication of where he was most of the race. But time, or elapsed time, Trent wanted no knowledge of until the finish line was reached.

The mountains surrounding the deep gorge the Lehigh snaked through looked foreboding, even though Trent had seen them countless times. Then again there was a majestic grandeur in their presence; after all, the town of Jim Thorpe was nicknamed the Switzerland of the Americas. He wondered who had coined the phrase, as he exited off the gravel trail next to the railroad tracks, and got back onto the asphalt of the roads again. A nice sized crowd was gathered to spectate in the downtown vicinity, which served to re-energize Trent as he let the boisterous noise wash over him. Just then he heard someone actually yell out his name. It was Keith, who was standing in front of Molly Maguires Bar with one of his kids, Ronald. Trent waved and hollered thanks. I guess Suzanne must be running this as well, he surmised.

Ron had a solid year wrestling. Made it to states again. Was ranked in the top two or three all year long in the district at his weight class. Think he medaled at some of the big tournaments as well. Really strong at escaping when starting from the mat. Trent realized a few blocks up the road, as he neared Saint Jerome's Catholic Church, that he had completely drifted off into a tangent about Keith's oldest kid; he was pleasantly surprised to suddenly see the sign for ten miles almost right in front of him. Five kilometers left, the thought of which seemed doable, yet daunting. Trent knew it was time to really dig deep, with a clear-eyed, steely focus.

What was ahead was another part of the Switchback Trail; again, his pace slowed some, as the single-track trail had many roots and rocks that needed to be continually navigated. Trent almost fell, for the second time. His brain and legs weren't as synced as they should be. He tried shortening his stride a touch, but that only seemed to aggravate the quad muscles more. Trent felt a little frustration seep in, along with a few crumbs of panic. Why, he wondered? He was wary of how thirsty he was, and now hungry too. Almost to the point of wooziness, when a real pronounced wave of hunger hit. He should have eaten something before the race. And taken Jill's advice. Negative thoughts kept coming at Trent. What he needed to hear was the music. That would help.

The Switchback Trail terminated on the right side of the road, by a small wastewater treatment building that was fenced off at the edge of the woods, and abutted the precipitous incline up the Broad Mountain. The course, however, crossed onto the road. Trent took notice of the eleven-mile mark sign, stuck in the ground just in front of another aid station, the final one of the half. He grabbed a cup of lemon-lime flavored Gatorade from the hand of a young girl, and forced a few big swallows into his throat. For some reason he thought about the orange flavored drink McDonalds used to sell; there would always be big portable jugs filled with it during knee-hi football practices at Baer Memorial Park. But you'd have to be careful not to chug too much when it was really hot out, or it made you sick. Trent recalled how he puked once at the end of practice, in the back of his older brother's Camaro. Rick was pissed, and almost wailed the tar out of him in front of half the Army team.

On the much wider, double track section of the Switchback Trail, Trent tried to summon the pace to where it had been a few miles ago, but the legs just didn't seem to want to cooperate and turn over fast enough. He felt like he was barely moving, though in reality a rather respectable speed was still being maintained. The terrain was at a slight incline too. And would be for the most part until Mauch Chunk Lake, where the finish line was. His right hamstring started to send out shooting pains, joining the rebellion the quadriceps had fomented. Trent began to question his ability to make it all the way, or if the body would give out short of the destination. And then he remembered the music.

Trent queued Led Zeppelin's *Kashmir* on his phone. As if by divine intervention, the twelve-mile sign appeared. Little over a mile to go. Perfect. For he was a traveler of both time and space. Trent briefly debated checking the run-time on his phone, but opted not to. He would know soon enough. The trail emerged out of the forest; Trent could see the lake across the brownish green, barren meadow. The sun, which had risen above Flagstaff Mountain to the south, sent golden shafts of light onto the fields and the water. "Oh father of the four winds fill my sails, across the sea of years."

After looping along a dirt road adjacent to the shoreline at the far end of the lake, the course entered one last section of woods. Two runners were about thirty, forty meters up ahead of Trent, and he decided to try and catch them and latch onto until the end. One of them he did manage to reel in, a young female who didn't look to be much older than his daughter, who was seventeen now. The fellow competitor had two black pigtails that bobbed back and forth across her neck and upper back as she ran. Trent started to draft her, like in a track race. A step or two back, off one of her shoulders. In the slipstream. Like Dick Semmel taught us. He hoped she wouldn't mind. Trent knew once they got out of the woods the finish line would be maybe fifty meters away. Up ahead he could see a spot of light, like the light at the end of a tunnel. Come on legs don't fail me know, Trent prayed. For everything felt like it was going numb.

But he still heard the music. "My Shangri-La beneath the summer moon, I will return again." Before he knew it, Trent had smashed into the light. Out of the woods. On to the macadam. Crossing the parking lot. He could see cones. Ribbons. The finish line stanchion. People. Cheers. He saw Jill. And heard her too. And then he glanced at the electronic clock above the finish line. On the PA system it was announced, "Trent Zeigenfuss from Lehighton in a time of one hour thirty-two minutes and fifty-seven seconds." It all blurred into one joyous moment of triumph. The slow walk through the chute. A medal placed around his neck. A bottle of water handed to him. A huge grin spread across Trent's face, even though his legs were cramping like all hell. Jill rushed over and gave him hug.

"I'm so proud of you," she said, as her husband almost collapsed into her arms.

Chapter 33

"Look," Denny said again. "It's freaking snowing!"

This time several of his running companions assured him they saw the snow as well, that had begun to lightly fall, in very fine flakes. Perhaps none of them wanted to acknowledge aloud how ominous the weather situation was, twenty-four hours shy of the race's gun time. The assembled group of runners, about ten or so members of the Wilmington Road Runners Club, headed out along the banks of the Charles River. In the more exposed spots, the wind coming off the water made it feel downright frigid. All were dressed in long pants and many layers, plus gloves and knit hats. Some like Denny's friend Jackie, had opted to skip the traditional club shakeout run and stay warm in their hotels.

"This is sort of crazy," Sylvester, or Sy as he was called by most, admitted. "I guess there's a first for everything." He was the resident Sherpa of the coastal North Carolina contingent; tomorrow would be his twelfth Boston, and eighth in a row.

Briana pulled up beside Denny as they ran; both sensed the anxiety in each other in lieu of the forecast, and just how cold it had already gotten. "Have you decided what to wear?" she asked, not attempting to shield the nervousness in her voice.

"I keep wavering between pants and shorts. And whether to wear some kind of rain jacket too." Every half an hour Denny changed his mind, as he would mull over some new kernel of information.

"Yeah me too," she replied.

"I'm afraid anything extraneous will get too heavy and act as a drag," Lee offered. "Though I do not enjoy the thought of freezing to death in a cold rain," he added, with a somewhat forced chuckle. He had run several Bostons; ironically the last time he was here, it was too warm for his tastes. Temperatures were approaching seventy by the time wave two started, he shared with them.

"God that sounds so amazing right now! Seventy..." Denny remarked, as he let the last word linger in the shivery air.

"Look, it's not really that big of a deal," Sy said, from the front of the pack, as many of them slowed and stopped to take a few more pictures. "It may mean wearing more clothing. And adjusting goals. If the current forecast holds, we're also looking at a nasty headwind too for most of the race."

"I don't mind rain. But rain and thirty-six degrees?" asked Natalie, who was also there for the first time.

"They are now calling for two to three inches of rain. And snow and ice near Hopkinton and points west," Lee added.

"Welcome to the Boston Marathon," Sy said, as he busted out in a wide grin. "We all get to be a part of another chapter in the ever-growing lore of this most prestigious of events."

Denny felt a little more at ease after hearing such sentiments verbalized. He realized too that they were all in this thing together, for better or worse. Not just the small group shivering along the river, but the entire field of thirty thousand runners. And all the volunteers. And fans. The weather would not be indiscriminate; the same conditions would have to be braved by all. Denny mentioned such thoughts to Natalie, who was huddled beside him.

"Let's do this man," was her response. A little fire was in her watery eyes. Apparently, she had received the message too.

It had been a mental process the last few days whereby Denny gradually released any attachment he had on obtaining the goal of breaking three hours. He wasn't falling prey to a defeatist attitude; a more realistic mindset was being adopted. Under ideal conditions, and in a state of maximum fitness, Denny figured he could come close to running a 2:55 marathon. But he had lost a few weeks in the training cycle, and the nature gods were apparently not in the mood to cooperate Monday. And even on a good day, Boston could be a bitch of a course. Several people had cautioned him during the past few months about the inherent challenges to perform supremely well there, though to a person, none discouraged him from trying. The later start times, the net downhill, the Newton Hills, and now the weather. It all was like one big riddle, that apparently was not easy to solve.

As the Wilmington gang ran the famous last two turns in the world of marathoning, right on Hereford, left on Boylston, Denny felt like an injection of adrenaline had been stuck into his veins. It was fucking Boston, and he was ready for whatever she would throw at him come tomorrow. He couldn't wait to get to the starting line, and see the dream that he and so many others had worked so hard for finally take flight. It was almost showtime. The whole world would be watching.

~

Denny was lying on the bed absentmindedly watching an NBA playoff basketball game on the television when his cell phone rang. It was Uncle Mike calling. But when Denny answered, Mr. Hackenberg was the voice heard on the other end of the line. He explained that Uncle Mike had been in and out of consciousness all day, and that all parties figured the end was imminent. His immediate family were all present at the farmhouse, and Mr. Hackenberg was happy to report that relations had been mended between him and his son Roger, of which Denny knew how vital such a thing was to his uncle, who was relatively lucid at the present time, and asked that his nephew be phoned.

"Hello," Uncle Mike said into the phone, which was being help up to the side of his head.

"Hello Uncle Mike," Denny replied. He had muted the television, and sat up in bed. Jennifer watched him, from the chair in the hotel room.

"Denny?"

"Yes, I am here," Denny assured him. It sounded like there was some confusion in his uncle's voice.

"Good."

Denny could hear shallow breathing in the phone. He heard Roger say something, but couldn't quite make out the words. So, Denny started to talk into his cell phone about the shakeout run earlier, and how cool it was to run down Boylston Street towards the finish. Then about what time he was going to leave out to catch the busses downtown tomorrow, what the latest forecast was, and where Jennifer was going to try to be on the course.

Uncle Mike seemed to perk up, or become a little more alert. He spoke again, and said, "I love you Denny. I'm so proud. You'll do great."

"I love you too."

"Just remember," Uncle Mike began. Once again there was silence, except for the sound of breathing. "That tomorrow..."

"Are you trying to tell me to win one for the gipper?"

Woven into the noise of human breathing, was the unmistakable sound of laughter. It was ruffled, faint, and likely painful. But it was laughter. Denny pictured the old love-soaked smile appearing in the middle of that shaggy grey and white beard on Uncle Mike's wrinkled face.

Into the phone came the voice again, the voice of one standing on the threshold of the next dimension, where God's angels deliver mercy, and we can relax and let go.

"Just remember. To enjoy every step of the way. Tomorrow. And every day. Thereafter."

Denny hadn't noticed tears had welled up in his own eyes. But he smiled, and said, "you've had one hell of a ride. Thank you for allowing me to tag along for all of these years."

And that was that. Denny rolled off the bed and put his head in Jennifer's lap. She rubbed the back of his head softly with her hands, and told him about the conversation in the art gallery last month, and how she planned to honor Uncle Mike's wishes for as long as the days may stretch out for her and Denny.

"His message was simple," she said. "Just be there for each other."

Chapter 34

Denny woke up several times in the night; the rain and wind continued to lash against the windows, like an acoustical accompaniment in a bad dream. Each time he glanced at the alarm clock on the bed stand it was as if only another fifteen minutes or so had passed.

Finally, he got up, and brewed himself a cup of coffee. Everything needed for the day ahead was neatly arranged on the floor, against the front wall of the hotel room. As Denny sat in the dark and sipped the hot coffee, he checked the messages and well wishes and good lucks he had received via text and on Facebook and Instagram. This was a big deal, and not only for him. So many others scattered about, whether friends or acquaintances from years past, or people who were currently a part of Denny's social fabric, were invested emotionally in the day's outcome themselves. As he looked over in the bed where Jennifer slept, he was nearly overcome with gratitude to be a small part of so many human lives.

Denny slowly dressed and finished the coffee. Jennifer woke up and joined him for the walk across the street to the T station. Several other runners were bundled up, desperately trying to stay warm and dry on the platform, which had only a small shelter for a lucky few to stand inside. The train came rolling in right on schedule; Jennifer and Denny parted ways, as she wished him good luck, and promised to have warm, dry clothes for him beyond the finish line at their designated meeting spot.

"Take care of yourself too," he said. "It's going to require a heck of a lot more courage to be a spectator in this thing."

"I'll be fine," she assured him with a smile and wave.

Denny struck up conversations with some of the other runners on the ride into downtown, before he and thousands more boarded school busses in Boston Common park for the hour ride west to Hopkinton. It was almost surreal; a mass of finely tuned athletes about to plunge headlong into the jaws of a nor'easter. No one knew how it all might turn out. Or just how dangerous the day could become. Denny admitted to the lady sitting on the bus beside him that he was actually a little scared. His new found friend was too.

It was hard to fully appreciate the specter of being in the renowned Athlete's Village; like many things associated with the Boston Marathon Denny had read about, and had formed mental images of or had seen photographs of, the emotional reactions could not be fathomed until one was actually physically present. Like landmarks to be run by on the course, god willing over the duration of the next several hours. But so much of his psychic energy had been devoted to battling the elements, that Denny was skeptical of his ability to fully absorb the significance. All he could do was try, and take the day as it came. The village was an abject mud pit from hell. Denny's shoes were quickly soaked, and caked in mud. Despite all the layers of clothes being worn, he was cold and damp. It was almost impossible to move, since everyone was trying to remain under the tents. Stay present he told himself. Stay positive.

As soon as the announcement went out over the public address system for wave one to leave the village and head to the start line area, Denny left out. He had yet to find French-fry or Colby, who were both also in wave one. But he figured at this point it wasn't all that important. What was important, was to get himself to the proper starting corral, which awaited him about three-quarters of a mile away. Denny used the portable bathrooms one last time, that were set up in a parking lot next to a big drug store. It was like halftime of a football game, when the whole stadium simultaneously descends upon the restrooms. Which was a bit unnerving. He was also engaged in a final hour game of second guessing what to wear when the gun went off. Should he just keep on the cheap poncho picked up at a department store? But then Denny would have to take his bib off and pin it on the thing. And his hands were already so numb and raw inside two pairs of gloves, that he doubted his ability to be able to take the bib off a shirt and reattach it to the poncho. The last thing he wanted was to be fumbling around with the single most important item that was needed to be worn.

    The national anthem started to be sung as Denny got himself safely ensconced in the correct starting corral. He took his right hand and placed it over his heart, and tried to lose himself in the words of the song, even silently singing along to one of the stanzas. As soon as the anthem ended, Denny started to shed clothes and discard garments over the railing. A squadron of fighter jets flew overhead. A man beside him wished him good luck, which was returned in kind. The field of runners were instructed the race would begin in two minutes. Up ahead, but out of Denny's sight, stood many of the best male distance runners in the world. The elite women were already out on the course. The exact course that Denny was about to also run. Every dip, turn, incline; it was twenty-six miles to Boston for all of them.

    Suddenly Denny recalled Christmas night. Uncle Mike was telling the story about the Philadelphia Marathon, and how it was pouring down rain at the start. An indescribable feeling welled up inside Denny; all of it seemed to merge together, that is today, Christmas, and the race forty years ago. The barriers had dissolved. Denny began to walk forward with the tightly packed crowd around him, then slowly jog. It was like the body was floating along, removed from the laws governing the natural world. He crossed the threshold, that famous start line painted in yellow and blue on the road, and then Denny was off, running without a care in the world.

Mr. Hackenberg had the phone propped up on Uncle Mike's chest, but he kept his hand on the back of it as well. Roger sat on the other side of the bed. A few minutes past 10:00am, a message appeared stating that Denny Defilippis had crossed the start line, and had begun running the Boston Marathon. And a few minutes past that, the blue stick figure moved. Very slightly, but it moved. Mr. Hackenberg looked at Uncle Mike; the pale glimmer that appeared in his eyes confirmed he had seen it move as well.

The End

Special thanks to all the first responders in Boston and the surrounding communities, who work tirelessly to keep everyone involved with the Boston Marathon safe.

For Notes

II

III

IV

V

Thank you for reading.

Made in United States
Orlando, FL
30 April 2025